THE *Wizard* OF WOZZLE

The TWITH LOGUE CHRONICLES

KENNETH G. OLD
&
PATTY OLD WEST

Volume One

THE WIZARD
OF
WOZZLE

Adventures with the Little People

TATE PUBLISHING *& Enterprises*

Published by Tate Publishing & Enterprises, LLC
127 E. Trade Center Terrace | Mustang, Oklahoma 73064 USA
1.888.361.9473 | www.tatepublishing.com

Tate Publishing is committed to excellence in the publishing industry. The company reflects the philosophy established by the founders, based on Psalm 68:11,
"The Lord gave the word and great was the company of those who published it."

Book design copyright © 2010 by Tate Publishing, LLC. All rights reserved.
Cover design by Lindsay B. Behrens
Interior design by Jeff Fisher
Author photo by Karin Spanner
Poetry excerpts from Footprints in the Dust by Kenneth G. Old
Map design by Rich and Lisa Ballou

Published in the United States of America

ISBN: 978-1-61663-888-7
1. Juvenile Fiction, Fantasy & Magic
2. Juvenile Fiction, Historical, Europe
10.08.30

DEDICATIONS

The Glassman Children with Ken
Ruth, James, Daniel, and Stephen

Dedicated to the children who first heard these stories
at the boarding school in Murree, Pakistan.

OTHER BOOKS BY KENNETH G. OLD

Walking the Way
Footprints in the Dust
A Boy and His Lunch
So Great a Cloud
Roses for a Stranger

OTHER BOOKS BY PATTY OLD WEST

Good and Faithful Servant
Once Met, Never Forgotten

EAGLE'S FLIGHT

Better grasp at a flying star

Than seize the sweet fruit on the bough.

Better than walking tall, by far,

Is to soar with the eagles now.

When there is a chance to choose

There are things only birds can see.

Better by far wings than shoes.

Alas, earthbound mortals are we.

Better a child's mind set alight

With fantasy's call to be free

Than a hundred facts put right

To maintain its captivity.

ACKNOWLEDGEMENTS

Ken Old was a man of many talents. The Lord endowed him with the ability to see beyond the everyday and gave him the creative writing talent to put those dreams and visions onto paper. His unique way of looking at things opens up new vistas of imagination beyond the ordinary. It is my hope that while reading about the Little People you can capture some of that same exciting, vibrant, carefree way of living and seeing.

Special thanks go to Margaret Spoelman, Patrick Wilburn, and Kim Dang for kindly making copies of the first chapters Gumpa sent by e-mail. After being entered into the computer, Gumpa's creative genius generated more than would fit into one book. It was split and the two smaller stories were expanded once again. Those also became too large and had to be divided. Eventually the initial few chapters became twelve volumes known as *The Twith Logue Chronicles*. They chronicle the adventures of the Little People as they are exiled from their homeland until they are able to return many centuries later.

My good friend Lisa Ballou graciously agreed to do the initial editing of this book. It was not an easy task, and I am most grateful for her expert help. Briana Johnson was responsible for the final editing. She gently guided me and taught me new ways of looking at things. With the help of these two beautiful young ladies, the story has taken on new life and vitality.

It is with deep appreciation that I acknowledge the proofreading skills of my three precious daughters, Sandy Gaudette,

Becky Shupe and Karin Spanner who have spent endless hours reading and re-reading the manuscript to ensure there are no stray errors.

Finally, I must give credit to my dear, sweet, kind, considerate, thoughtful and wonderful husband, Roy. At times he must have felt like a widower once again as I spent so many hours with my nose pressed up against my computer screen. His patient, loving, support has allowed me to continue the process of sharing these delightful stories with others.

Principle Charachters

The Beyonders

King Druthan (DRUH thun)	King of Trevose, Cornwall
Griswold (GRIZ walled)	The future Wizard of Wozzle
Glug	Griswold's brother

The Little People (Twith Logue)

Munro	A Twith sea traveler
King Rufus and Queen Sheba	The royal family of Gyminge
Princess Alicia (Ah LEE shah)	Their daughter
Dayko	Court High Seer
Gerald	Dayko's apprentice
Gareth (GARE eth)	The Earl of Up-Horton
The Countess	His wife
Taymar	Their oldest son
Ambro	Their second son
Fyrdwald (FIRD walled)	Count of the Dark Forest
Cleemo	The Woodcarver
Cymbeline (CYMBAL een)	Cleemo's niece
Barney	Cleemo's nephew
Jock	A Scot Twith who comes to help

Jordy	Another Twith who comes to help
Zaydek (ZAY deck)	A seer who betrays King Rufus
Haymun	Another seer who is a traitor

THE BIRDS

Rasputin (Rass PUH tin)	A raven, friend of the Wizard
Tuwhit (Too WHIT)	A barn owl
Crusty	A golden eagle

PLACES

Ben Armine	Mountain in Scotland
Gyminge (GIH minge)	Land of the Little People
Lyminge (LIMB hinge)	Capital of Wozzle
Wozzle	Kingdom of the Wizard

PREFACE

Gumpa loved to tell stories to children. It gave him a chance to be a child again himself. *The Twith Logue Chronicles,* which just means "Little People Stories," are fanciful, imaginative fairy tales that he told over a period of more than fifty years to children from ages five to fifteen. He just made them up as he went along, and the children always wanted to hear more. They would ask, "Will you please read some more out of your head?" The heroes of these stories are the Little People, only half a thumb high, known as the *Twith Logue* or just plain *Twith.*

When Gumpa retired, there weren't so many children around, so he began writing the stories to send to children. The stories are a mixture of reality and fantasy, and sometimes it is hard to tell where one leaves off and the other begins. I think that sometimes he didn't even know himself. The reality part is the old Tudor farmhouse and the surrounding area known as Gibbins Brook in Kent, England. The fantasy part is the Little People—Jock and Jordy; Taymar and Gerald; Cleemo; Barney; and his sister, Cymbeline. The adventures they have with Gumpa are where reality fades into fantasy.

So picture yourself sitting on Gumpa's knee or gathered with other children at his feet. Listen to Gumpa put you into the world of the Little People, challenging you to *always tell the truth* while he takes you into strange and exciting adventures.

PROLOGUE

A prologue usually tells what has gone before. Since this is the first of the stories (or chronicles), there is nothing that has gone before; but there are a few things you should know before the story begins.

There is no Wizard of Wozzle in the beginning. But just so you know, the odd little boy named Griswold will become the mean and nasty wizard. And when he does, he is an enemy of the Little People.

We are on the side of the Little People. They are far older than the English and have their origins in myth. These tiny folk are very wise and know many things we do not. They have senses we don't have. They understand and talk to animals and birds. They do *not* use magic, and they *always tell the truth.* The Little People can only be seen by those they want to be seen by. Even though they are only half a thumb high, they have managed to survive for many centuries. Winning battles doesn't always depend on how big you are. These wee folk live in the east of England in the kingdoms of Wozzle and Gyminge, just on the north edge of Gibbins Brook.

The people who live outside the land of the Little People are called Beyonders. The adults and children you know are all Beyonders. Very few Beyonders know about the Little People, so you are privileged to be learning about them.

One more thing before you begin reading about the adventures of the Little People: this story takes place long before

Gumpa was born. In fact, it begins five hundred years before Columbus discovered America. In a later book, we will find out how Gumpa first meets the Little People in Cornwall.

Now let's get started. Enjoy the fun of Gumpa's overactive imagination.

THE GREEN BOTTLE

The tide is coming in fast. The beach is empty of people, save for two boys messing around on the rocks. The leading edge of water spreads steadily across the gold sand between the two short headlands and into the pools where the boys are exploring for tiddlers and crabs. The sand where they stand momentarily dries off as the water retreats in great, curving swirls behind an edge of foam. Farther out, great arcs of breaking surf throw unseen rainbows into the sky.

Soon there is no drying off of the sand as the foam edges farther up the beach. The boys' feet are caressed continually by moving water tickling their toes. They have no jars to hold what they catch. The fish and crabs are too small to eat and are not wanted at home anyway. Realizing they have the power of life and death over what they have caught, they know it's not good to kill things, so the boys release the frantic sea creatures back into their pools after a moment or so of holding and studying them.

The boys hardly notice they are hungry, although they have been on the beach since before noon. As soon as they arrived and felt the trickle of sand between their toes, they ate almost all of the food they brought with them. They saved only one muffin each for later. They are ragged and barefoot and wetter than any mother would want her sons to be outside of a bathtub—that is, any mother except their mother. She believes that sea water is better than fresh water. The salt makes it antiseptic; it cleans off dirt without the expense of soap or the energy of scrubbing, and it doesn't have to be pumped. Instead of bathing her boys, she sends them off to the beach with strict instructions not to go into the water. That is enough to bring them home clean.

The boys are completely happy, even Griswold, who is rarely completely happy. There is no one else on the beach. Beaches have not yet been discovered as a destination for tourists. They are merely a source of sand for builders, but there are no carts today interrupting the boys' solitary use of their domain. Beaches are designed and intended for boys. Sometimes they might choose to permit the more tomboyish of their sisters to accompany them. But anyone else is an intruder and not welcome.

Earlier, they had been searching for ambergris. They found some of the grey, waxy matter and stacked it in their secret cave for recovery later. Ambergris is from whales, sperm whales, and is washed ashore on these north Cornish coasts where the boys play. In the shop down by the dock, they can swap the ambergris, and the occasional little knobs of amber they also find, for things to take home. A growing family can better use things like fishing lines and hooks.

The two boys are not twins, although they are clearly brothers and close in age—somewhere about twelve years old. They are both of a skinny build. Obviously, their parents, in order to produce such results in their sons, must both have large ears and long noses and somewhat pointed chins.

Glug has been named by his father, and the mother has chosen Griswold's name. It will be his father's chance to choose a name with the initial "H" for his next son. The parents are wisely doing the naming of their children alphabetically. Two sons with each initial, one named by Dad and the next by Mum.

Dad can't spell as well as Mum, so the names he chooses are usually shorter. They have space for fifty-two sons and fifty-two daughters in their system, and it is unlikely they are going to go beyond the letter Z except in an emergency—like triplets or quads. Dad wants to manage a hockey team of his own sons, and the fourteen he now has will allow for a referee and two reserves as well. His mother calls her youngest son Grizzie, but to his friends, he is Griz. His father doesn't bother with names and just calls him and all his brothers, "Hey, you."

On the beach, Griswold tries to take leadership, but Glug is clear about his seniority as the older brother. He is not going to be bossed around, and it is he who straightens up, sees the water at the mouth of their cave, and yells, "Come on. Let's make a fire."

They splash into their cave. To get through a small opening, the boys have to duck down, but it is high enough inside for them to stand upright. It is a small cave, and it is *their* cave. No one else has any right to their cave. It faces seaward but cannot be seen from the shore. Only the boys and those who walk the beach at low tide know it is here. Even their brothers and sisters do not know. They move their treasures, including the two remaining muffins their mother baked, back into the cave above the high tide level.

Glug goes farther back into the cave to their secret hiding place, a shelf high up and to one side where they keep their flint and tinder. These words tell us that Glug and Griswold live in a world where matches and cigarette lighters and other sources of instant flame have not yet been invented. So that means it is a very long time ago. Boys themselves never seem to change whatever the year's date is. Probably Adam, the one who married Eve and who was never lucky enough to be a boy, is the only man who never squeezed mud between his toes, climbed trees until the top swayed with him to and fro, or swung from branches upside down while his pockets emptied themselves into the dead leaves. Boys are the same the world over and throughout time.

The tinder is easy. There is always plenty of suitable dry material left behind by a retreating tide. Once it is dry, it only needs a spark from a flint to be coaxed into a smoking glow and then a flame. As the boys add small twigs and Glug blows, the flame builds into a small fire. Griswold notices that suddenly, his hands are cold and his fingers need warming. More wood is piled on, and now a fire begins to blaze. The boys warm their hands. There is something about a fire that stirs a boy's blood.

Eerie shadows race up and down the black, damp walls of the cave. The water halts its rising, steadies, and struggles to hold its level. The tide is on the turn. The boys could paddle out to the beach if they wished. The water might be up to their waists, though, and it could be a bit tricky keeping their balance on the wet sand. They prefer to wait and enjoy their secret isolation and pretend they are pirates or explorers from Norway or Roman invaders shipwrecked in a storm.

The two boys lie on their backs with the soles of their feet towards the fire. Between their feet, they see the mouth of the cave. Beyond that, the quiet surface of the water throws flashes of reflected light towards them in response to the firelight. They eat their muffins slowly, trying to make them last as long as possible. One or two seagulls float on the water. Others swing in the distant sky.

Glug and Griswold know that their time for enjoying their cave is coming to an end. It's time for the two boys to start earning their own living. Dad, who works as a stable groom at the castle up on the cliff, has got them both jobs in the castle kitchen. They start in a day or so, and then all this—beach and cave—will be over. Mum will be glad to get them out from underfoot. Their father has managed jobs for all seventeen children. The boys and also the three girls will work in the castle in various jobs from chambermaid to furniture polisher to groom to kennel boy. The highest job goes to Axelgris, the second son, who is steward of the bedchamber. None of the children is yet married. Weddings cost too much for a poor family to afford.

Glug plans to work hard to keep his job in the kitchen and not get pushed out, like Dad, into the stables. He certainly doesn't want to eat straw! He knows that when he is at work there will be plenty of food to eat, and he intends to take full advantage of that. He is never going to be hungry again, but he's not going to be fat either. Lifting weights should turn what he eats into muscle. Glug tells Griz, "Once I start work, I want to become a bodybuilder and develop huge muscles. I mean *all over*, not just my arms. And I figure on doing height exercises as well to make myself taller. I want to be bigger even than Axelgris. I never knew why he got to be the biggest in the family. Maybe I'll join the weightlifters' club and aim for the top. Girls like muscles on a boy, and I'm going to have them. They'll be falling all over themselves just to be near me." He flexes his unimpressive biceps as he talks and imagines his empty hands are holding huge weights high in the air. They are the same weights Axelgris had previously tried to move from the floor and totally failed to budge. Glug staggers as he pretends to jerk and lift a barbell high above his head. He can even hear the king breaking into spontaneous applause at what has just been accomplished. It has never been done before—it's a world record!

Glug comes back to earth and remembers his brother. "What about you, Griz? What do you want to do?"

Griswold sits up. He is about to answer, but something on the edge of the water catches his eye. He climbs to his feet and walks over to the water lapping into the cave. He bends down and picks up something he sees floating. It is a small bottle, a broad-necked, green, glass bottle about as long as his thumb. Looking at it closely, he sees it is sealed with a cork. He wipes it carefully on his trousers and lifts it up so that it is silhouetted against the outside sky. Looking and looking again and yet again, he studies the contents of the bottle.

"Hey. Look at this, Glug. There's something inside, and it's moving. Wowee! It looks like a man, a tiny man! Careful!"

THE WEE MAN

Glug stuffs the last three bites of his muffin into his mouth at once, almost chokes, and jumps to his feet. He forgets his job of keeping the fire loaded with fuel. He skims with his eyes the waters in the cave in case another such bottle might be floating, but there is none to be seen. He takes the bottle that, upright and with great care, Griz hands to him. The glass of the bottle is only partially clear, and its contents are difficult to make out. He cleans it again on his brother's trousers, cautiously and slowly, and then lifts the bottle to eye level. The features of the little man within are hazy, but he appears to be bearded and dressed in a countryman's tunic. A tiny hand waves to him, pointing above his head.

"I can't believe it, Griz; I can't believe it. It's alive; I'm sure he's alive! Shall we let him out? I think he wants to get out."

Griz firmly recovers the bottle from his brother. If anyone lets the little man out of the bottle, he is going to be the one who does it. Besides, he wants to keep the bottle. He doesn't want it broken. He looks carefully down on the top of the bottle. It is not the shape or size of any bottle he has seen before in his part of the country. The glass looks thinner. The bottle is of finer quality than their own bottles. It is a wonder it has not been broken at sea or when the waves washed it onto the rocks and into the cave. Where has it come from? It looks as though a regular cork has been pushed down into the opening and then covered with wax. Perhaps it's ordinary candle wax to make it waterproof. The wax comes to the top of the bottle and is smoothed off, maybe by the wear of the sea.

The two boys sit down again. The tide is beginning to recede. Their sense of wonder and surprise is being replaced by practical considerations. First, the wax. Griswold picks up a splinter of seashell and works away. A little of the wax scrapes away with every stroke. Glug is jealous, and he wants a go. Griz warns him to be careful. They don't want to push the cork in on top of the little man. He hands the bottle over with reluctance.

While his brother works away at the wax, Griswold searches among the shells and pebbles on the cave floor. He looks ahead to the time when the wax is removed and wants to find a particular type and shape of shell. He has several at home in his collection. Soon, he spots one, a spindle shell. This is a long, brown, spiraling shell of small diameter. The first one he finds has a broken top, so he stays on his hands and knees, searching. There will be others for sure; and now he finds several of them, finely spiraled, unbroken, sharply pointed, long, and thin.

He looks up, anxious lest his brother spoil things by his clumsiness. "How're y' doin', Glug? Be very careful not to push. Just clean around the top of the cork. That's all, and then I'll get the cork out."

Glug is not anxious to hand the bottle back, but he too wants to see the cork lifted and discover whether they can talk to this little man who is now seated on the bottom of the bottle, waiting. He hands the bottle back to Griz. The boy is slow and painstaking. He knows that it is best when the corkscrew goes into the exact center of the cork. Using the thinnest of the spindle shells he has found, he takes his time and makes sure to place it right in the center of the cork. He turns it, being careful to push just hard enough to help the spiral cut into the cork. He is relieved that the plug does appear to be cork, and it is allowing the shell to penetrate. He holds his breath, and Glug, desperately wanting his chance to turn the shell, holds his breath as well. He hopes that Griz will remember he has a brother who shares things with him. Well, sometimes he shares things, so he deserves to have a turn too.

Griz asks his brother, "Glug, see if you can find a long strand of seaweed that we can lower into the bottle if we have to. We may need to give him a rope that he can climb up if turning the bottle on its side doesn't work."

The spindle shell is in as far as it is wise to screw. Any further turning might break the cork. He pulls on the shell without pressing sideways. He doesn't want it to break. A moment's hesitation, and then, as he feels the cork give, Griswold begins to smile. Success. The cork moves up the stem of the bottle neck and plops into the open air.

The fire burns steadily. More firewood has been added. The tide continues receding, and soon, the water will be back at the opening of the cave. Glug finds a tiny seaweed rope, but Griz wants to try and pull the wee man out first.

He sets the bottle on its side, level on the sand uncovered by the retreating tide. Both boys are leaning over, watching intently. They wish they could see better through the sides of the glass. They have no need to worry. The little man inside is quite capable of working out what he needs to do. He wastes no time and lies on his tummy with his hands above his head like a swimmer about to dive. With his toes, he is now edging his body forward. His hands are first into the neck of the bottle. He continues to inch ahead. His fingertips are getting closer to the bottle's rim as he pushes with his toes. At last there is enough of the little man's hands outside the bottle for Griswold to be able to give him a pull. He reminds himself he must be gentle because he could easily hurt the little creature. With his fingertips, he catches hold of the hands extending from the bottle.

WHAM! BANG! OOPS! DOINK! Griswold wonders, *What on earth has happened? WOWEE! The world's turned upside down! Where am I?*

Glug seems to have fallen backwards, and at the same time, with the speed of a runaway horse heading for the barn, looks like he is growing into a giant. His head is almost out of sight. His voice booms like a foghorn, "Griz, where are you?"

Griswold lets go of the hands of the little man as all kinds of things happen around him and to him. The fire has enlarged to a blazing inferno. The end of the bottle has a huge glass mouth with a pair of hands the size of his own sticking out from the center. The cave has suddenly become an immense cavern. The pebbles on the cave floor are suddenly boulders on which he awkwardly balances. The small ripples of water have become great, crashing waves.

Griswold realizes with horror there has been a disaster. Something has happened that could not possibly happen. He has *shrunk*. He has hardly summed up for himself what has happened, let alone how it has happened, when a voice from inside the bottle echoes out at him.

"Give us a pull, will ye?"

Griswold grabs the wrists protruding from the bottle and, moving backwards, pulls with all his might. While Griz is pulling, Glug is in shock and cowering against the wall of the cave as he watches one midget man being removed from a bottle by another midget, a midget who used to be his brother, Griz. He thinks, *I knew I should never have gotten up this morning. I wasn't through with my sleep.*

Out from the bottle emerge arms, then a head and shoulders, and then a chest and hips and legs. Finally, as Griswold falls backwards and the stranger falls in a heap on top of him, the bottle is empty.

"Wha's yur name?" the tiny, bearded man asks as he picks himself up, dusts off his tunic, smoothes his beard, and offers a hand of help. "I'm Munro."

Munro

Griswold has no idea whether he will ever be able to regain the size of his giant brother. He is also aware that when the tide is out a little farther, Glug is likely to tear across the beach and off home. If that happens, Griswold knows what will happen next. Glug will not want to be blamed for what has happened to his brother and will deny he ever went out with him. He is sure to tell his mother, "No. I've not seen him since breakfast, Mum. I've been down at the beach all day. Griz went off by himself to climb trees in the castle woods. He was after birds' eggs. I told him to come with me, but you know what he's like." Griswold can't worry about that just now. He has shrunk to the size of a mouse, a very small mouse, and maybe not even a mouse, a cockroach more like it! He has to take care of first things first. He has to be able to get back up to the size he had been.

He takes a long, searching look at the little man in front of him. The man is bareheaded and barefoot, stocky in build with long, untidy, red hair and a matching shaggy, red beard. His full, humorous face is brown and weather-beaten; and he has a twinkle of fun in his bright, blue eyes. He wears a plain, brown, leather tunic. His forearms and calves are strongly muscled. Griswold feels he can have confidence in this likeable little man. He seems not at all puzzled by either his surroundings or his present company.

Griswold says, "My name is Griswold but my friends call me Griz. I'm pleased to meet you and I look forward to a long friendship. But could you please help me sort something out before we talk further? I used to be the size of…" He points up at Glug, whose eyeballs are popping fit to play marbles. "And now I'm the size of…" He points to Munro, who seems untroubled by his own small size. "Is it possible that I can get back to where I was if, as seems likely, I will, later on, want to?"

"It will nae be any trouble at all, me lad," answers the little man, smoothing first his hair and then his beard once again. He speaks with a strong Scottish accent very different from Griswold's rolled Cornish, but he is completely understandable.

Pointing to the huge Glug, who looks as though he might burst into tears, Munro says, "Ye 'ave ta know this. That one's a Beyonder. Beyonders cun nae understand wee folk except with great difficulty, a' least nae while they stay tha' stupid size. Ye may be a Beyonder, but when ye becum me size ye cun understand me easily, aye, 'n' other creatures o' me size too. Tha's why ye cun understand wha' I'm saying ta ye now. I doubt 'e cun, e'en if 'e could 'ear me."

Munro seats himself on a pebble and motions to Griswold to do likewise. "Me own people know 'bout changin' size only cuz we 'ave already met Beyonders who wan'ta 'elp us. There be nae many o' them, but there be a few. I'm grateful fur yur 'elp. We cun change Beyonders into our size by 'oldin' thur 'ands. Tha's wha's jus' 'appened ta ye. Ye 'eld me 'and 'n'—*DOINK!*—ye 'ave becum me own wee size.

"Should ye wish ta go back ta yur Beyonder size, tha's easy too. Cross yur first two fingers like this," he demonstrates, "'n' then 'old me 'and. Th' 'ole thing goes in reverse. Cum 'ere. We cun try it now if ye like. No matter wha' ye do, ye cun nae get any smaller than ye are now or bigger than ye were afore ye shrank. We've run inta a magician who could change 'is size, e'en withou' our 'elp. That one's been a lot o' trouble to us; 'e's dangerous and 'e's very powerful cuz o' all 'e knows."

Griswold holds off for a while on accepting Munro's invitation to get back to size. He is intrigued by this whole shrinking and growing thing. It is something that definitely needs further investigation. He likes the news about the magician. It sets his thoughts churning. *Curious. Just imagine what I could do if I were a magician like that. Intriguing. He said magicians are powerful and dangerous. Good! That's just what I want to be.*

"Now that I'm your size," Griswold asks, relieved that there's a way back when he is ready to use it, "can I shrink my brother if I hold his hand?"

"Sure thing," says Munro. "Go ahead, 'ave a try! But ye will 'ave ta 'old on ta me 'and too. It will be nae good me askin' 'im; 'e probably won't understand a word I say."

"Glug! Can you hear me?" Griswold yells at the top of his voice. The giant boy is still cowering against the cave wall, staring at his tiny brother. He nods his head.

"Come over here and hold on to my hand! You can come on down too."

Glug is having none of it. He shakes his head vigorously from side to side. He has seen what has happened to his brother, and he'd rather lose his brother for good than have the same thing happen to him.

Griswold tries to encourage him, "Come on! It's alright. We can get big again afterwards. Come and meet Munro."

Glug showed interest in the little man when he first arrived, but he has now reached the limit of his interest. He thinks, *By no means am I going anywhere near either Griz or that little man until Griz is back to the size he was when we started out this morning. If I shrink too, it will take several days for us to get home. I imagine that once we get there and try to get heard banging on the front door, it is quite likely that one of our clumsy brothers will step on us while going for firewood. No. I'm staying where I am!"*

Glug watches the retreating edge of the water. The thought crosses his mind, *I could make a break for home and get some help, except… except no one will believe me. Whoever heard such a stupid story? No. I'd better just stay where I am and see what happens,* Glug decides. *But come what may, I'm going to be off for home when it begins to get dark.*

Griswold gives up on Glug, but he is reluctant to lose sight of his new friend, perhaps for good. Besides, Munro has some questions.

"Griswold, me lad, I'm pleased ta meetcha, too. Now, would ye please be atellin' me where exactly I 'appen ta be? I've cum frum Scotland 'n' 'ave been travelin' fur many, many years now tryin' ta get ta Spain. Fur Little People, time does nae matter much of anything, if at all. We live fur centuries, 'n' our seers cun foretell th' future. So I'd like ta know if this is Spain 'n' whether it's fourteen ninety-two yet. Cun ye tell me?"

"No, this isn't Spain, and it certainly isn't fourteen ninety-two yet. That's more than five hundred years away. This is Cornwall, and we are a long way away from Spain. People here don't really like the Spaniards, you know. Wild bulls chase them through the streets, and their fishing boats catch our pilchards and mackerel. I wouldn't go there if I were you. All you'll get to drink is olive oil."

Griswold's reply seems to persuade the little man he needs to catch the outgoing tide and be on his way. Munro asks Griswold, "Do ye 'ave a moment or so ta spare? I will need th' 'elp o' ye 'n' yur brother if ye do nae mind. I 'ave nae gone fur enough yet. I'll 'ave ta get back in the bottle ag'in, 'n' th' cork will need ta be sealed with wax ta make it completely waterproof. This is only a short stoppin' place fur me, 'n' I need ta be on me way withou' delay if I'm ta get ta Spain in time. I do nae want ta mess around 'n' arrive a day after th' ships 'ave sailed. If ye boys will please put me back in th' water—somewhere where th' tide will take me ta me destination—I'll be very grateful."

Griswold thinks to himself, *I'm not letting Munro go back into that bottle before I cross my first two fingers and hold his hands one more time.* He wants to be sure Munro's explanation for enlarging him back to his normal size is true. He yells to Glug, "Put more wood on the fire. We're going to need to melt some of the ambergris to seal the cork." Griswold wonders whether the little man gets hungry while he bobs up and down for centuries on the waves but doesn't ask. But he does have one last question for Munro. "Why don't you stay here with us? We could take care of you and bring you something to eat every day. My mum makes good pasties!"

Munro laughs at his new friend's concern for him. "Nae, lad. I need ta get goin'. I 'ave a dream, 'n' I'm on me way ta fulfill it. Our seers tell o' a land across th' ocean tha' one day will becum a powerful nation, 'n' I wan'ta be there when tha' happens. They will need someone wise 'n' discernin' ta 'elp make decisions. There's time yet fur me ta get there. Aye, well I know they are Beyonders, 'n' some o' them might be twice as tall as yur brother. But, well, one has ta start somewhere, 'n' I like a challenge ta be a challenge, something worthwhile. I'm pretty determined. While I am in me bottle, I keep sayin' ta meself, 'I can! I will!' Wha's a man withou' a challenge? I reckon th' most impossible task a man o' me size cun 'ave is ta becum a hockey coach fur some o' th' tallest 'n' most muscular Beyonders in th' world. But, truth be told, me lad, they will certainly need some good coachin', 'n' I reckon I'm th' man. I keep goin' over in me 'ead plans fur attack 'n' defense, but I 'ave nae been ta many games, so I'm 'ampered a bit by tha'. First, I need ta get ta Spain ta get a lift ta tha' foreign place, so I reckon I'd better be on me way agin.

"Are ye ready, Griswold? I'm pleased ta 'ave made yur acquaintance. Maybe we'll meet ag'in some day. Cross yur fingers now, 'n' 'old me 'ands." Griswold quickly obeys and—*DOINK*—he is relieved to be once again as tall as his baffled brother, relieved but also wondering why he feels a bit disappointed.

The two boys drop the resealed bottle carefully into the water at the point of the rocks and watch it swirl away, bobbing up and down in the receding tidewater. They watch until they can see it no more and then turn for home.

They walk home slowly across the beach. Griswold muses to himself, *What a day! It's been an absolutely brilliant day. It seems there may be untold possibilities for my future.* He and Glug agree that since no one will believe them, they will not tell anyone about Munro. Glug strangely appreciates his brother beside him, which is unusual. Griz is a nuisance more often than not, but there are a few times, like now, when Glug is glad even for a nuisance brother.

Griswold thinks about Munro's ambition to be a hockey coach when he is only half a thumb high. The casual mention of a powerful magician who can switch sizes to and fro by himself flicks again and again across his mind. He remembers the little man's words. They are like poetry that he will repeat word for word to himself a thousand times.

"You have to start somewhere, and I like a challenge to be a challenge, something worthwhile. I'm pretty determined. I keep saying to myself, 'I can! I will!' What's a man without a challenge? I reckon that the most impossible task a man of my size can have is to become a hockey coach for some of the tallest and most muscular Beyonders in the world, but I reckon I'm the man."

In his heart and soul, it seems that Griswold is finding a goal for his life. Inside his mind, everything is sorting itself out and falling into place. *Not a bodybuilder like Glug, I need to think big. Not a hockey coach like Munro either. I don't even like the game. Dad wanted me to play, but it's just a bunch of smelly bullies shoving each other around to keep anyone from making a goal. What sense is there in that?* He does not share his thoughts with his brother, but thinks to himself, *I am going to become a magician, the best there is. I'll be able to swing my size to and fro like a yo-yo. I'll be able to change from one thing to another, and then I'll go straight to the top. I'll replace the king. It'll be just too easy. I'll become the master of Trevose. Why stop there? More than that, master of Cornwall. Think bigger—even more and further than that: king of England! Why stop there? I'll be master of the world! That's what I'll be. I reckon I'm the man! How about that, Munro? Check that for size!*

GRISWOLD SETS

HIS GOALS

The kingdom of Trevose meets the sea on the north Cornish coast, about halfway up. High above the boys' beach and cave is a castle where the beloved old King Druthan rules with wisdom and justice. The castle of the great king is built on a cliff edge overlooking the Atlantic Ocean. Waves dash against the foot of the cliff at all stages of the tide. Spray reaches high into the air, catching rainbows.

The king is so old that he seems to have been on the throne forever. No one can remember, or has even heard tell of a time, when he wasn't there. Not even Mrs. Rodda, who is one hundred and twelve and no longer able to climb stairs or ride sidesaddle, can remember when he wasn't the king. He was there when her grandfather was a boy.

Much of the time when the king sits on his throne he appears to be dozing, but no one is fooled by this. He can be asleep twenty-three hours a day and still know more than anyone else. The king is famous for his wisdom and his great powers. There is nothing the king cannot do. If he snaps his fingers and says, "So be it," it is done. As far as the castle servants are concerned, Solomon, in all his wisdom would have had to sit in the corner wearing a dunce's cap if compared to King Druthan.

There has never been a king so wise, and there never will be again. He seems to know the answer to everything, and he has complete control over his kingdom—over everything except, perhaps, a boy helper in the kitchen.

That boy, Griswold, would never have won a prize in a baby show, even if he was wrapped in blankets up to the eyebrows and the lights were out. It was his looks that finally put his mother against boys. His features are odd. As a baby, he looked older than his years, shriveled and sly. He has large ears and a huge nose. His mouth matches his nose in size, but is fitted sideways. His small, brown, beady eyes beneath a large forehead dart to and fro constantly and are placed fully halfway down his head. His jet black hair is thick. His father cropped his boys' hair the way he groomed and trimmed the horses in the stable. Griswold, like his brothers before him, was hardly able to walk when he learned to cut his own hair, and his appearance then improved—at least the boy thought so.

As the final boy of fourteen brothers, Griswold bears the stigma of having to wear hand-me-downs from those thirteen bigger boys. He goes unnoticed among his crowd of siblings with his messy hair and tattered clothes. That is bitter medicine indeed for a youngster so gifted, so ambitious, so steeped in *envy*.

While he cleans pots and pans down in the kitchen, this growing boy dreams. *My ambitions are never going to be satisfied here in the kitchen. One day, I will be as powerful as the great King Druthan himself and even wiser. I'm going to live in a castle of my own, bigger than this one, and have even more servants and soldiers to do my bidding. I'll always have enough to eat and still discard leftovers from my plate for my brothers. I'll have a hundred differ-*

ent suits of clothes and fifty pairs of shoes, and I will have my own personal barber.

In the meantime, Griswold shares a room with his brother Glug high among the roof timbers of the castle. To encourage himself, on the door of his attic bedroom, he scrawls in red crayon, "I can! I will!" This is the first thing he sees as he sparks the flint to his tinder each morning and sets a flame to the wick of his candle. It is the last thing he sees at night before he blows out the light. The wind off the sea rattles the shutters, squeezes through the cracks, and tries to get under the blankets as Griswold curls up against his brother for warmth.

Griswold rises early, long before Glug, and he works hard. Amid the greasy dishes in the kitchen, Griswold hears all the gossip and remembers all he hears, scrubbing all the while. He knows that to succeed he must put in longer hours and work harder than anyone else. He will not yield to the tiredness he feels. He drives himself to the point of exhaustion and excels at his job. The plates and saucepans have never glistened so brightly. Even the pastry cook notices.

He learns also worldly wisdom, the wisdom of agreeing with his superiors. This pleases them, and they excuse any mistakes he might make. He learns to hide his inner feelings and to tell those above him what they like to hear. This brings promotion. He learns to disguise his inner anger and dislike. He watches and imitates the way those in charge behave. He says "Please" and "Thank you" at every opportunity. He accepts insults and criticisms with a smile, as though he absolutely agrees with everything being said. He praises to the other servants the actions of those above him in position and authority. Those words, he observes, carry upwards and sometimes bear fruit. He learns never to rock the boat by contrary opinions. He is available for any duty, twenty-four hours a day. If someone wants a willing worker, Griswold is there. Throughout the busy hours on his knees, scrubbing floors, he repeats to himself words no one else hears. *I can! I will! I can! I will!* If trying can help him succeed, he will rise to the top.

Slowly, as the months pass, his efforts are noticed and appreciated. He rises through the ranks of the lower court servants. He is dishmaster over the other dishwashers, and then all the kitchen equipment is placed under his charge. He leaves Glug behind at the vegetable bench, competing to peel the longest potato skin and find the most peas in a pod. Such childish exercises are not for him. He no longer prepares vegetables himself but supervises their preparation and cooking by others. He moves on to the meats and poultry and finally the pasties, pies, cakes, and other pastry.

King Druthan's favorite dessert is a trifle, cool and tasty to the tongue. He can never decide whether he likes the creamy custard or the fluffy sponge cake best. Griswold is great on trifles. He is inventive in the design and decoration of trifles never before heard or dreamed of. Although trifles are usually made with fruit, Griswold ventures further into the world of cooking. His seaweed and cabbage trifle, sweetened with honey and decorated with clotted cream and strawberries, is famous beyond the bounds of the kingdom. It is Griswold who first puts saffron into the rolls the king has for the royal tea time. The king has noticed him and knows his name. Then Griswold advances to assistant kitchen steward. He oversees the quantities used and exercises thrift. He becomes kitchen purchaser, checking the market purchases for price and quality and quantity. He carefully examines each bill so every penny is accounted for. He rises now above his brothers. Only Axelgris is above him.

In his spare time—there isn't much of it—Griswold reads. Few of his brothers and sisters can read, but Griswold is fluent. He is too poor to own books, but he borrows where he can and reads rapidly. He is prompt to return the books once he reads and memorizes the important matters within them. He trains and develops his memory, locking into his mind facts and figures. Later, he challenges his recall with questions to himself throughout his day. Reading and knowledge are steps to power, and he is going to get there, come what may. Although he is the youngest son, his parents and brothers and sisters come to him when they need help or information or a letter written.

Griswold delivers a bowl of parsnip trifle garnished with honey to the library. Book duster number four, a small, trusting soul heavily spotted with face pimples, having unkempt hair, a simple mind beneath it, large hands and a larger appetite, has unwisely accepted it. He is unaware that certain powerful herbs have been added. The effects are somewhat embarrassing, and the disgraced duster is demoted to underdishwasher. Shortly afterwards, Griswold is moved upstairs as book duster number four. He moves in higher circles. Using a feather duster, he spends all his spare time going around flicking all the books in every bookcase scattered throughout the castle halls and corridors. He reads the titles of all the books searching for a dictionary—the key to knowledge. Words are power. When he can discover the meanings of words, he will know everything, but he will have to remember what he has learned.

Griswold is frustrated when the only dictionaries he can find are in Chinese, Arabic, Greek, or Latin. Since he has not yet learned these languages, they are of no help to him. He determines to write his own and compiles an alphabetical list of words and their meanings in Cornish. He is before his time. The first English dictionary won't be written for another seven centuries. When it is, it borrows from Griswold's masterpiece without giving credit for the help it offers. It is obvious to every scholar that the very first word, *aardvark,* is a word borrowed from the Cornish, though few know it first appeared in Griswold's dictionary.

Above all, as his immediate goal, Griswold is bound and determined to gain access to the books on magic housed in the castle. There are many of them, but they are locked up because the court does not have a magician. His present aim is not to become court magician. That long-term goal will come later if he can persuade the king that one is needed. For now he wants to be the court librarian, and his foot is on the bottom step of that tall ladder.

All the time Griswold goes around dusting books and extending his list of words; he is memorizing and thinking. He nurses his dream. His day will come. He repeats to himself, *I can! I will! I can! I will!*

GRISWOLD

EXPERIMENTS

Winter is over for another year. Already, it is spring. The March winds blow strong off the sea. A year or so has passed since Griswold moved upstairs.

Griswold is now the chief librarian. Suddenly and mysteriously, his superiors in the line of library staff have dropped by the wayside, stricken by strange diseases that have made them incapable of work. Their disabling maladies have not come to the notice of King Druthan or his senior staff. No one has made the connection between the meals the library staff have recently shared with Griswold and the onset soon thereafter of various symptoms such as cramping pains, spots before the eyes, temporary blindness, toothache, earache, ringing in the ears, headache and bellyache, hair loss, facial spots, boils, rashes and pimples, housemaid's knee, and kitchen elbow, not to mention gout and locked knuckles, constantly blurred eyesight, and confused thinking.

Griswold keeps details of the effects of his potions and the size of his doses in a book he hides in a corner bookcase on the second shelf behind other books. He is anxious not to overdose. Just enough to gain the effect he needs is what he uses.

This has all been achieved without the use of magic, a skill that still lies ahead for the ambitious young man. Griswold is biding his time. He is preparing the foundations well. His main present interest and weapon is botany and the use of plants in medicine and otherwise. He needs to know their various mysterious qualities, even qualities not yet discovered by others. He usually experiments on animals but occasionally, when necessary, on Glug. He does not tell his brother that he is playing a key role in the advancement of science. Glug is often quite unwell and experiences very strange symptoms that he cannot understand, such as walking on his hands or mooing like a cow. He appreciates his brother's care and concern without suspecting that Griswold is the cause for his sickness.

The potions are derived from plants gathered from the fields and hedgerows and from the edges of the sea. The Cornish lanes are profuse with flowers that are seldom found elsewhere. Griswold can identify and use over two hundred wildflowers and plants. The most rare and most useful he recommends to the head gardener of the castle as herbs for the kitchen. Once they mature, Griswold helps himself. From the stems and leaves and roots, as well as from the flowers, he extracts everything they have to yield. Some plants are poisonous, but Griswold is careful to apply only small enough doses that will disarm, disable, and cause discomfort rather than upset the routine of the castle. Multiple funerals would possibly attract the attention of the king, who would most likely be suspicious and take steps to discover the cause.

The king does not approve of magic. The schools of magic that operate along the north coast from Towan Blystra to Tintagel are doing so without royal permission and contrary to the rules and laws of the land. In order to oppose these illegal activities, the king has collected all the known wisdom on record about magic and its practice. There is in no other place a greater array of knowledge about magic than in the library at King Druthan's castle. These books are, by his royal order, kept locked up in a reference cupboard to which, as chief librarian, Griswold alone now has the key. This is a position of great trust. He is answerable to the king for their safekeeping.

Griswold reads almost continuously. Even so, it will take years of reading. He stays after work until the light has at last faded in the sky, reading and remembering by rehearsing in his mind what he has read. It won't be any good just reading without remembering. He is going to be a self-taught magician, drawing from all the wisdom in the library. Nothing is going to miss his eye or slip from his mind. He allows no one else access to the books except by the king's direct order, and even then he does so reluctantly. He is not eager to share access to knowledge that he feels is intended for him alone.

He has become aware of other ingredients of spells and potions apart from plants and has been gathering a stock of supplies for the future. He has collected birds' nests, the egg-shells of wild birds, varieties of seaweed, snail shells, horse hair, cat and dog fur, sheep and lambs' wool caught on thorns and brambles, cats' whiskers and cats' claws, mouse and rat tails, frog and toad spawn, and the castoff tails of newts. He must be sure that he has every advantage for progressing towards his goal of ultimate influence and power. He does not intend to be short of anything that will be needed if he can help it. As he acquires fresh items, he crosses them off his checklist, but always there are others to add as his knowledge of magic grows.

He has healed the mysterious face spots and falling hair of the daughter of the castle jailer with a mix of marsh marigold petals, lesser spearwort leaves, and poppy seeds steeped in saffron juice. His reward has been the use of an unused corner dungeon cell as storage. It is steadily filling up, and it may soon be necessary to inflict the little girl with corns and bunions to acquire yet another empty cell.

Griswold has awakened to the fact that he needs an assistant—not an assistant librarian but an assistant magician or, at the least, a magician's helper. But this raises the question of who he can trust. Certainly not his brothers or sisters. He decides that he can trust no one, but he does need an assistant.

Much magic requires a second person, someone in another place or even alongside, helping things to work out to their desired end, someone he can send on errands instead of doing everything himself. Before he can rise to the top, he will have to find someone. It will need to be someone he can rely on completely, through thick and thin. He could marry, although he doubts if there is a woman smart enough. And the thought of possibly having eighteen children resembling his brothers and sisters to bring up as a result is not attractive. There must be a better solution. He will look around for an alert, capable animal, some subhuman that will be completely loyal to him and capable of being trained. It will need to be a young, intelligent creature of strong character that will follow orders well.

This thought fits in well with Griswold's present attempt to acquire new skills. He realizes that if he wishes to progress, the ability to understand and talk to creatures other than people is essential. He begins with cats and dogs. Some of them already understand human conversation. He needs to learn to also understand them when they meow or bark. With determination, he steadily makes progress by using the castle animals, including the kitchen cat, for practice. Sadly, though, none of them is "personal assistant" material, added to which they already belong to someone else, so their loyalties would be questionable. He will need from his selected assistant unswerving personal loyalty to himself.

Griswold finds that a drink of marsh lousewort tea improves his understanding of animal language, although it tends to make him giddy. He finds he needs to hold on to the back of a chair as he continues a conversation. Sometimes he hiccups, but the hiccups are in the pursuit of knowledge and worthwhile.

Once he has mastered dogs and cats, talking with other animals becomes easier. He considers and rejects for his job vacancy a rat, a mouse, a ferret, and a bat. He seriously considers a viper but decides that snakes are insufficiently intelligent. If they were smart, they would have grown legs by now. He practices constantly at his language study; and all the time, his knowledge of animals and the way they think grows. The animals, not as crafty and deceitful as Griswold, openly share the secrets they have learned. He gets information of what goes on in the king's councils behind locked doors. He is aware of matters even the chief counselor does not know.

It is time now to work harder at mastering the next step: bird talk. Already, only the king himself is better than he at communicating with animals. Griswold starts on ravens, the most available species other than seagulls, which stink of fish and cannot be considered.

There are many ravens along the north Cornish coast, where they love to soar and glide as the rising winds off the sea hit the cliffs. The castle ravens are cocks of the castle roost. There are more than a dozen of them, each of them numbered and named. Noisy and bossy, the ravens are protected and fed by order of the king. No one is allowed to harm them. Griswold has known the family of ravens since he started at the castle. The castle servants also know them. He selects one of the plump female ravens and tries to strike up a conversation. She is not talkative. He holds out a worm. She is interested and hops nearer. He asks, "Would you like another one?" He has a pocket full of worms and tries to avoid squashing them as he removes them for the greedy creature. The bird pays no attention to where Griswold is leading her as they walk and talk. He has more food in his room. It is Glug's day off, and he has gone down to the village beach to bounce stones on the water at high tide.

Using a towel, Griswold fashions a sitting place for the bird inside the bedroom. As she picks at a bowl of hazelnuts, he asks, "How are things going for you?" The raven tells him in very basic caws, "I'll be glad when my eggs are laid and hatched. They are due any time. I really don't enjoy the time I have to sit around waiting. My nest is on a cliff ledge below the castle, and it won't be any fun in these winds. A girl gets cold sitting around doing nothing. Feeding the little brats once they hatch is no fun either. After six weeks of the greedy monsters, all my motherly love has gone, and I can't wait to throw them out of the nest."

Griswold wastes no more time. He pours some of the lousewort tea for the raven and takes a big swig himself to increase his fluency and understanding. He hiccups. He tells the raven, "I sympathize with your problems. I'd like to be helpful. I have a deal to propose that would benefit us both. I have a ledge just inside the attic window that I can make very comfortable, a mansion among ravens' nests. If you are willing to teach me your language to fifth-year level in a crash course of study, I will undertake to feed you and your brood until the fledglings are ready to fly."

The raven is interested. "What kind of food are you thinking of?"

Griswold is full of ideas, which he shares. "First off, the room has mice; and I will scatter crumbs on the floor to draw them out. There will be leftover food and raw eggs from the kitchen: snails, worms, hazelnuts, and wheat and barley grains. You will find me as devoted a father as any male raven and far more reliable. All my life, I have loved baby ravens above all other birds. My word is my bond." It isn't of course. He will break a promise without hesitation. The bird isn't really listening. She wonders, *Did I eat too many hazelnuts? I'm feeling quite uncomfortable. My tummy is rumbling something fierce. I don't think I'm going to make it back to my nest on the cliff before the first egg arrives.* She decides to move in. *The man is a fool. I'm on to a good thing,* she thinks.

RASPUTIN

The clutch of fledgling ravens has been large. Six eggs have been laid in the nest on the sill. The distinctive, greenish blue shells dotted with brown spots are almost as hard as ostrich shells. The one that rolled off the window sill onto the floor just bounced and rolled under Glug's bed, giving its female contents a permanent headache that lasted from the date she broke into the fresh air until she died of old age.

Baby ravens need beaks designed like jack hammers to break out of the shell that confines them. From the moment they see the light of day, they are on the attack. With this particular batch, even half the number would have taxed the energies of two able-bodied and busy parents to keep them fed. It is clear the word *ravenous* derives from the appetite and behavior of raven fledglings. The six birds have such huge appetites that they might have been vultures dressed in black fuzz. But they are merely the largest members of the crow family and are all mouth all of the time. Beak and body are merely boundaries to gaping, gulping, pink holes that never close—yelling constantly that death from starvation is approaching faster than a runaway train.

Six mouths clamor for survival, determined to be the first to snatch whatever approaches. Once or twice, Griswold has narrowly wrested a finger free before it has been mistaken for offered food and swallowed. He now uses a long, thin stick as a tool for transferring food. He wants to keep all of his fingers for the days to come. Griswold never imagined the demands that six fledgling ravens would make upon him. He wishes now that he had been more careful in making the contract for language study. Feeding them is almost a full-time job, and he also has his job as librarian to do.

The largest bird and the first out of his shell uses his size to grab advantage over the others. Who cares whether his brothers or sisters survive? He doesn't. All the more for him. He is also helped by the preference that Griswold shows to him. He gets the longest and fattest worms. He gets the greasy bits of fat and gristle from the kitchen scraps that build muscles while the others get the fried bread and parsnips that never did anyone any good.

Griswold has had his eyes fixed on the eldest raven from the start. He likes the streak of ruthlessness as well as the little bird's determination to have his own way, even when he can't yet fly. One might say he is a bird after his own heart. An assistant is at last on the horizon, even nearer, on his windowsill. Griswold decides that Rasputin will be a good name for his assistant.

Glug also brings scraps from the kitchen every time he returns to the room, but he is not allowed to feed Rasputin. Only Griswold does that. The librarian is building loyalty. Rasputin knows that he is nothing special to his mother. She shares with his siblings what Rasputin feels is rightfully his. Without question, the aggressive little bird knows he should have the right of first choice. He is, after all, the firstborn and senior fledgling.

Rasputin develops associations. He can work out what is good for him. Griswold alone is his true parent and provider. The man might not be a raven in appearance, but for sure his heart is comfortably black inside—a real raven at heart, even if he doesn't have feathers, wings, and a tail. Who would not wish to have a father like Griswold? He is a role model to the next generation. Rasputin grows to love this odd-looking, intense, little man who thinks of a helpless bird's welfare and the rights of the firstborn even before his own needs. Why, they would make a good team once he is grown and flying and able to contribute his share to the common good.

Griswold's fluency in the language of ravens, crows, jackdaws, and rooks grows. He can even make himself understood, although not as well as he wishes he could, to magpies. He lets the library more or less run itself under his team of hand-picked staff which, to please his father and make things easier at home, includes two of his brothers and his crippled sister. When he isn't catering for the fledglings, he reads through all the books on magic he can find—one right after the other. As he reads, he memorizes everything word for word. When he recites spells over and over, he is doing memory exercises. He spends time listening and talking to the ravens in the castle, trying to pick up slang words and different ways the birds have of saying things. He proves an excellent student and, by the end of the fledglings' flight training, should easily be through grade five of fluency.

Time passes, and the birds are growing away. The fuzz begins to transform itself into feathers. Rasputin's mother has never had it so good. She fancies herself as an excellent teacher and thinks she would look well with glasses. Griswold was fortunate to choose the only raven in the flock with high teaching ability and broad understanding of language and grammar. She would rather talk and teach than train her babies, and she takes off for her flights around the castle only for exercise and a change of scenery rather than foraging for food. The other ravens are envious. She knows that the easy life cannot continue indefinitely, but she delays the first shove of her children out of the nest and out of the window as long as possible.

In fact, she does not have to shove. The kitchen cat sees to that.

Griswold is at work in the library. Glug has climbed back upstairs to the room with his midmorning snack for the birds culled from the leavings on the breakfast plates. Without thinking, he has chosen as the bowl to carry the scraps in the same bowl that the kitchen cat considers to be her very own, specially selected food bowl. Initially, she is not alarmed. She observes lazily from her position on the kitchen hearth her least-favorite servant filling her bowl. He has not done this for ages. *Well*, she thinks, *Good-oh. He obviously doesn't know I have already had my meal. He thinks I haven't been fed yet!* She watches with approval the addition of various greasy bits of rind, sausage, potato, and egg that make up bubble and squeak. She runs her tongue around her lips.

To her surprise, even anger, Glug takes *her* bowl, brimful of goodies, and departs from the kitchen towards the servants' quarters. *What does he think he is doing? This is intolerable! He has already eaten with the other servants. He eats twice as much as any of the others, so he can't possibly be that hungry. I wonder if he has a cat or some other creature that he's feeding. He better not have! That is just not on. Well, if he wants a fight to the death, so be it! No dirty, lazy, scrounging pet is going to invade my territory and eat out of my bowl.*

She is in attack mode as she slinks along on soft paws, unobserved, behind the poor, clueless servant. As he climbs the stairs and unlatches the door to his room, the cat is close behind him. She is through into the room before he can turn to close the door. She has seen enough. The windowsill is filled with ravens. She understands all. There is a natural animosity between ravens and cats. She is but a pace into the room when she launches herself in a tremendous leap towards the window. The fight is on.

THE TALE OF THE CAT

The cat is not high bred. She is neither Siamese, nor Manx, nor Persian, nor Calico, nor Tabby, nor yet a Cheshire. She is not anything a cat fancier would notice, not even with a free ticket to a cat show. No one would buy her even if she was being given away free with a bowl of goldfish. She is a vicious-looking, dirty grey alley cat accustomed to living by her wits. She has been brought up without table manners and bred to the law of the jungle. One of her ears is torn, and she has claw scars across her forehead. She is a fighter from the tip of her nose to the tip of her tail. No other cat dares to venture into the kitchen. The moment she sees those birds in the window, she sees red. All reason goes out of the window. She knows only one thing: ATTACK!

She has never liked ravens. The law of the jungle says, "To each her own," and, "Defend your territory to the death!" It is unfair that within the castle precincts, these drab, black birds, with nothing in their favor except that they can fly, are protected by King Druthan's decree. Kings should not play favorites. There have been many times when, lying motionless and unnoticed on some branch or wall, she has paid attention to the rules of the castle and had mercy on ravens nearby, even small ones. Had they been any other kind of bird, they would have vanished in a flurry of scattered feathers. No longer is she going to have patience or obey the rules.

The attic window is, as usual, wide open. Wide eaves above prevent most rain from blowing in. All seven birds, the six fledglings and Mama, are on the sill, waiting for their meal. Glug does not reach them. The squawk of the mother is hardly needed to alert her young. A glimpse of an airborne, dirty grey blur approaching them is enough. Mama throws herself backwards out of the window without bothering to turn.

Five of her flightless young, with unused wing and tail feathers, throw themselves after her, trying to sort out what to do as they fall. The mother forgets all her other concerns and tries to catch the ones nearest the ground before they crash. The upwards draft of the wind from off the sea is helping, together with the height from the attic to the ground. She caws frantic instructions: "Flap, child! Flap! That's it. Harder! Flap for your life!"

Instead of training her fledglings one by one, as she expected, this is a class of five fighting for their lives at one time. They try to find air solid enough to support their weight. For the smallest of them, it is a close-run thing. Only his mother beneath him saves him from collision with the ground. She pushes aloft again with a passenger on her back, yelling orders to the others. All around her is a flurry of falling and twisting fledglings. Other ravens rally to her cries and come to help where they can. They don't know what has caused this sudden exodus from the attic window; but they are all one family, and this is an emergency where explanations can wait. They swoop below the nestlings, between them and the ground. Although the little birds are tiring and are wobbly and unsure, they begin to get the hang of flying. They look for some safe place where, without knocking themselves to bits, they may land and rest. Matters are sorting themselves out.

Back inside the room, it is a far different matter. Rasputin has jumped down onto the table from the sill as soon as the door latch is lifted. He sees Glug enter with the bowl of food. Before the kitchen helper can place it on the table and get the serving skewer, there is chaos. An enemy flings herself into the air. Rasputin has never seen the creature up close, but he has seen her parading in the yard below on occasion. His mother has warned her children of the treachery and evil intent of the kitchen cat. Rasputin, forgetting he has never flown, launches himself towards the enemy like an aerial torpedo. His motives are unclear. It could be he is trying to help his siblings or his mother, but they are already beyond the cat's frantic snatch. It could be he is following his instincts and defending himself as well as he is able by attacking. It is more likely he is defending his dinner. He is hungry. My, is he hungry!

His black beak, designed like a spear point, catches the cat just above the tailbone and cuts a path along the fur towards the right ear. The cat lets out a scream that echoes down to the kitchen itself. Her front paws barely reach the sill before they are caught by the rear paws following rapidly behind them. At the same moment, the back of the cat curls into a spring and straightens in a flash, propelling the cat upwards. At the top of her orbit, she feels the titchy raven coming in clumsily for a second attack. Rasputin's tiny claws catch the torn ear of the cat who is wondering how to get outta there quick. She doesn't like the window option. There would be a long way to fly, and the enemy is better equipped for aerial combat than she is.

Glug, more quick-witted than usual, flings the door open, but in the process is caught off balance by the fleeing cat. Glug falls to the floor. As he does so, his foot slides forward and catches the cat on the side of her head, giving her a terrible thump. The cat gets a double thump as the other side of her head hits the leg of Glug's bed. There is a moment when the cat, half stunned, is stationary.

Rasputin, although young and not fully formed as a fighting machine, is not going to allow chances for advantage over an enemy to slip away. From the edge of the table, he launches himself forward with barely enough room or time for more than one flap of his wings. His powerful beak, closed tight to a point, pierces the cat's ear, the right ear, which has previously suffered no damage in combat. For a moment, the two adversaries are locked together. Rasputin is suddenly left behind as the cat takes off through the door and down the stairs, four steps at a time, screeching like a banshee all the while. The boy raven returns the screams from deep within himself, cawing threats to anyone who tries to steal his meal.

Rasputin begins to get the hang of this flying thing now and moves his wings more efficiently. He focuses on catching the cat and, once again, running his beak along her back from rear to front. He has enjoyed the feeling of the first attack and would like to taste it again. It is like the taste of blood to a lion cub that has gone out for the first time into the jungle hunting with his mother. All sorts of stored-up instincts are released. In order to catch the cat, Rasputin will have to move faster than the cat. Fat chance. He flaps his wings wildly, but there is little hope of catching up. However, the thrill of the chase grips him.

The cat moves as though she is pursued by a dozen hounds, all intent on her blood and all accomplished sprinters in the bargain. But Rasputin is the only one after her. He is learning, by tilting and twisting his wing and tail feathers, to steer and to rise and fall while in rapid forward motion. Rarely can a raven have had such a speedy introduction to the art of flight upon

which his future life will depend, especially all indoors and not
in the open air, where such skills are usually developed. It is like
a toddler rising for the first time from the crawl position, putting one foot in front of the other and then covering one hundred yards in ten seconds flat before pausing for breath.

Flying unsteadily, but not being a bit cautious, Rasputin
banks sharply around corners as he chases the cat down the
stairs. He does not forget to caw loudly. He cries the battle song
of the ravens that his mother has used as a lullaby to her children when they were restless. This is full of clashing discordant
caws that terrify the cat ahead. She is not yet traveling at the
speed of sound, so she can hear what is happening behind her as
she reaches the ground floor and races wildly down the hallway.

The cat misses the turn down to the kitchen but doesn't
pause for a stride. She heads for the upper rooms, hoping to
find a cupboard in which to hide. She is, at this point, even
willing to risk attempted flight through an open window, but
all the windows are closed. Fortunately, the library door is open,
and there is Griswold, standing in front of the tall bookcases.
He has opened the glazed door to withdraw the next volume
he needs in the series he is studying. The book is in his hand
when, bursting past him and knocking the book sideways, a
frenzied cat in a panic launches itself into the space vacated by
the book. It is, fortunately for the cat, a thick book. A narrower
book could have meant problems. The desperate creature, her
head and body disappearing into darkness, is suddenly brought
up short by the back of the bookcase. With a brilliant flash of
thinking, she hooks her tail around the door and pulls it shut on
herself to exclude the pursuing raven. Unfortunately, the door

swings shut tightly, trapping the tip of her tail, and leaving it exposed to attack.

Rasputin, imagining nutcrackers clamping tightly upon a walnut, takes only one bite before his friend and ally, the chief librarian, takes him onto his wrist. Griswold is stroking the bird's head to calm him down and stop that awful cawing. He congratulates Rasputin on mastering the art of flight and asks, "What are you doing out of the nest so early in the morning?" He also thinks to himself, *At last I have found the assistant I will need, one who has proven himself battle worthy at the very first test.*

GRISWOLD,

MASTER OF MAGIC

In the world of King Druthan, time has little significance. Days and hours are useful to count by, but not really important. There is little to disturb the steady passage of hours. Many months have passed since the kitchen cat learned her lesson never to tangle with ravens. The scars of her encounter remain. They run deeper than just her wonky tail. Winters and summers have come and gone, but she still refuses to go outside except after dusk and never up to the attic.

Rasputin's brothers and sisters have long since left home, courted, married, and produced generations of other ravens. Rasputin himself has never moved. He has grown up but has stayed close to Griswold. In a strange way, the two creatures—the ugly, little man and the tough, black bird—are fond of each other. They are not always polite to each other, but they know that they are going to journey together to the end—wherever that end may be. Both are selfish, yet they know that their selfishness must be inclusive of the other if they are to prosper. And while Rasputin is not ambitious, Griswold retains his intense determination to get to the top. It is this difference that makes possible the harmony between the odd pair.

Rasputin is content to be alongside Griswold as helper and

assistant. He is not personally interested in what magic can make possible. Leave those dreams to his boss. The librarian has agreed not to practice on Rasputin, although in his heart he knows he might do so—but only if it were necessary in an emergency, and he wouldn't tell the bird. Rasputin tends to agree with Griswold's suggestions, whatever they are, and does his best to make them come true. He feels that they are a two-man expedition with the librarian as the general and himself as the full total of troops under his command. The two of them make a formidable army.

Griswold has progressed in his studies of magic until now he is well into the practicing of it. The years of intense study are over. The books have been read and their lessons learned and memorized. He has little need to read more. When he reads, it is merely a refresher. Griswold considers that he is working on the leading edge of discovered magic. Most of what he does not know has not yet been discovered. Still, there is much yet to learn, even though no one is ahead of him. He now believes he is even ahead of the king in both the knowledge and practice of magic.

He has had a few narrow escapes when he changed himself into something else and for a while was unable to change himself back. That was scary. Fortunately, no matter what form or shape he takes, his memory and intelligence remain intact. His ingenuity has been tested in the past and has saved him more than once as he has had to improvise his return back to his original appearance in stages.

He can now transform himself into a wide range of living creatures. He does this, without potions or brews, by uttering one or two special key words followed by, for instance, the word *spider*. The first time he did this and used the word *spider*, he took more than an hour to change, probably because he had neglected to include the word for the shrinkage factor. He ended up hairy and red-spotted and multi-legged on his bed, a full two yards across. Rasputin hopped high on the back cupboard, hoping he would not be taken as a fly. They had both had to push against the door to prevent Glug getting in when he came up from the kitchen unexpectedly. It would have been difficult for Glug to understand what was going on. He might well have passed the news on to his friends in the kitchen, and that tidbit would have gone up the chain of gossip to King Druthan himself.

Once the ability to change his appearance has been mastered, Griswold concentrates on speeding up the process. Hours are reduced to minutes and minutes to seconds and seconds reduced to whatever is shorter than seconds until a transformation is almost instantaneous. Quicker than you can say, "I'm hungry," Griswold can change into a mouse or a bat or a raven or a frog. He has even, while in the woods alone, done a small pony, which took a little longer than usual. He has not, up to the present, tried an elephant, and probably won't. After all, there is no place to appear as an elephant. Certainly not in the attic, and there are no menageries nearby.

Quicker than you can say, "More! More!" he can change himself back again, and no one knows that Griswold has ever been absent. He practices over and over again. He can apply the shrinkage factor to himself and be as small as half a thumb high without changing into another creature. Then he can make himself big again. So far, he hasn't discovered how to make himself bigger than he starts out. None of his attempts have been successful, although he has tried very hard. Perhaps it is just not possible. Munro had said that it couldn't be done and he must be right. Otherwise, the world would soon be run by a race of giant magicians pushing everybody around. There has to be a limit somewhere, and perhaps Griswold has reached it.

Another barrier for Griswold is that he has not yet succeeded in making himself invisible. This could be very useful, but there are still some details to work out, both in becoming unseen and then in being sure he can return to visibility. It would be difficult to rule the world with an iron hand if one could not be seen. Meanwhile, he can achieve almost the same result by turning himself into something very small. He is nervous about being too small though. People are clumsy and don't look where they are going or care what they step on. In a quiet part of the library, when he was alone, he changed himself into a beetle and then quickly changed himself back again. That was just to see if he could do it if necessary and he succeeded.

He is also only partially successful in moving himself in an instant from place to place. Sometimes he succeeds, but more often than not, it doesn't work, and he has wasted valuable time. When the distance is short, it seems to work better to change himself into a bird and fly. The swallow is his favorite speed bird. It has few enemies and doesn't attract a lot of attention.

Griswold continues to work at this problem of moving himself. He usually tries it when he is in bed beside Glug, who is snoring away and clutching more than his share of the blankets. Even if he is successful, he needs to get back before dawn because Glug will see his brother's clothes hanging at the foot of the bed and wonder why he is missing. He is sure to panic, either because he thinks his brother has jumped out of the window, or he will begin to put two and two together, which would be even worse.

Although Griswold is successful in changing himself into something else, he isn't as good at changing other creatures. He doesn't work on people lest he encounters resistance, which will mess up his magic. And there is a fear their absence or change of appearance will be noticed. He prefers to work on four-legged creatures or insects or birds—at least for starters—until his technique is perfected. Occasionally, something does work, and a mouse will change into a lizard; but it is unusual when this happens. Unfortunately, they don't usually stay around long enough to be changed back. The number of transformed creatures wandering around the castle in a daze, not understanding what has happened to them, continues to increase.

Another of his experiments that pleases Griswold immensely is the cherry tree in the herb garden. Griswold's favorite fruit is the cherry, lots and lots of them, juicy, white and red and purple bunches. There is no better fruit when they are ripe and sweet. Everybody knows it is extremely difficult to harvest cherries from any tree because the birds get there first. How do you ensure the cherries get into the hands of those they are intended for? Griswold is close to success. The cherries are not yet fully ready, but they are ripening fast. The tree is loaded. More and more birds are attacking as the clusters of fruit develop. Blackbirds, magpies, crows, ravens, and thrushes are all trying to snatch the fruit, but totally without success. The tree repels them. The marauders fly in with outstretched claws, beaks open to gulp, wings in the half-folded position and—*CRASH!*—they tumble down the outside of an unseen something before they ever touch a twig or taste a cherry.

The librarian has achieved a first. He has created an impenetrable bubble that no one can see. It completely envelops the tree. By patient testing and improving, it is now completely invisible and almost indestructible.

In the earliest model, it was possible, if someone was really determined, to kick a hole through the bubble or cut it with scissors. Not now. The material, invisible to the eye, has become tougher and tougher. Even a blue heron bounced off. When it tried a head-on attack with its beak as a spear, it almost stabbed itself in the throat. Griswold plans, one moonlit night when birds are roosting and no one is awake, to carry a sack down with him to the garden, open by a spell a slit into the bubble curtain, slip inside and pick away to his heart's content. He will, of course, share with Glug and Rasputin, but few others are going to benefit from his ingenuity. The kitchen servants are all waiting with hungry lips for the cherries to turn ripe. They do not know that one night before they get there, the fruit will all disappear.

Griswold sees a great use for his bubble, which is not even hinted at in any of the books of magic. This is *his* brilliant discovery and his alone. He has not shared his most secret thoughts about the use of the bubble with anyone, not even Rasputin. Just suppose, for instance, that King Druthan were to awaken one morning inside a bubble. That would rather cramp the king's style. The bubble could be soundproof. He might be seen, but he couldn't give orders except by writing them down. Then if there were to be a small rebel assault force—led by himself, of course—how could the king handle that?

Griswold supposes he could do the whole thing, from bubble to surrender, in one night. He would have to get into the king's bedchamber of course, but that should be no problem. The king trusts him, so he wouldn't even have to change himself into anything small. He could just walk in boldly. After encasing the king in the bubble, he would summon the rebels he had gathered and take over the castle. One of them would hoist the new flag; that would please his troops. He has decided it will be all black (his favorite color), the color of a raven. The castle staff will be assembled, and he will declare, "The king is no longer king. *Long live King Griswold!*" Just to impress them, he will perform one or two feats of magic. He might even go on to terrify the populace; that should keep them under control. Maybe he'll turn the lord chamberlain into a chicken, plucked and ready for roasting. He chuckles to himself at the thought. He can almost hear in his mind the screams of terror, the shouts of awe and amazement. Slowly, there is a gathering swell of noise.

Long live the king!
Long live the king!
Long live the king!
Long live King Griswold!

There is only one thing that begins to concern the librarian and cast a shadow over the rosy pictures his mind creates. He has a persistent infection in his right eye that none of his potions or spells are able to cure. It is getting worse rather than better.

THE TWITCHY EYE

When his eye had first become infected, Griswold had no idea that it was more than a minor problem. It should have cleared itself up with an eye salve derived from the usual ground-up buttercup petals and bee saliva. It didn't. Steadily, he works through the complete range of remedies, even trying as a last resort the one for ingrown toenails and athlete's foot. Nothing works, absolutely nothing. If anything, the problem just gets worse.

In addition to the infection, Griswold has also developed an annoying twitch of the right eyelid. His left eye is perfectly okay—no trouble there. It is just his right eye. His vision does not appear to be affected. He can see as clearly as ever. But about every two or three seconds—occasionally the time is a little longer—his right eyelid twitches. Sometimes, the upper lid will start it; sometimes the lower lid. When the twitch is at its worst, it even affects the right corner of his mouth, which lifts as the eyelid twitches. He looks as though he is perpetually winking.

He tries controlling the twitch by will power, but that is like trying to control blinking when you are trying not to blink. You can only not blink for so long before you blink again, even though you don't want to. Even raising a finger needs a thought to a nerve to set the finger in motion. Without that thought, the finger doesn't move. Blinking and twitching, on the other hand, seem to work on their own without requiring an order from the mind. Griswold wonders whether he twitches even while he sleeps. He can't find out for himself, although he tries. Rasputin, who watches carefully, reports that Griswold does indeed twitch while sleeping.

There is little doubt about what has caused the problem. He has the magician's twitch. In his heart, Griswold knows that most likely he has an incurable ailment. It is going to severely hamper his plans for the future if he cannot find a cure. There is no value in changing his appearance if his twitch gives him away to every enemy pursuer. Even disguised as a dog or a cat, even as a mouse or a snail, or even as small as a spider or a beetle, his twitching eye is a dead giveaway to those in the know about twitching. He can see the messages being spread by his future enemies. As Griswold's armies gather for battle, the word goes out. "Watch out for his twitchy eye. Don't worry what kind of a creature it is. If the eye is twitching, it'll be Griswold the magician for sure. No one else has a twitchy eye such as Griswold has. It's him for sure. Stamp on him. Jump on him. Sock him in the eye. Go get him. Bring him in chains."

The books he has read have warned against it. Everyone who uses magic gets a twitch somewhere. It goes with the trade. When you venture into magic, you *will* end up with a twitch. It is as though when you start the alphabet with an A, for sure, the B will follow. Very often, it will be a mild twitch like a finger, or in a place covered up where it is unseen. Sometimes, only a single hair twitches. But an eye! There can't be a more obvious place! It is a disaster. There is no one from whom to seek advice. King Druthan probably knows the remedy, if one exists, but he's the last one to think of asking.

Griswold goes back into the books of magic. There are plenty of warnings that it will happen to every magician in some form or other. Frustrated, Griswold finds that none of the books offers a remedy or even suggests there might possibly be a remedy.

No remedy yet, true, but there is a hint—just a hint and no more—in one of the oldest and thickest volumes. It is the last of all the books that Griswold has been working frantically through, looking for answers. Because it is the biggest and thickest, it has been at the bottom of the pile. His eyes are aching with reading. Way at the back end of the book, he comes across just a short reference in passing. The writer, who's spelling is awful, has heard that the Twith, who live far to the east in Gubbins and Wozzle, have an answer to the twitch. Sadly, the writer has no knowledge of it, cannot confirm it, and expresses doubt that it can be true. Griswold is disheartened. *Not much help there. Who or what are the Twith? There has been no mention of them in any of the other volumes. Are they a race of super magicians? Are they human, or are they some other type of creature? Where are Gubbins and Wozzle? Are they different countries? I've never heard of either place.*

Griswold has taken to wearing an eye patch. He is afraid his twitch will be reported to or examined by King Druthan. Dark glasses are more dangerous than an eye patch. They are too easily removed, and one glimpse of his right eye is going to give the game away. The only references to the twitch he is aware of are in the forbidden books on magic in the library. No comfort in that. The king will know at once what is going on, even if no one else does. It is also likely that his counselors know about the malady of magician's twitch and are alert to detect it. Fortunately, the king himself rarely visits the library; and his counselors come round only seldom.

Griswold tells himself, *I either have to find a remedy before the king finds me out or I'll have to lead a surprise attack soon to replace the king. Perhaps there is time for a delay of a few days. I can plead sick if necessary and not go to work, but I sure don't want the healers coming round. It can't be very long before something happens. The clock is ticking. Time is short to find a remedy.*

It is during the night, and Glug is snoring away to an irregular rhythm. Light from the full moon is streaming brightly into the brothers' room when the obvious next move comes to Griswold. He has given up trying to control his twitching and lets his eye twitch away while his mind thinks about the future. *I have not come this far from being the fourteenth child in a stable groom's cottage at the foot of the hill to be stopped by such a thing as a twitch. Surely, I'm big enough for any problem I face. After all, the whole world is my doorstep. Knowledge is power. Remember, I can! I will! I am unstoppable!* He sits up suddenly in bed and smiles to himself. He has the answer.

He must send the raven to find the Twith, if they exist, and have him purchase a bottle of the twitch remedy—if indeed they possess it. If they do not possess it, at least Griswold and Rasputin will have tried to secure peace in the land for awhile longer. But then there will be no other course open to them but an immediate attack on King Druthan and his followers.

If, however, the Twith do supply a remedy, then his preparations for taking over the throne can proceed as planned. The king alone will pose a threat. It will remain only to overcome him. Later, there will be time to move beyond the present boundaries of the kingdom. He will be immensely stronger than previously. No other magician adversaries will be able to penetrate his unbreakable disguises while their own twitches will be their betrayal. They will be fried eggs—fried both sides please—on the plate for Griswold's breakfast. He chuckles to himself.

Glug hears him and stirs uneasily. Griswold now makes plans for the gold pieces Rasputin will need to take with him. His mind never rests—the mark of a true leader. Griswold chuckles again. Glug, disturbed a second time, falls out of the bed and continues his sleep on the floor without fully waking. The mice run over him, but he does not know.

Rasputin Sets Out

Griswold has informed Rasputin of the journey the raven will be making to obtain some eye ointment. His assistance will not be needed to obtain the gold coins he will take with him for the purchase. Griswold will take care of that. The bird is out foraging when the librarian moves to get things underway.

Griswold watches intently from the attic window until he sees that the window of the chamberlain's office has been opened. Soon, a sparrow with a twitchy eye flies across the courtyard and looks inside the office. The room is empty. The bird hops in and flies around, checking things out. All is safe for the moment. Suddenly, the bird is replaced by the chief librarian, who bolts the door on the inside. He searches the desk. Sure enough, in the top, left-hand drawer is a money bag with a knotted drawstring. As he unties the string and opens the mouth of the bag, he finds that it is full of gold pieces. Taking only five of the precious coins, he puts them in his pocket. Gold is heavy, and the raven will find it difficult to carry more than that. He reties the bag as it has been tied before and replaces it in the drawer.

There are sudden noises outside, and the handle of the door turns. The librarian does not panic. He remains cool and calm. Cucumbers may be cool, but Griswold is cooler. The door does not open. There are more noises outside. Again, the handle turns, but the door still does not open. It's time for Griswold to disappear quickly. A spirit of daring—the mark of a leader— seizes him. This will be a mere dress rehearsal for his much more exciting future. He will give them a puzzle to exercise their minds. He bolts the window also from the inside, very quietly so that no sound carries, and changes himself into a bee. The gold coins shrink in size along with him. All this requires but a mere moment to a man of his ability. He hides himself on the decorated ceiling cornice in the corner near the door and waits.

There is more than one voice outside, voices of several men calling and shouting. Someone attempts again to open the door and gives it a half-hearted shove or two. "Break it down." This is the voice of the chamberlain himself giving orders. On the second shoulder charge, the whole room seems to shake with the impact of the collision. The door bursts open. Two of the castle servants stumble into the room and fall spread-eagled in front of the desk. The chamberlain strides in behind them, looking around curiously.

He is mystified and wonders, *How has his door become locked?* He examines the tower bolt, still in its locked position. The hasp on the door post has been torn away and is still on the bolt. He looks at the window. He is unsure. He questions in his mind, *Did I close the window before I left the office?* He cannot remember that he did, yet it is now closed—and not just closed by a draft of stray wind playing strange tricks because it is also bolted.

He shares his puzzlement with the three men with him. He goes to his drawer, pulls open the top, left-hand drawer and removes the money bag. He balances it on his hand, testing the weight of it. It is clear he does not know how much money was in the bag. He examines the knotted drawstring closely. He does not untie the string but replaces the money bag in the drawer. He appears satisfied that nothing has been taken from it. He sits at his desk and looks around the room curiously. Something odd is happening. A window and door, the only window and door, are both bolted from the inside. He does not remember locking either. In fact he could not have done so because if he had, he would still have been inside the room instead of outside. He passes his hand across his forehead and thinks, *Is something happening to me?* He goes slowly through each of the desk drawers. Nothing appears to be missing. He leans back in his chair. He is worried, and he is perspiring.

One of the servants opens the window for fresh air, and another fetches a glass of water. The chamberlain is confused. *How can a room be locked on the inside and yet have no one inside?* He decides he needs to share this mystery with King Druthan. He will surely know how it happened and whether he, the chamberlain, is in some way responsible. Maybe he is getting too old and should be thinking of retirement. Perhaps he should be spending more time with his grandchildren. His wife has been telling him so for years.

He rises slowly and instructs the servants to stand guard in the corridor while he goes to inform the king. They are to stay alert and not allow anyone into the room. The men all leave and a single pair of hurried footsteps echoes down the corridor. There is the murmur of voices as the servants take turns offering explanations and just as quickly discard them. The bee, buzzing towards the window, is unnoticed.

The insect checks the sky through a twitching eye before launching back into the open air. It is well known that birds eat bees, and Griswold certainly wants to avoid having that happen to him. The sky is clear. He makes a quick flight across the courtyard and in through the attic window. The bee and the raven are alone. Rasputin has been wondering where the librarian has gone. Griswold reappears—the bee is no more—and shows the raven the coins he will need. Griswold wraps the five coins in a clean handkerchief and ties a couple of knots. He then ties the handkerchief to the raven's left leg and thrusts the bundle of wrapped coins into his claw. He doesn't want the coins in the room in case there is a search by the castle guards. He instructs Rasputin, "Bring back as much salve as the money will buy, and don't delay for any side trips. Things are developing here at the castle fast, and your help is sure to be needed. Now get on your way without delay."

The raven asks for clear directions. Griswold is patient with his explanations but anxious for the raven to be on his way. "I don't know any more than that the Twith live in the direction where the sun rises and that it is said to be far away. Whatever the Twith might be, I have no idea what they look like or how many they are or what language they speak. I found only two places where they might be living." He thinks, *Is it Gubbins and Wizzle? No. Wrong. It's Wozzle and Gubbins. That's where they live, according to the book.* Griswold cautions Rasputin, "They live in lands called Wozzle and Gubbins, but they might have moved by now. The book with the names is a very old one.

"Just inquire around, my good fellow. Ask some of the ancient residents, old birds you meet along the way. Get all the crows in the district on your side, and you will soon have all the news that has happened in the area for the last fifty years. Don't give up easily, young friend. Know that I'm relying on you. If there isn't enough money for the expenses, just sign an IOU. I'm sure to be back for more if the stuff works. If you need me alongside to interpret, then you'll just have to come back and get me, but I am confident you will succeed on your own. You'll find a way. I am expecting great things of you. It will be a great test of your own initiative. Good luck, my lad. Off you go."

Summons from the King

A whole week passes and Griswold begins to miss having Rasputin around. It is the first time they have been separated since the raven struggled out of the shell and opened his eyes to see a strange little man looking at him with great glee and approval. Given the time that Rasputin left, Griswold had been thinking that the raven's very first pause for a rest would be just over the border into Devon. There, the bird would be gaining news of the mysterious Twith in the lands of Wozzle and Gubbins. That should surely have allowed his return in, say, four days or even five. The return of the bird is long overdue. His absence is worrying. Griswold's mind is full of nagging questions. *How far has Rasputin had to go? Could something awful have happened to him once he was away from friendly Cornish skies? The weather has been fair, and there have been no signs of distant storms or strong winds. Could the bird have lost his way? Suppose he can't find his way back home? Perhaps he has reached the end of his journey, succeeded in buying the ointment or medicine, and then dropped my precious eye salve in some sky accident. He could even be afraid to return and admit failure.*

Griswold is busy working at his desk. Over his right eye is a black eye patch. If he has to wear an eye patch, it might as well be in his favorite color. He takes his work seriously.

He has been having his staff make lists of the books in each of the fifty locations in the castle. The titles have been copied and are arranged in alphabetical order. He knows the titles of every book in the castle and in which room and storage place each is to be found. He is now compiling the various pages in order, and then he will have them bound by the bookbinder. Because of the smell of the fish glue he uses, the bookbinder works alone in one of the cellars.

It is eleven in the morning on the twelfth day after Rasputin's departure. Again, Griswold's thoughts return to his missing assistant. The bird is worth two of any of the assistants he has in the library, even including his own relatives. Griswold is concerned. *What has happened to Rasputin? I probably should have sent a companion with him. But who would I have sent? I could hardly have gone myself; my absence would have raised far too much curiosity. After all, I am indispensable. The library couldn't function without me!* He finds himself looking out the library window a dozen times a day, hoping against hope that he will see a familiar black bird flying around outside or perched on the window sill. It has not happened yet.

There is a knock on the door of the library office. *I am expecting no one. Who can it be?* The door swings open. In comes a court messenger, one of the new, recently appointed young men that Griswold does not know. His black and gold uniform shows that he is from the lord chamberlain's office. He passes a sealed envelope to Griswold and stands, waiting, expecting to convey an answer back to the sender.

The envelope is addressed to "Mr. Griswold Beswetherick-Jacka, Librarian." Griswold lays down his pen and leans back in his chair so that the curious young man leaning forward shall not have his curiosity satisfied. He breaks the seal. The note inside, written in the lord chamberlain's own hand and with his scribbled signature, is brief.

Report to the audience room immediately upon receipt of this note. Do not delay. Bring your keys.

Griswold has a sense that he is in trouble, but he will not betray what he feels to this insolent teenage ruffian standing before him. "There is no reply. I will go myself."

He pulls the black cloak of his office around him, hangs his two large rings of keys on his tasseled girdle, runs a hand across his hair to smooth it, and moistens his dry lips with his tongue. For some encouragement, he thinks, *I can! I will!* to himself several times as he follows the young man striding ahead of him along the corridors. He is in trouble. He is sure of that. He wonders, *What have they found out? I mustn't give away anything they do not already know. I'll have to lie as necessary to keep them in the dark. Have they found out I've been reading the books on magic without permission? Could it be the mysterious promotions I've received on my* way to *becoming chief librarian? Can it be the five missing gold pieces, or merely the prank of the locked door? Or have the lizards I changed into rodents ratted on me? Can it be the cherry tree? Maybe they just fear the extent of my knowledge. I doubt they have any idea at all of what I can really accomplish.* He thinks of possible changes he might make to himself if things get too hot: *a bird, a bee, a mouse, a snake. I might need to make a quick escape. Where can I go?* He wishes he had a few more friends he might turn to, but he does not. His only friend is Rasputin, and he is lost and might be dead.

The audience room, towards which Griswold is headed, is the largest room in the castle other than the banqueting hall. It is actually the great hall where King Druthan meets with his officials and with the public. It is where he dispenses justice and issues decrees. The floor has four distinct levels. The golden throne is at the highest level. It sits alone on a dais in the center of the longest wall, with a great canopy over the throne and the upper platform. Ascending steps to it rise on all three sides. Two broad steps below the throne is the floor of inner audience, where only those welcomed forward by the king may stand. Two further broad steps below is a wide platform where those appointed and authorized by the king may take their seated places at the sides, leaving the space in front entirely clear. These upper three levels are lavishly carpeted with woven rugs of bright colors and varied design.

The lowest level has a floor of plain brown and white tiles and is where any member of the kingdom with a complaint or plea stands. It is also where witnesses called upon by the king stand. And this is where prisoners and their counsel stand. It is where the accusers throw their accusations against a prisoner and the prisoner makes his equally passionate defense. Here, at the lowest level, there are no seats and everyone must stand. All weapons are forbidden within the audience room. All who enter are given a silent visual inspection by the guards, looking for hidden weapons, but there is rarely any disturbance. King Druthan's kingdom is a peaceful kingdom, and there is nothing to fear.

As Griswold arrives at the left-hand entrance door to the audience room, he is shocked to see that the chamber is completely full and the whole of the king's court is present. The buzz of conversation stops as he is observed approaching. All heads have turned towards him. The hollow echoing of footsteps—both his and those of the chamberlain's messenger ahead of him—are the only sounds to be heard before the buzz of animated conversation recommences. He is the focus of all eyes.

The king himself, crowned and fully robed in regal splendor, seated upon his throne, watches him enter. He is an old man, white haired, of a little over average height. His long face has a high forehead, and his eyes are a clear, light blue. The king's beard is neatly trimmed. He looks sharp and alert for his age. He sits behind a small, cloth-covered table on which rest certain books and papers and a bell. His hands, clasped, rest upon the table. His face is stern and unsmiling.

The sides of the councilors' floor are packed with seated officials wearing robes and chains of office. They also have turned to stare at him. The floor of common audience is filled, crowded to the back and side walls with castle servants and people from outside who have come to see a spectacle.

One space alone at the common level is empty. It is a large, clear space nearest to and in front of the throne. It is marked off by a red line painted on the floor. People are crowding up to the line and standing shoulder to shoulder all the way to the back of the hall. Those in front are down on one knee to give those behind a better view. Griswold has never seen the audience room so full or so many of the highest officials of the land present and waiting, apparently waiting for him. He wonders to himself, *Can they all be waiting for me?* He realizes with an inner dread that they are. There can be no doubt about it.

The crowd divides to allow him space to walk forward and take his position in the red-lined area before the throne where the accused or plaintiff stands. As he does so, he spots on the level between him and the throne a jumble of items he recognizes.

His collection from the two dungeon cells that the jailer has been allowing him to use for storage has been retrieved and is now prominently displayed on a low table. Those precious secret stores of his—the birds' nests he has climbed trees for, the eggshells of wild birds that he has so carefully guarded and identified, the varieties of seaweed that he has gathered between tides, the various snail shells all piled together as though their differences didn't matter, the horse hair from the stables—are all there. To one side are the smaller items: the cat and dog fur, the sheep and lambs' wool in neat little bundles, the cats' whiskers and cats' claws collected with such difficulty, the mouse and rat tails, the frog and toad spawn separated into brown and green bottles, and the castoff tails of newts in little boxes that he has spent years gathering. All of these treasures are spread out for foolish eyes to gawk at, eyes that have no idea of the power or significance of this invaluable collection.

Yes, there is no doubt at all what this gathering is about. The summons he has received by order of the king is to his own trial. *Griswold,* he thinks to himself, *you have problems. Boy, do you have problems!*

Magic? Who, Me?

The crowd settles down. The buzz of conversation stops. People are looking first at Griswold and then back at King Druthan. Griswold halts in front of the throne and two paces back from the nearest step. He raises his right hand to his forehead to acknowledge the summons he received, but he does not utter a word. Let the king make the first play.

King Druthan speaks. He instructs the librarian to give his keys to the attending steward and asks, "Do you have any other keys anywhere?" Griswold shakes his head as he removes the key rings and hands them to the steward, who comes forward to take them. For years, those keys have been the sign of his charge and responsibility. He feels strangely stripped of authority and power without them. Anyone who matters has keys, and now he has none. Now he is a nobody.

"Mister Beswetherick-Jacka, before we explain to you why we are gathered and why we have called you here amongst this assembly and before we seek from you answers to certain questions we have, we must point out to you a device that assists this court to know if you are telling the truth. There is upon this table a brass bell which serves as a lie detector. You will observe that its striker hangs at its side. It will remain silent while you are being questioned. When you give your evidence, however, if you should fail to tell the truth before this court, it will strike loudly and clearly to inform us that your answer is untrue. We trust it will not strike during the time you are before us.

"If it should strike three full times, indicating that you have lied to this court three times, then the judgment of guilty is given without further delay, and you will be subject to the full penalty of the laws of this land. Is this understood?"

Griswold looks to see whether the bell striker, a horizontal bar which appears to swing loose, is connected by a cord to the king's foot or to the foot of anyone nearby. But the fringed tablecloth falls to the floor, and it is not possible to see if the bell is connected in any way to someone who will decide whether he is telling the truth or not. There could even be a second hidden striker.

He wonders whether he could insert an unseen bubble (such as he has put around the cherry tree) between the striker and the bell. However, surely the king would see what he had done even if no one else could, and then he stands condemned before he even speaks. There is too great a risk for that to succeed. He decides not to try. On his forehead, little beads of sweat are beginning to appear. He thinks, *This is not fair. The trial has been rigged against me from the start. How can I possibly prevail against so many gathered against me? It seems the decision has already been made to find me guilty.* Griswold bows his head in acknowledgement that he understands.

The king continues. "It is the opinion of this court that magic has been introduced into this kingdom in the recent past, and its presence is now evident among us. The court considers this to be a most serious crime, threatening the safety of the realm and the safety of each person within it. No one is safe now that magic is released among us. Furthermore, the court considers that you and you alone are responsible. We are gathered here as a royal assembly to consider what needs to be done to rid the kingdom of this danger if this is so. Are you guilty or not guilty?"

"Not guilty, Sire!"

For only a short moment is there a hush. It is as though people, the whole chamber of people, are waiting. They have not long to wait. There is a single, low-pitched *Ding!* from the bell on the table. The sound reverberates. It is so very loud and so very clear that it could well be the ringing of the town hall bell instead of this small one before him that could easily be held in one hand. It has been struck just once. Griswold did not see the striker move, but it must have done so.

As if rehearsed, the councilors and those below them count a sonorous "One." They are counting. The sound moves across the whole room, and all assembled appear to join in, all except the king and Griswold.

Griswold's eyes are haunted. He looks desperately around him. He sees some of his brothers scattered among the crowd, but he does not know whether they are also counting. Towards the left door, he spots the rest of his family: his father and mother; his brother, Axelgris; and his three sisters. His mother and the girls have been crying. They are likely wondering who is going to write their letters now.

Griswold puts up his hand respectfully. He has a question he wishes to ask of the court. The king nods for him to proceed.

"Sire, I am aware that magic is forbidden by the laws of the kingdom. I stand before you accused of introducing magic into the kingdom. I am unaware, however, of the penalties for doing so and would request information from the court."

The king responds. "There is such a thing as good magic, magic intended for the benefit of people other than the one who practices it. Such magic may have the sanction of this court and, once given, there is no penalty to the user. Such a sanction is only rarely given, although I am aware that in the times of my predecessor, it was given more than once. This court has never sanctioned magic of any kind and is unlikely ever to do so.

"For other magic, which increases the power of the user and can have consequences affecting the whole nation and people everywhere, the penalty is death or banishment to some place where there are no people—some lonely, wave-washed island; some empty desert; some undiscovered mountain cave—for at least one thousand years. Those who use magic can learn to extend their lives long beyond the normal span of years. Others yet unborn must be protected against their evil power. Do you understand?"

Griswold nods. He is not going to say more before he needs to. The strikes from the bell are limited to three, which is a very small number, and one has already slipped by.

The king has another question for the librarian. "You see before you on display on the table a certain collection of objects. Do you recognize any of them, and do you know where they have come from?"

"Yes, Sire. These are part of my collection of natural history specimens. By permission of the chief jailer, I have been allowed to keep them in an empty space in the dungeon. I have long been interested in botany and natural history. I can identify for you all of the objects on display, for I have collected them personally over many years."

So far, the bell has not rung a second time. *So far so good,* thinks Griswold.

"Will you please come forward and identify to those present the various objects on display?"

Griswold steps up onto the councilors' platform and then up onto the next platform. He wonders whether he might quickly throw a bubble over the king, but discards the idea. It cannot possibly succeed in an arena so filled with the king's followers and friends. Besides, he is uncertain as to the king's own powers.

"Sire, these are birds' nests. Here is a robin's. Here is a thrush's. Here is a blackbird's. And this is a swallow's, gathered from atop the coach house eaves. These here are eggshells of various small wild birds." Griswold points out the various species of birds as he identifies the shells by their colors and markings. People are patient, and he is being given all the time he needs.

He describes the varieties of seaweed that he has gathered between tides, passes by the snail shells all piled together, explains the horse hair came from the stables. Although the items strike the listeners who can hear him as a strange assortment, Griswold is anxious not to trigger the bell again, so he sticks to the truth. He points out, without explaining, the cat and dog fur, the bundles of sheep and lambs' wool, the cats' whiskers and cats' claws, the mouse and rat tails, the frog and toad spawn, and the castoff tails of newts.

He steps back down to his place and looks back up at King Druthan. He has not triggered the bell yet. He is fearful though, *What is the next question going to be?*

THE BELL STRIKES
AGAIN

"Are you aware, Mister Beswetherick-Jacka, that all these items you have collected and explained to us can be used in magic spells and preparations?"

Griswold thinks hard. He must avoid the trap of the bell striker.

"Yes, Sire. It is well known among scholars that magicians use many strange objects in their spells and potions. Undoubtedly, these will all be part of the variety of substances they use for their wicked activities. They will certainly use many other items also. However, these items in my collection are also of considerable interest to a botanist and a student of natural history."

The hall is silent. King Druthan is not finished. "Have you ever used any of these items displayed before us in a magic spell or potion?"

"No, Sire." Griswold shakes his head and is emphatic. If he had used any of *these* items, then there is no way they would be here now.

The bell does not ring. The king is thoughtful. He puts his question in a different way. "Have you ever used any items like these displayed before us in a magic spell or potion?"

"No, Sire." Griswold again shakes his head and is emphatic.

There is a single *Ding!* from the bell on the table, pitched low as before. The sound reverberates once more, loud and clear. The bell has been struck just once. This time, Griswold has clearly seen the striker move, unaided and of its own accord. There is an indrawn gasp of breath from the assembly, and then, as if rehearsed, everyone in unison shouts, "Two!" Griswold looks at his parents. There is no rejoicing in their appearance, but they too are counting, counting with dread and fear not only for Griswold but for themselves.

Now the king asks, "Do you like cherries?"

This is an unexpected question. It is not dangerous, but danger can soon follow. He must be extra careful here. "Yes, Sire."

"Have you observed the cherry tree in the garden?"

"The cherry tree in the herb garden, Sire?"

"Yes, that is the one."

"Yes, Sire."

"This morning, I rose early to walk in the garden and went across to examine the fruit on the cherry tree and perhaps select some for the breakfast table. They are about ready for picking and such a wonderful crop this year. I found that I could not approach the tree. I could not even touch the branches. The fruit has been protected by some kind of barrier that I have never before experienced. Can you explain this to me?"

Griswold begins to realize that he is trapped and the questions are being carefully woven like a spider's web around a fly. He makes an attempt to avoid the last gong. If he had had more time and warning, he could surely have worked out a bubble or a curtain that would stop the striker hitting the bell.

"What you relate is truly amazing. I believe, Sire, that it might be that someone, some inventor wishing to benefit mankind, someone with an immense untapped and unique creative ability, has devised a completely new means of protecting the fruit of the tree. This is but one tree, the first. Think ahead, Sire. Our farmers have tried natural pesticides such as dusting with sulfur, but they have been no more successful than the ancient Mesopotamians were. Who has ever thought or heard of such a device as this unseen protective barrier before? It is a remarkable invention unheard of in the history of man. It is also of desirable low cost. The mind boggles. Think. It can increase the harvest of orchards across the world and be of immense help to hungry people. Think of possible benefits, Sire, if this can be successful and applied not only to fruit but also to berries and grains and vegetables. Think of the starving multitudes in other lands beyond the seas. The country that fosters such a development will become truly renowned as a benefactor throughout the world. Why, the process could even be patented. It is clear that much work still needs to be done. You will need to identify who it is that has achieved this superb breakthrough of guarding the fruit of the cherry tree. He should be given the opportunity to control development. There will need to be a special research establishment with adequate funds and long term security for the staff, good health arrangements, and controlled agricultural and orchard plots ..."

The king holds up his hand. The librarian is getting carried away with his own ideas. The man is fighting back. "Was it you who placed this protective barrier around the cherry tree?"

"Yes, Sire." Griswold is not apologetic. He looks around. He is proud of his achievement with the cherry tree.

"Did you do so by means of a spell?"

There is only a small hesitation from Griswold before he replies, "Yes, Sire. I have been researching how the use of magic can be applied for the benefit of men and women everywhere."

There is a single and final *Ding!* from the bell on the table. Griswold realizes he has said too much, as the bell, unaided by human hand, strikes for a third time. The sound echoes across the audience room. The bell is loud and clear. There is an indrawn gasp of breath from the assembly, and then, as if rehearsed, everyone in unison shouts, "Three!" Their heads turn towards each other, and a burst of chattering breaks out.

Griswold looks around desperately. He has said too much and is convicted by his own mouth. His denials that he has been involved in magic and that he has used spells and potions have both been revealed as lies by the bell, and now his false claim that he has used magic for the benefit of mankind and not for himself has completed the trial. He has been found guilty of magic. He looks desperately around him for any sign of mercy or understanding. He sees none. His mother and the girls have burst into loud wailing. They are warned to hush by the guards at the door. As two of the guards approach and stand beside him for his sentencing, he spots one slender, very slender, sign of hope. Silhouetted against the sky through the upper window, high above the throne is a bird, and he knows birds well enough to recognize that the bird is a raven.

THE SENTENCE

Griswold's heart has lifted, but he has no time to reflect upon the late, though encouraging, arrival of Rasputin. He doubts the bird can see into the audience room well enough to understand what is going on. Meanwhile, his own problems are most pressing. His right eye twitches furiously under its black patch. It must be the stress.

He pulls himself together. His thoughts are resolute. *They shall not see me crumble. I will accept the judgment of the court with dignity. The people here shall see, the whole world in time to come shall hear, and all will applaud how a Beswetherick-Jacka can take his medicine. Future generations shall not talk about me with scorn and contempt but with grudging admiration and mayhap even envy.* He imagines them saying, as they talk about him over their cucumber sandwiches while enjoying the finest Chinese tea in china cups, "He went down to his destiny with his head held high. They could not break his spirit though they tried hard. He met his end with a laugh. What character. What vision."

With some remorse he thinks, *If it had not been for the bell, I would have survived. No matter. Adversity builds strength. I will not crumble into a mess of jelly. I will be rock hard and as strong as iron. They cannot make me flinch. I'm not finished yet, no matter what they might do to me. My spirit will be unbroken, even to the bitter end. The way of victory is through the fields of defeat. I will find compensations even in disaster.*

At least I will finally be away from sharing a bed with Glug, even if I have no bed at all where I'm going. No more of his wrig-

gling and snoring and keeping me awake at night. Thank goodness for that.

He wishes he had a handkerchief to wipe his nose, but he forgot to put one in his pocket when he left the attic for the library. He sniffs instead.

The king raises his hand for silence. The buzz of conversation subsides. Within the hall, there is no movement at all. Fidgeting and shuffling of feet stop. This is the crisis of the trial. Out of his own mouth, the defendant has admitted his guilt. Everyone is wondering, *Will the king exercise mercy or not?* The crowd cannot remember a death penalty during the reign of the present king, but rarely has there been such a serious charge as this brought before him. If he does decide on the death penalty, it will be the first of his reign.

"Mister Beswetherick-Jacka, you stand condemned out of your own mouth. Three times you have lied to this court. I have no doubt that, had our questioning continued further, you would have lied yet again and again. The evidence against you has only been lightly touched upon, but we are fully aware of the extent of your activities.

"You are guilty of introducing and practicing magic when it is completely forbidden in our land to do so.

"We judge you to be ruthless and dangerous. We have stopped you on the edge of a criminal career you are determined to pursue. You are cunning, and you will stop at nothing. You have spent many years acquiring a wide range of the knowledge and practice of magic. You are determined to gain your ends no matter what the cost. We can only surmise what those ends might be. We should rightly fear for the peace and prosperity of our country if you could have had your will upon it. Have you anything to say before sentence is passed upon you?"

Griswold does have something to say. He sees out of the corner of his eye his father comforting his mother, and Axelgris comforting his sisters. He cannot see Glug. He must do what he can for his family. He owes them this. He will be gone—that is sure—but they will be staying. While he speaks, he must be sure the bell does not ring. Otherwise, all that he says will have been of no purpose. To make his point, he will need to admit his own guilt. Well, it is too late for any denials to matter.

"Sire, I do have something to say. I admit to having a deep interest in magic. I admit to the charges made against me, but you should know that there is none other who has conspired with me. What I have done, I have done alone. I have had no other person knowingly helping me or assisting me. Yes, indeed, I have used my brother, Glug, the dishwasher, to do errands and perform tasks for me in my pursuit of knowledge and magical power, but he has not had even the slightest thought of my true intentions. I have kept everything hidden from him. It would be wrong to punish him. Neither have my parents nor any other members of my family been aware of my interests, nor have they ever encouraged me in any way. I have no friends who could have been engaged with me. I do not stand before this court as the first of a group of conspirators. The court need have no concern that there are others yet to be brought before it upon the charge that I face. I stand alone."

King Druthan nods, and the chamberlain looks relieved while the spectators stir and murmur. The bell has not rung once during Griswold's brief speech. The king holds up both his arms, commanding silence. He looks first at Griswold and then slowly around at the whole assembly. It is a solemn moment.

"Mister Beswetherick-Jacka, and all those here present, hear the judgment of this court.

"You are, first of all, relieved of all your duties within the castle effective immediately. Your duties will be taken by another.

"You will not be allowed to return to the library or to the room in the castle you have been using as your home. All your private papers, notes, and records are to be brought to my chambers for my review. They will then be destroyed.

"In view of your remarks, we can advise you that the court anticipates no action against other members of your family because of your activities.

"We must assume that in the future you will continue to lie to us and to others as you have done here today, so no reliance can be placed upon any promises that you may give. We can thus assume that a sentence of banishment will not be effective, for you will break any promises that you might make before this court. The alternative sentence to banishment is that you shall, without further delay, pay the cost of your crimes with your life." A collective gasp goes up from the assembly.

"However, we are moved to show mercy to you. The sentence is that you shall be banished from the realms and habitations of ordinary people for one thousand years. You are allowed two days to identify and notify and receive approval from the court for your preferred place of banishment. If you fail to make such a choice, the court will make the choice for you. Should you be apprehended in breach of this sentence before the period of one thousand years has elapsed, then the alternative sentence of death shall be carried out upon you without further action by this or any other court.

"The guards will remove you to the dungeon to be held there until the sentence of banishment is carried out and you are escorted to your destination. You will wear prison apparel and be in the custody of the chief jailer, who will be responsible to the lord chamberlain for your custody. You will be permitted no visitors.

"Do you understand the sentence that has been given?"

Griswold looks at the seated king and slowly takes a long look around the hall. He thinks sadly, *My life, all of my remembered past, is ending. I've grown up among these people—played with them as a boy, studied in school with them, worked with and for them in the castle, risen through their ranks to a position of authority. Now I'm left with nothing, absolutely nothing. In one brief hour, my whole world has collapsed about me.*

Well, at least my life has been spared. I still know what I know, and I'm sure—at least I hope I'm sure—that I still have the friendship of a black bird. Perhaps though, Rasputin won't be willing to go with me. To lose the companionship of the raven would be the last straw. It's rather strange that a man of my high character and quality shall have become so dependent on the company and friendship of a mere bird. But I don't know whether I have enough strength to continue the struggle by myself.

"Yes, Sire."

"The court is adjourned."

The king rises, and so do the courtiers and officials. The monarch proceeds down the steps past them, towards the door on the right without a further glance at the prisoner, who is flanked by two guards. The officials follow the king. When they are gone, but before the rest of the hall empties, Griswold is on his way, escorted down the stone steps to the lower dungeon. He has been this way many times before when adding items to his collection and knows all the hallways and passages well.

THE DUNGEON

The suit he is wearing fits badly. Griswold tries to decide whether it is blue with white stripes or white with blue stripes. It is hard to tell which; the colors are both the same width. The suit includes a too-small, round hat of the same striped material that perches on his head like an upturned cup on an upturned saucer and never reaches his brow. The suit must have been made by a tailor's apprentice for a misshapen dwarf with a barrel chest and very tiny arms and legs. It has, for a very good reason, never been previously worn. No self-respecting prisoner, however much deprived of rights and privileges, would have allowed it anywhere near his body. It has never been washed, and the cloth, stiff and starched, is making him itch all over. He still wears his eye patch. He ignores the rats and pretends to himself that they are only mice. Rasputin would soon see them off if he were here. Around Griswold's ankles are manacles chained to a ring in the wall. These were put on before the escorting guards left. His hands have been left free.

The jailer is being as kind to his new prisoner as he dares. His daughter is showing signs of strange green spots on her face and considerable hair loss, and he may need the ex-librarian's help. He explains, "I want you to know that I did not betray the stores of your treasures displayed in the audience room. They were found by the search party of guards who had been ordered by the chamberlain, on King Druthan's instructions, to search the castle from top to bottom." Unfortunately, they started at the bottom, and all the severe consequences for Griswold have flowed from the discovery in the dungeon.

Griswold sits on his low, wooden bed with his head in his hands. The jailer continues, "I was questioned first by the chamberlain and then by the king himself. With that bell waiting to ding at the slightest slip of my tongue, I could not avoid saying that the supplies belonged to you. My wife and I are personally deeply grateful for the amazing cures you accomplished for our daughter. She is our only child, and is greatly loved."

Griswold takes advantage of the jailer's gratitude. "I wonder if I could be permitted a visit by my small pet raven? I know the king has ordered no visitors, and I have no desire to put you in difficulty. However, a pet is hardly a person, is it? You couldn't call a goldfish swimming around in a bowl a visitor, could you? That would be ridiculous. Then neither could you call a raven a visitor. After all, they are both the same thing, only different, aren't they? One swims, and one flies; but both are the same: pets. You've already met my raven and know what a mild-tempered creature he is. What harm can a raven be? He is probably off his feed and pining away for me. It would be a shame to see the poor, wee bird die of a broken heart. Are we not taught and trained from childhood to be kind to dumb animals and especially birds?"

The jailer is not sure how strong the argument is that a pet is not a visitor. He is also not sure that the description, "poor, wee bird," fits the bird he knows as Griswold's companion. He does want somehow to show his gratitude for the medicines and his regret that the librarian is now in such trouble. He must at all costs avoid getting into trouble himself. Griswold is his only prisoner.

The jailer tells Griswold, "I will have to keep your dungeon cell locked. However, when I go out in the courtyard to eat the sandwiches I brought for my evening meal, I will leave the outer door to the dungeon slightly ajar. It will be fading light, almost dark, and I wouldn't notice a tiny bird hopping in behind my back. After all, I don't have eyes in the back of my head, do I? That is as far as I dare go in assisting you. Since your pet is black, when the night guard comes on duty, the bird will remain unseen unless he moves. Your raven, if he does come, could hop through the bars and stay all night and leave in the morning."

Griswold has been thinking hard since the jailer left. When Griswold thinks hard, the wheels turning inside his head can be heard clear across the room. He thinks as a leader should think. *Defeated? Hah! Condemned? Hah! Banished? So what!* His mind is a factory of ideas, a launching pad blasting off hundreds of new thoughts each hour. There are scores of wheels turning, cogs rolling, ratchets clicking, wires humming, connections overheating, keys tapping, shelves stacking, files filing, and memory cells memorizing.

Already he has his priorities sorted out for the moment when the raven arrives. *I have no doubt that Rasputin will soon be here. There will be no time for idle conversation then. First things first. Chit-chat can wait. I'll give him one or two quick orders, and then, while the door is still open, I'll be out of here like an arrow from a bow. I'll get beyond the castle walls, and then, only then, will I look for a comfortable place to rest. Only then, not here in the dungeon, will be the time to hear Rasputin's news, scrounge a meal, and make plans for a new future in some more hospitable land and place than the kingdom of Trevose.*

I've been fed up with Cornwall, anyway. There must be a place somewhere in the world where people speak without steamrolling their "r's" into the ground and murdering their personal prepositions by misuse. Refined people like myself need an environment of culture to flourish. A man needs to venture far beyond his birthplace if he is to truly taste adventure. It's time for a change. Why has it taken me so long to see it? I'm amazed I haven't acted earlier. Why, this whole affair is just the spur to action that I needed.

Rasputin had seen his friend on trial in the audience room and watched as Griswold was escorted across the courtyard to the dungeon by his two guards. The raven couldn't understand what was happening or what might have happened since he left, but things have clearly gone wrong for his boss. This means that everything is up to him now. He must forget, for the time being, the news he has brought and instead concentrate on his master's rescue from the dungeon before it is too late.

He checks around with the other ravens for the news. They have freedom of movement within the castle. They are trained from childhood that all their mess stays outside; they make no mess inside, and they stay silent indoors. They also pick up and carry outside fallen feathers, leaves, and petals and help to keep the castle tidy. This has, over the centuries, given them access even to council rooms. The ravens are well informed.

Few of the people in the castle know the birds understand their conversation. Only the king is fully aware how much the animals and birds around the castle know. He alone was able to communicate with them until the librarian learned. Several ravens have been in the audience room, perched high and unseen, and they have all been listening carefully. From them, the full story emerges. Griswold has been brought before the king and his council and has admitted being involved in magic. He has been sentenced to be banished from the habitations of ordinary people for a thousand years. He has two days to decide where to live out his banishment before the court makes the decision for him. Rasputin realizes he needs to get into the dungeon and find his master.

A Daring Escape

Rasputin has been down to the two storage cells in the dungeon many times, sometimes by himself. He knows there is only one entrance, and that is from the castle courtyard. Rasputin stations himself close by the door. He finds an empty dovecote above the servants' kitchen and wriggles himself in backwards. The roost is too small for him to turn around inside. He settles down to watch and wait. He wants to get in unseen. Otherwise, guards might be called to locate and eject him.

Hours pass. The long afternoon begins to slip away as the light starts to fade. Rasputin does not move. He knows well the routine of the dungeons and that the chief jailer hands over to the night guard when darkness falls. He does not have to wait that long.

The door of the dungeon opens and remains ajar. The chief jailer, once regarded by Griswold as a friend, comes outside and sits on a low wall. He looks around the courtyard and, seeing nothing, scans the upper storeys of the castle buildings. However, Rasputin is certain that he has not been spotted. He watches as the man unwraps a sandwich and takes a huge first bite. It reminds the raven that he too is hungry and probably Griswold as well, but finding something to eat will have to wait.

Time to move. The jailer looks towards the castle gate, where someone from outside is banging to get in. The raven wriggles out through the roost hole and slips into the air with a quiet glide low to the ground, behind the jailer. Flying sideways, he slips through the slightly opened door and into the complete darkness of the dungeon. As he lands, he stumbles forward a few unsteady paces, and then runs into the darkness, heading for the steps down to the lowest level. His eyes slowly adjust to the darkness ahead. He does not allow himself to look back. The brightness of daylight would blind him.

Rasputin halts on the edge of the stone steps and gives a low whistle, barely audible. No answer. He whistles again, slightly louder than the first time. From the darkness behind him, to the left, comes an answering low whistle. The bird swings around and retraces his steps. Griswold must be at the upper level. The bright sunlight streaming through the open door makes him squint. He hears another low whistle to his right, and Rasputin knows he has found his boss. Using smell as well as vision, the raven wriggles between the vertical iron bars and caws quietly. "Hi, boss. How're things?"

Griswold is glad to hear the bird's greeting, although it should be obvious that things aren't going well. His reply does not betray the relief he feels at the arrival of the raven.

"Welcome back, lad. I knew you'd make it. No time to get your news just now. We'd better get outta here while the door is open. When it closes, who knows what might happen next. Any ideas?"

Rasputin has. "Don't waste any time, boss. Change yourself into a mouse, and climb on my back. I'll get us out. Hurry."

Griswold dismisses his own idea of becoming a second raven, although he has the spell ready in his mind. Maybe one bird coming in and two going out might be noticed. He'll give Rasputin's idea a try. Griswold wonders, *Will the manacles around my ankles shrink with me, or will they stay unchanged because they're attached to the building and thus part of it? Well, there's one way to find out.* He closes his eyes and concentrates.

DOINK! He is furry and four-legged, and he has a tail he can swish. His ankles are free, and his feet can move. Good! He jumps over the manacles. He can feel his whiskers twitching. He smells something, something frightening and ominous. It's the kitchen cat, out after dusk, prowling in the courtyard. He has never liked that cat. He scrambles onto the back of Rasputin, who is flat on the floor.

"Be careful. The kitchen cat's out in the yard. Get outside before it comes in. Don't on any account go for the cat. You might spill me off. Just get out beyond the castle walls as quickly as you can, and then we can talk."

Rasputin is ready for a fight, especially with this enemy, and is tempted to head for the cat as soon as he sees it. He can still taste that run of his beak up the cat's back when the animal had tried to steal his food. However, first things first, as his friend would say. He can settle scores with the cat some other time.

The bird squeezes between the bars of the dungeon. They are not wide apart, and there is little room to spare. Hopping down the corridor towards the door, he goes through and out into the open courtyard. The jailer is standing up, bending over and collecting the trash from his supper, almost ready to go back inside. His back is to the door as he talks to the kitchen cat. He gives her his last crust, and does not see a raven leave the dungeon. Neither does he see, snuggled down in its back feathers, a bump that could be a mouse hiding himself.

The cat does. She looks up and sees, through the legs of her benefactor, her arch enemy: the attic raven. If dirty grey kitchen cats could go as pale as a ghost, then she would have gone whiter than snow. She stands for a moment petrified, and then *Flash!* The cat tears towards a disused mouse hole on the other side of the courtyard that she foolishly thinks is big enough to let her inside to hide.

The jailer has to come across and help extricate her backwards. Her face is badly grazed. Her whiskers are bent double. Busily helping the cat, the jailer has no eyes to spare for the raven that climbs into the air from the dungeon door, gains height, and disappears over the castle wall.

Neither the bird nor the mouse upon his back are near enough to hear the ringing of the alarms in the castle when the jailer realizes that his prisoner has escaped. They do not know that the castle is being searched once more by the guards, personally supervised by the lord chamberlain. And they are unaware that the jailer himself occupies the dungeon cell so recently vacated by the prisoner. Eventually, the king decides that Griswold has used magic to assist his escape, and the jailer cannot be held responsible for the effects of magic. Besides, he has a sick child.

The two friends are far away. They have first settled on a ledge of the slate quarry across the river north of the castle. Griswold has changed from a mouse back to himself. Seeing himself dressed in prison garb, he realizes that he needs to get rid of these ridiculous clothes. He flings the hat into the air and watches it fall towards the blue pool in the bottom of the quarry. So much for that stupid thing. He would like to do the same with the rest of the outfit he's wearing, but before he gets rid of that, he will need to find some other suitable apparel. However, that will have to wait awhile. They must first find a place to settle for the night, and Griswold is getting hungry. There is nothing in the quarry to make a meal from and nothing nearby that he can see. He decides that Rasputin is used to foraging and fending for himself. He can do no better than to become a second raven and turn himself over to a master of the skills of looking after himself. He informs the bird, who smiles and waits. The two birds climb into the air. Griswold has tried out being a bird before, so he has a rough hang of how to handle wings and tail. Rasputin flies around while Griswold practices climbing and swooping, as well as turning and gliding. After all that, he does a landing or two and finds that takeoffs are actually easier than landings. He tries a somersault and nearly crashes. His beak scrapes the ground. He needs to be higher before he tries that again. Griswold begins to appreciate the freedom of the skies, and is strangely happy to be away from the routines that, for years, have confined him to the castle. He is going to learn a whole new way of living.

The sun has set over the sea, and the light is fading fast. Rasputin asks his master, "What would you like for supper, boss? Fish or meat?" Rasputin has sometimes brought his meals home. On those occasions, his meat menu has typically been scraps from the castle kitchen, small birds, snails and offal, and an occasional worm. Such a menu does not appeal to Griswold, but neither does he fancy sea fishing while he is still getting accustomed to wings. He could get swamped by a wave. Instead, he will go vegetarian for the evening. With all the strenuous flying about that he has been doing, his stomach is a bit tender. In the dusk, the pair of ravens takes flight, heading for the fields. To look at the two, you'd never guess which is the true bird and which is the shape-changing wizard.

Rasputin's Journey

The two birds have eaten well, and their stomachs are full. There have been plenty of seed grains in the fields. It is good that the weather is mild and dry. Also, the moon is full and there is a pleasant, pale light flooding over the landscape. They are lying under the shelter of a hawthorn hedge. Fallen leaves provide mattress and pillow. Griswold has folded his claws behind his head. It would be nice to have a good cup of something hot to drink like lousewort tea, but this luxury must wait for better times.

Strangely, he is not all that tired, although he should be after such an exciting day. It had begun as usual with getting out of bed while Glug snored on. At some time in the future, he will share with the raven his experiences of the worst day of his life. But first he would like to hear the whole story of his companion's past twelve days.

"Leave nothing out, friend. Every scrap you tell me might prove to be very important in the days to come. Take your time."

Rasputin too has had a long day. He had rested last night on the far edge of the Dartmoor Park. He had a strange urgency pushing him homewards and had rested little. His flight back had been over land the whole way, more direct than his earlier flight in the opposite direction. Coming back, he knew where he was heading and could take a shorter route, but he is still very tired and badly wants some rest. However, Griswold needs to know at least something of what he has discovered before the man will be able to sleep peacefully.

"Boss, we are both exhausted. Your day has been completely full and mine also. Let's take a nap for an hour or so first and then I'll tell my story. That way we'll both be refreshed and alert instead of fighting sleepiness. But I will tell you that I did find Wozzle. Gubbins I could not find. And I did find the Twith. Their home is a long way away, in a land called Kent. Apart from Wozzle, they also live in another place next door called Gyminge. They are tiny people, just half a thumb high. I met them, and they understood me when I talked to them, so there wasn't a language problem. I did not buy the eye salve because I could not find out whether they have it. Perhaps they do. Perhaps they don't. I came back to fetch you. I buried the gold pieces there to save bringing them back. I know where they are and can easily find them again. You can think that over while I take a rest. Good night."

Rasputin yawns, rolls over, and is soon asleep. Strangely, soon after, Griswold is also asleep and dreaming that Glug is snoring beside him while gold pieces like snowflakes drop on them from the skies. Neither stirs until the dawn chorus of the songbirds wakes them just before daylight. Griswold finds that the gold pieces he has been dreaming about have been raindrops and he is wet clear through.

After a good rest, Rasputin is able to give his master a full report. "Boss, after I left you, I headed east, as you told me. There wasn't too much left of the day. The land was new to me. Much of it was hilly moorland, higher than here and not as pretty. After a while, I guessed I was out of Cornwall, so I landed in a wood and met some crows who were coming back to their roost. They were really friendly and offered me an empty nest for the night. They had never heard of the Twith or the two places I was looking for, so clearly, I had to go farther.

"I left at dawn and went across wooded land before I started flying over the sea. There was no help from the birds on the coast. Some seagulls flew alongside and wanted to know why a raven was flying over the water. I told them I was looking for Wozzle and Gubbins, but they knew nothing. They advised me to fly a little to the north, stay below the clouds, and keep the coastline always in sight. Otherwise, I would end up in France, where people eat ravens for breakfast and frogs for supper. They told me the coast goes on and on and on and when I got to white cliffs, I would be getting near the end, but there would still be a long flight over the sea. I said I didn't know whether Gubbins and Wozzle are in England or not, but I hoped they were. One of the seagulls dropped down and caught a fish and gave it to me, which was good of him because I was beginning to feel hungry. They were ever so much more friendly than the seagulls at Trevose.

"I veered north and began to follow the coastline just above the cliffs and beaches. It was beginning to rain, and the clouds were low. That made it easier for making inquiries along my way, but I was getting no sign at all whether the places I was looking for even existed. From then on, I stayed with the coastline. I thought that coastal birds would also know about things inland, and there was no point flying over the sea because the land I was looking for wouldn't be there anyway.

"That night I spent in a castle something like our own. The ravens in the castle thought that they had heard of Trevose, but they had never heard of Gubbins or Wozzle, nor had they heard of the Twith. One of them told me that there was a large island

with white cliffs ahead of me and things there were a bit mysterious. There were dragons guarding a castle in the middle of the
island, and strange things happened. I should be careful with my
inquiries. From then on, I hardly saw any more ravens, although
there were plenty of crows and magpies. And there were always
plenty of seagulls. I kept north of the island. The birds I asked
said there was no Wozzle or Gubbins in those parts, so I passed
by and flew over a big river and kept on going east.

"The land was becoming very different from our own land
of Cornwall. There were more trees, and the land was softer.
There wasn't any flint and not so many rocks. There were many
more fields and towns and villages than here. The houses were
different too. There were very few homes with slate roofs but
lots of thatched cottages. I saw many more people on the
ground than we have here. The roads were wider and better
kept, and they were crowded with carts and wagons and walk-
ers heading for market.

"Some were out fishing in boats very much like ours. I slept
in the woods the next night. I'm glad you tied the coins in cloth
and tied them to my leg. Flying for days with a load like that
was beginning to tire me. Several times, I switched the coins
to my other claw. I watched out for farmers plowing with oxen
or horses and dropped down on those fields with the seagulls.
They didn't seem to mind an odd raven hopping among them,
looking for worms.

"It was on the fourth or fifth day, towards evening, that
things began to happen. Soon I knew that my long journey was
not in vain. I had been flying over a very flat marshland at or
below the level of the sea with the hills to my left when a seagull

caught up with me. We were both flying the same way, although she was flying faster.

"She saw that I was tired and asked me if I was a stranger and whether I was hungry. She was a kindly creature, for she swung away several times and each time brought me a small fish, fresh from the water and still wriggling. She didn't bother to land, but transferred them to me while we were still flying. Once, I dropped a fish, but she dived and caught it still in the air and brought it back. That snack really revived me.

"She had never heard of Gubbins, but she had heard of the Twith. Hurrah! She was friendly with them. One of them had pulled a thorn out of her foot. She told me that they are tiny little people who live on their own, away from people like you. And she knew where they live, in a place called Wozzle and a place called Gyminge.

"Was I happy! Now I could buy the salve to get your eye fixed. Then you could carry on working in the castle without anyone ever finding out that you were working with magic. I asked her if she could tell me how to get there. She said that since I was a friend and a stranger in the area, she would take me there. Wasn't that good of her? Talk about going the extra mile.

"Far ahead of us were tall, white cliffs, but we did not continue towards them. She swung around and flew due north. While we flew, she told me about the Little People. They are not as tall as her beak is long, and they can talk to animals and birds. They are people with their own language, but they can understand the language of others without the need for translation. 'They are good people,' she said,' who keep to themselves and think no harm of others. They only speak the truth, and they are healers. Injured birds and animals go to them for help. They have very few enemies among wild creatures and are friends to all.'

"This sounded perfect for our needs. Surely they would sell us salve for your eye and I could soon be on my way back. It took a little longer than I thought though and didn't quite work out as easily as I was hoping."

Rasputin Inquires

Around

Griswold waits patiently for the raven to nibble at a hawthorn berry or two hanging just above his head. He does not interrupt the story at all. He listens carefully. Questions can come later. Refreshed, Rasputin continues.

"The seagull and I touched down near a cattle pond on the edge of a bog about three or four miles inland from the coast. Some cows were drinking, and they had a herder with them. His large dog seemed to have a thing against birds even though we didn't do anything to him. He was noisy, so we moved out on the bog. The dog didn't dare venture out there, although he barked at us from the bank. We made faces at him, which made him frantic. Served him right.

"The seagull told me, 'Just beyond the bog, where the hedge and fields begin, is where the Twith live. They look just the same as humans, but they are very much smaller. They avoid people, and people can't see them even if they are straight in front of them. But birds and four-legged creatures can see them, so you'll have no trouble.'"

Rasputin offers a word of explanation to Griswold. "The Twith seem to be able to decide who can see them and who can't see them. Strange. They can see each other, of course, so you may have to become their size in order to see them."

Griswold nods. He is listening very carefully, remembering all that he is hearing, and is ready for the raven to continue.

"Her last message to me was, 'I'll be on my way now. I have young ones at home. I hope your errand will be successful and you'll be able to manage. Beyond the bog are the fields of Gyminge, and just a little farther on are some low hills. That's where you'll find Wozzle. You won't have any trouble now. I'm sorry I couldn't help you with Gubbins, but I have just never heard of it.' I told her that she had been a great help anyway. I shall think better of seagulls in the future. I was sorry to lose her company. She was so much more helpful than the seagulls in this part of the country.

"I decided to rest the night where the seagull left me and start fresh in the morning. There were lots of crows about, and many headed for a barn on the edge of the bog to roost for the night. They knew I was a stranger but made no trouble when I joined them, and they shared what they knew about the Twith, so the time with them was useful.

"I spent the next day or two just looking around. I did not see a single Twith those first two days. I talked to the crows, and I talked to other kinds of birds that weren't too frightened to share what they knew. The magpies were the most helpful. They are always ready to talk.

"I buried the coins you gave me. There was no point in carrying them around until I found someone who would sell me the medicine. Shortly after that, I found a weasel who knew a lot more than I had learned so far. Being a trader, he had connections with the Little People, and he was willing to talk. He even made a few inquiries to find answers to some of my questions. He seemed not to have many friends. I buttered him up and offered to take him for a ride on my back, but he thought he might fall off. Just as well really. He would have been heavy to carry, although I could have done it.

"He was the one who told me that the wisest of the Twith, their seers, had just put out a warning that the Little People should stay indoors and keep away from strangers. They foretold that an enemy was approaching from the west. They did not know what form the enemy would take, but he, or they, would be wearing black. I wonder who that could be and what they might be up to. I can't see why anyone would want to attack them. They don't do anyone any harm.

"Boss, I can tell you what I found out about the Little People, or I can tell you about what I did when I got to the bog. Which do you want to hear first?"

Griswold is in little doubt that he'll take the first option. Once he knows all there is to know about the Twith, he can be planning his strategy for the future, wherever it may take the pair of them. It is just a matter of the most efficient use of an exceptional mind that is capable of proceeding on more than two tracks at the same time.

Under the patch, his eye is twitching as though to remind him he is not going to get far until this problem is solved. "Tell me about the Little People first, my lad. It will provide the background for your own story, and I'll understand that better."

Rasputin is expecting this response. He is intense and wanting to share the news he has found. This is, after all, why he has hurried home. "Once, the Little People were the only people to inhabit the land of Kent. There were many tribes of them, each ruled by its own king. Because they were so small, there was plenty of space for everyone. Then invaders came across the sea, people your size, your kind of people. This was long, long ago. They pressed in upon the small folk causing most of them to flee and resettle far to the north or the west. They went off on birds, and some even crossed the sea. Our own Cornish pixies down by Lands End are probably from the Little People that fled from Kent centuries ago.

"The weasel thought that nowadays, probably only two kingdoms of Little People, Wozzle and Gyminge, are left in all the country. They share a boundary line, and the people are all close friends. Many are related to each other. The land in Gyminge is more flat, with a large pond in the middle that the local Twith call a lake. Wozzle, to the north of it, is not quite so large but has more hills and more people.

"I spent most of the time I was there in Wozzle. An elderly king, King Leo, governs from Lyminge Castle on the hill. He isn't in good health, and people have wondered whether when he dies, the two kingdoms will merge into one. The weasel thinks people would find that arrangement beneficial.

"The Little People, he said, are happy people. They envy no one. There are no quarrels over land or property. They are contented and industrious and live in peace and prosperity. There is enough for everyone. They are accustomed to harmony. They have lived by the rules of truth for centuries. They never lie to each other, and when they make a promise, they keep it. This makes them good to trade with.

"There is one strange thing about them. It might have to do with their small size. Maybe being small is wiser than being big. They grow older only when they want to. They choose the age they want to be and just stay there for as long as they want.

I asked about whether the Twith ever die, and no one I asked had clear memories of that happening. They all remembered their kings doing so and occasionally old relatives, but it doesn't seem to be a very frequent event. They don't have wars, and there seems to be little or no sickness. They just seem to go on and on.

"All their farm animals are very small too. Their barnyards and pastures are full of tiny horses, cows, pigs, dogs, chickens, rabbits, ducks, geese, and turkeys. The wild birds are normal size, very much bigger than the Little People. This is probably because they range over territory far larger than the two kingdoms and many migrate overseas in winter. They wouldn't survive if they were as small as flies. Toads too are full-sized. They are special and exceptional, and that's because they migrate between the bog and Gyminge Lake each spring to have their babies. They were probably doing so long before the Little People themselves arrived.

"I didn't spend long in the other little kingdom, Gyminge, but the weasel knew a lot about them too. That country is governed by King Rufus and Queen Sheba from Gyminge Castle. It is situated on the edge of their lake. He and his family are much loved by their people. The king's father only recently died after a very long reign.

"The king of Gyminge is advised by a select group of men. They must be like King Druthan's council. They are said to be wise people. Some of them are seers and soothsayers and can foresee future events. But they do not use magic. They think magic is bad.

"The Little People have recorded all the knowledge accumulated in the past into one book, the Lore. It's possible that might be where the cure for the twitch could be found, but no one could tell me. The weasel understandably didn't know very much about the Lore. The birds I talked to about it also didn't know very much. Apparently, though, in addition to storing the wisdom of the past, it talks about the future yet to come. It says that one day, when the people depart from their old traditions and begin to tell lies and practice deceit, the way you Beyonders do, the Twith will be defeated by conquerors from outside Gyminge. Many will be captured, but a few—only a handful—will escape into the land of the Beyonders. They will have to live there until they find a way to defeat those who conquered them. But they can only use the weapon of truth. One day, they will return. That's all far in the future."

Griswold Plans

Action

With every explanation by Rasputin of the Twith and their way of life, Griswold sees clearly how these stupid Little People have deliberately gotten rid of the very weapons with which they can defend themselves. The weapons of deceit, discord, and division are the essential tools of the victor in any struggle and become the tactics for any dictator, any leader. It is a wonder they have not already been taken over. He is only just in time.

The campaign, for he has already decided upon his course of action, is going to be a pushover. A leader does not need to wait for all the facts to be at his fingertips. Additional facts will just fill in more details. A few essential pieces of information and Griswold, the general—maybe he should promote himself to field marshal—is at work planning an attack. Inspired and possessed by an inner force, he pictures battalions of soldiers on the move, striking like lightning where least expected. He chuckles. The current is flowing, gaining force and speed within him. The excitement is building. General Griswold is leading his troops, and their march is unstoppable. He'll show King Druthan yet. The king may think that banishment is a punishment, but Griswold will turn it into an opportunity.

Even though Griswold is still a raven like Rasputin, how different the two of them are. As his companion has been talking, Griswold, behind his closed eyes, has been elsewhere. Oh no. Do not be fooled. He is not sleeping. In his mind, he is ruthlessly executing a campaign against an increasingly helpless enemy whose retreat is turning into a rout. He yells at them, *Run for your lives! Run! Run!* He remembers Munro and the challenge he has made for himself. *Hold on to your dreams, wee man. Mine are beginning to come true.*

Griswold is meeting his destiny. For this, he was made. He might look like Rasputin, a mere raven in appearance, but he is so different within, a coiled spring full of energy, awaiting release. He is as different from his friend as chalk is from cheese, as different as real pasties baked in a Cornish kitchen in a Cornish range are from shop-bought ones. That thought reminds Griswold that he is hungry.

Sound the trumpets, sound the bugles, sound the horns, sound the whatever-you-will that makes a noise. He might have been born a stable groom's fourteenth son in a Cornish village that faces the sunset on the western sea, but his destiny—his role, his purpose—is to be master of Wozzle, master of Gyminge, master of Trevose, master of England, master of whatever-you-like-to-name!

History books will take his name as the focus, the hinge about which everything turns. It will be BG and AG, before Griswold and after Griswold. Baby children will be named after him. They will call the girls Griswolda or Griswoldine. He thinks he prefers Griswoldina.

Once again, he hears within his mind the cries that one day will be on a thousand lips:

Long live the king!
Long live the king!
Long live the king!
Long live King Griswold!

However, maybe he will give up on the king bit. After all, kings are only kings. Instead, he will be above and beyond mere kings, who are nothing more than overlords. He will be the great wizard, the Wizard of Wozzle or the Wizard of Gyminge. Wozzle sounds better, he decides.

Griswold continues to let his mind wander in wild imagination. *It will suit my kindly leadership style to have kings as vassals, begging for mercy, pleading for their lives, trading their wives and children for gentler treatment. I will be generous. After all, I am by nature a soft and kindly man averse to violence.* This is his own assessment of himself, so don't be fooled by what he is thinking.

I will give two sweets, not just one, to each child when I go to open orphanages for the children of my war veterans. My own immense talents, instead of being wasted on simply writing statutes and settling disputes, will be devoted to directing strategies behind the scenes. I will act as the conductor of an orchestra, the captain of a great ship, the benefactor of thousands, the master magician. I will out-think and know more than those who serve me as well as those who oppose me.

My court, my domain, will not be so foolish as to expect loyalty from those beneath, but will expect and give treachery. I will always be one step ahead. It is naive to expect the best of people. That attitude invites attack. "Expect the worst and be prepared," will be my motto—among others.

It will be important for me to be utterly ruthless in order to survive. Even simple peasants without an ounce of common sense should be able to see that a true genius, appearing like a comet in the sky, is now among them. Let them all tremble. I will outlie and outdeceive and outmaneuver all those around me. I must be prepared to outarm those who would attack and outmagic the magicians who oppose me. I will use every weapon at my disposal, including those in the hands of the enemy. It will be easy to promise the populace anything and everything. Griswold most certainly has no intention of ever keeping any promises he makes. Promises are weapons to be cast aside and forgotten when they have served their purpose. He intends to be their master. It is all sheer genius. For him, the end alone counts and justifies the means used to get there.

Griswold lets his mind penetrate farther into the future. *I must remember to write a manual of modern warfare when the campaigns are over and I have retired from active leadership. But,* he smiles to himself, *the clamor of my people will not let me retire. I am the father of the nation. They cannot go on without me. They will insist that I drop any thought of leaving them. They will be in tears, pleading on their knees. Reluctantly, I will accede to their entreaties. Though I'll be so very tired and aged, for their sakes, I will carry on.* He shakes his head and returns to more immediate plans.

The weapons of war, when one is determined to win, are broken promises, shattered agreements, lies, deceit, and betrayal. But, of course, it requires bigger, stronger, and better weapons as well. It will be essential to have a good herald with a loud voice to accuse my enemies of taking the same actions that I am. I will have to be prepared to pay the price that every ruthless leader must pay. I will discover that price and not hesitate to pay it every time. Add to that mix the fact that I will be a commanding general with a brilliant and youthful spirit, have outstanding leadership qualities, dogged determination, and extreme craftiness. Ah. With a combination like that, I cannot fail. Hail. The conquering hero comes—and his name begins with G.

I will talk peace but strike when the enemy least expects. Total surprise and total war is what will be required. I will stir up the people with stories of atrocities and terrify the enemy with stories of my anger. They will quake in their shoes and be afraid to get out of bed in the morning. World, begin to tremble!

It doesn't matter whether my attacking force is outnumbered. The history books of Wozzle are ripe for a rewrite. "An escaped prisoner in a prison suit too small for him, along with his raven, does battle with whoever dares stand against them." Beware. Wozzle will be overwhelmed first, then Gyminge, and then the world. The odds are all on my side. Sound the trumpets once more. Let battle commence.

The Twith have no idea at all of how to conduct a campaign of war. Well, I will have to teach them. My strategy will be simple. The plans that I worked through for King Druthan will adapt well for what lies ahead since the Twith have much the same foolish scruples as the king. Having two separate kingdoms to deal with, one after the other, rather than a single larger area, is going to make it all the easier.

Wozzle, the smaller kingdom with an ailing king, should obviously be the first target. I must first establish myself among the people and then locate allies within the court and gain access to the castle. I will ascend through the levels of the court until I am next to the king. Perhaps they need a new court doctor, perhaps even a new court jester. Simple. Next it will not be difficult to arrange a sudden vacancy, something close to the king. The idea amuses him, and he breaks into laughter. *I shall gain the confidence of all and then… and then… strike!* Again he laughs to himself, recalling the dishwasher's journey to chief librarian. *It is going to be faster this time, much faster. There is no need for reading the books along the way. The information is already all in my head. It's only the stage that is different.*

Griswold taps his forehead. *My brilliant mind is the force that is going to turn over the world. Soon my supreme leadership will be acknowledged—first by the Little People, half a thumb high, and eventually, as the conquests spread, even by King Druthan in his cliff castle in Cornwall. That pathetic king will plead for, but not receive mercy. What a struggle that is going to be. It will be the final struggle, the last battle. In order to keep the records straight, I will have to supervise the writing of the schools' history books.*

King Druthan has sentenced me to banishment for a thousand years. Well. Just watch out, tomorrow. It's coming sooner than any-one thinks. He laughs again. He laughs continually, surprising Rasputin, who is still waiting for some response to his story so far. He wonders which bit was so funny.

"Rasputin, my lad, we had better pick up some breakfast. And then we should be on our way. There's no time to waste. You can continue the story as we fly. Yes, we are heading for Wozzle, the fastest way you know. Ha, ha, ha. They're in for a surprise, and they have no idea what it is. It's us."

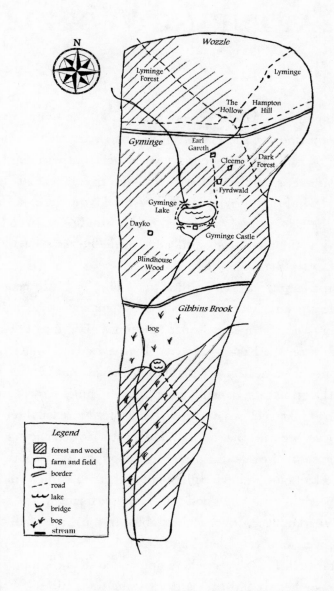

Wozzle and Gyminge, neighboring countries of Little People
The Brook (or Common), a new home for six of the Little People]

Capturing Wozzle

The kingdom of Wozzle extends south from the Lyminge Forest to the foot of the chalk downs that mark the bottom of Hampton Hill. At this boundary, with their southern neighbors of Gyminge, several small streams issue from the foot of the hill and wind through the Dark Forest to Gyminge Lake. From there, the lake water discharges through Blindhouse Wood into the bog at Gibbins Brook. The edge of the bog is the southern boundary of Gyminge.

On a sunny day, late in the afternoon, the Little People of Wozzle are surprised to see a stranger their own size clad in a blue and white striped prisoner "costume" glide into the castle courtyard on the back of a raven. The new arrival, quite comical from the start, begins entertaining the crowd that has gathered. The grimacing, dancing, hopping, twitching, somersaulting, gyrating fool of a clown makes everyone break into laughter. They have never seen anyone so funny. He must have been born laughing. He soon discards his striped costume for proper court jester attire, a half blue and half yellow suit with a red, ruffled collar.

Accepted as a jolly good fellow, he performs in the square of the marketplace, down at the stables, in the dining hall of the castle, even in private homes and finally before the throne of the king himself. He is everywhere applauded. King Leo, plagued with poor health and the cares of state, finds himself happily distracted by his new jester. The ministers of the court and the citizens themselves are more than merely amused. They cannot get enough of the jokes and tricks and stunts. And Griswold finds that he actually enjoys being just half a thumb high.

Many months have now passed since the new jester appeared. Few remember what life was like before he came round, and of those who do—well, they have gone off someplace far away. The jester is so well favored by King Leo that he is invited to step into the role of personal advisor to the king. *Marvelous, splendid,* muses the jester privately.

Griswold has now perfectly positioned himself to control every event, large or small, that takes place in Wozzle. Before long, the kind jester is officially standing in for King Leo, who's a bit under the weather more and more frequently. By cunning and deceit, the jester usurps the throne and grabs command of Wozzle's parliament as well as its humble military. Far too late, the king realizes that he has misunderstood the jester's laughter. While the court jester has been making King Leo, his court ministers, and the entire kingdom laugh, *he* has been laughing at *them.* The funniest jester the court has ever had is no longer funny anymore.

The court jester is deadly serious. He pursues his plans to usurp the throne and take over the kingdom, and no one is able to stop him. He may be the same size as the Little People, but he is always at least one step ahead of them. The king is already in his power. Now the Little People are wondering what has hit them. Ruthlessly and gleefully, Griswold and Rasputin do their worst. Their worst is not only bad; it is awful, awful not only for King Leo and the castle but for the whole of Wozzle.

The glass factory in Lyminge, which manufactures wine bottles and glasses for the wee folk, now works three shifts a day. It makes a new, larger product that Griswold has named "captivity bottles." Those ordinary citizens who insist on telling the truth and refuse to be subject to the wizard are being bottled and the stoppers sealed with wax. It's like the Egyptians keeping mummies in mummy cases, except that with the wizard, he can keep his captives alive. The victim is slid into the bottle, and a plug the size of a Beyonder's button is sealed over the top with candle wax. That person will stay there as long as the wizard wishes, for centuries and centuries if it pleases him. Scores upon scores of filled bottles are stashed away in the dungeons. Those willing to share the truth with lies and deceit are being changed into goblins and put into drab uniforms. Military service has become compulsory for all males over the age of eighteen, so women are compelled to replace the men and run the family farms, working as field hands.

It also does not promise well for Gyminge. The two masterful conspirators, the jester and the raven, are busy scheming and planning for further conquests beyond Wozzle. The Twith are living peacefully in Gyminge, but their peace is not going to last much longer. Gyminge is the next step forward in Griswold's plans, and he is not interested in wasting time. In fact, he is in a hurry.

North of the

Dark Forest

Although they still miss King Rufus's father, the old and good king who had ruled them for such a long while, the people of Gyminge are delighted with their new royal family. King Rufus and his beautiful Queen Sheba live in Gyminge Castle with their teenage daughter, Princess Alicia. Rufus has himself grown up here and knows every nook and cranny of the castle. A wise ruler, he and his family are wonderfully happy. His only sadness is that he does not have a son to succeed him.

The royal castle is set on the southern edge of a lake in the center of the country. There is said to be a serpent deep in the lake, though few in Gyminge, if any, have seen it. Gyminge Castle juts out into the water, but its main gate is easily approached by land. The castle needs no moat or drawbridge to defend it, for Gyminge is a land at peace. Or at least there *had* been no need until now. Suddenly, things are different, vastly different. Dark thunder clouds of war and invasion are, for the first time, beginning to sweep in and threaten the kingdom.

Soon after he comes to the throne, King Rufus becomes suspicious and wary of events taking place in the kingdom of Wozzle. What has happened to their good neighbors is serious and might well lead to dangers for his own land. King Leo has been overthrown in a palace uprising, reportedly led by the court fool. The king, people say without being sure how they know, is imprisoned in his own dungeon in a bottle tightly sealed with candle wax. He has been replaced by a wicked wizard. No one knows where the wizard has come from. He is not a native of Wozzle. There might be doubts about his origin, but there is none about his ability as a wizard. He possesses more knowledge of magic in his little finger than the wise men of Lyminge know with their heads put together. No one can withstand him or outwit him. Other magicians dread him and hide from him, lest he change them into worms or snakes, join their tails together, and use them for playing Quoits. There are some things he cannot do, but there are not many.

As soon as news of events in Wozzle reaches King Rufus, bringing with it the threat of attack upon his own kingdom, he is quick to take action. Beginning at home, the king speaks solemnly with Queen Sheba, who will not leave his side, come what may. He wants to be sure that she is aware of the risks of remaining in the castle, should attack and siege come. Without further delay, the king sends their beloved Princess Alicia off to a secluded cottage deep in Blindhouse Wood. He sends with her the nurse she has known from childhood and two trusted menservants. She has protested and is definitely not very happy. Hopefully, it will not be for too long a period of time. With the princess safely beyond the reach of the evil wizard, King Rufus turns his attention to military matters and sets about stiffening defenses throughout Gyminge.

The defense of the country is divided into three crucial areas. One of his most trusted and able friends is Earl Gareth. His estate, called Up-Horton, lies on the land northwest of the Dark Forest at the foot of the wooded hill that marks the boundary between the two countries. This is where the attack, if one comes, will most likely be launched, and the king assigns the earl the task of guarding all that area. Another trusted companion, equally strong and capable and wise, the valiant Count Fyrdwald, will guard and garrison the Dark Forest itself and prepare for battle in the forest. Attackers will have to penetrate the forest and overcome Fyrdwald to get to the center of the country. He, the king, as well as overseeing the whole campaign, will control the defense of the area from the northern edge of Gyminge Lake to the southern border on Gibbins Brook bog.

As the king begins to stir all of Gyminge to readiness, surprising news comes of a strange new barrier around Wozzle. The birds of Gyminge that fly northwards cannot penetrate beyond the border. They cannot even see what it is that is stopping them. It seems to be an invisible curtain that encircles Wozzle. There are no longer any birds inside Wozzle. They have disappeared completely. The barrier prevents the exchange of information between the neighboring kingdoms, but rumors spread as hot and fast as wildfire throughout Gyminge, changing and growing wilder as they pass from one person to the next. One person says, "The wizard can stun with a look from his eye." Another has heard that the wizard can change himself into a fire-breathing dragon! Frightened people declare, "He burned two oxen to a crisp with one breath." There is word that the birds have all been changed into ladybugs. It has been said that the wizard can hear conversation before it is put into words. No secrets are possible from the wizard. The town clerk exclaims, "The wizard can turn time forwards and backwards!"

Stories multiply throughout the bewildered populace, "The

wizard can move from place to place in the blink of an eye." One young lad tells his friends, "The wizard can disappear even while you are talking to him. You have no idea where he is or whether he is even there." They have even bigger news. "He has only to utter a word to make a giant out of you, or a dwarf!"

Most worrisome is the news that the wizard plans to take over Gyminge in the way he has taken over Wozzle. Some of the worst news comes from a visiting relative who is unable to get back into Wozzle, "All the able-bodied men in Wozzle have been changed into goblins and brought into the army. Only women and children now work the land. The men are needed to fight." The king himself has heard a rumor that the order to attack Gyminge at the next full moon has already been given. The goblin troops are moving up.

As rumors of the situation in Wozzle become more threatening, Earl Gareth requires the men of the north province to develop fighting skills. Instructors travel throughout the towns and villages, teaching the people and checking their weapons and the men's abilities to use them. The earl's two sons are tireless in helping him. Officers, sergeants, and corporals are appointed from among the farmers and their laborers. Training goes on through the late spring and early summer and becomes more intense. The men are not naturally fighting men. They are stonemasons, saddlers, thatchers, charcoal burners, woodcutters, and herdsmen accustomed only to peaceful pursuits, but they do not lack courage. Their fighting skills slowly begin to develop. They have staves, slings, bows and arrows, axes, swords, and lances. Earl Gareth begins to believe his men will give a good account of themselves.

At midsummer, King Rufus arranges to meet with Fyrdwald and Gareth at Fyrdwald's manor atop the hill in the middle of the Dark Forest. All paths in the forest radiate to and from the hill. The king and his escort gallop up from Gyminge Castle.

Before leaving home from the other side of the forest, Earl Gareth divides and delegates the watch of the border to his sons. He instructs them to be on full alert throughout the time he is away.

These two young men are both in their late teens. There are no other children in the family. Taymar is unusually tall, taller than his brother, who is himself well built and muscular. His tousled red hair droops around bright, blue eyes sparkling with mischief. Ambro, younger by a year or so, has brown eyes and light brown hair down to his shoulders. Since they were barely old enough to pitch a javelin, they have tested their strength and skills against each other. They are quick to anger and quick to forgive. Ambro is better at wrestling and weightlifting and the use of the staff. Taymar is better at running and wielding the sword and axe. He is capable with the bow as well. Both boys are self-reliant, enjoy being on their own as much as being with each other, and thrive on challenges. Their tutor is proud of them both and matches them against rivals with great confidence. One of the brothers might beat the other, but there is no one that can defeat either of them.

Their father is equally proud of both his boys. These are troubling times and, like the king, the earl is worried that the long, good times are about to come to an end. Either of the boys will fill his shoes well when it comes time for him to hand over his charge of the Northern Province. He and his wife, the countess, had hoped to see at least one of their sons married and settled before assuming the heavy responsibilities of governing the province, but no one knows how long they still have.

The Woodcarver's Niece

Ambro is in love. He has never been in love before, but he is certain he knows exactly how it feels. It's the way he feels just now. Almost every waking thought is full of Cymbeline, the brown-haired, bright-eyed, laughing girl who lives at the wood-carver's house where the path enters the forest. When wrestling with Taymar, Ambro is wrestling for her approval and praise, even when she is not present. He imagines her applauding every fall and every twist and then groaning as Taymar pins his shoulders. But the very next moment, excited and laughing, she's on her feet, shouting with joy as Ambro wriggles out from under his brother to be on top. When he is fighting with staves, every crack of the wood is an imagined blow from which he has protected her. He loses sight of his brother or his tutor in the fantasy faces of robbers in the woods trying to break in to his beloved's shelter. He can't get her out of his mind.

Although Ambro and Taymar are close, he can't share with his brother the depth of what he feels for Cymbeline. He hardly knows himself. He has no idea where his love begins or ends, for it envelops her. In happier days, before the Wozzle crisis, Ambro had spent many joyful hours learning from the woodcarver how to bring forth a bird from an ordinary block of wood. There is a wide variety of woods to choose from: oak or walnut or beech. Different birds emerge depending on the type of wood and the grain. After several lessons though, Ambro had to admit to himself that woodcarving, though enjoyable, was no longer his first excuse for slipping off to the woodcarver's house. Carving has been overshadowed by the irresistible Cymbeline.

Her Uncle Cleemo is a gruff old man with a white beard fringing his wrinkled, weathered face. He has never married and doesn't really understand children. The top of his head is usually covered by a red working cap. He has another like it, in better condition, for when he goes out to meet people.

Taymar has also been to the small cottage on the edge of the forest once or twice. He too has been asked if he wishes to learn to carve birds. Taymar, though, prefers doing something more active. If there is nothing better to do, he'd prefer to climb the trees rather than carve them. The more difficult the climb, the greater the challenge. If his brother wishes to carve birds instead, so be it.

Many years ago, Cymbeline's father and mother died, so she and her young brother, Barney, came to live with their uncle. They get on well enough together and love each other very much. In fact, Cleemo loves the two youngsters more than he can say. Sometimes he tries to say so, but more often, he is tongue-tied and uneasy when the children hug him and tell him they love him.

Cymbeline does the cooking and housekeeping and tries to keep Barney tidy. He keeps telling his sister he's not going to grow older but that he's going to stay as a boy all his life. Cymbeline hopes he will reconsider this idea and eventually grow up.

Cymbeline is not just pretty; she is beautiful. At sixteen, she has a natural grace and seems to glide rather than bounce along. She has a ready smile; deep dimples in her cheeks; laughing, light brown eyes; and shiny brown hair that falls down to her shoulders. She likes frilly, lacy clothes and yellow dresses. She has dresses in many shades of yellow but few of other colors. She loves embroidery and cross-stitch and needlepoint. When her housework is done, she will sit near her uncle as he whittles his wood and chatter to him as she busies herself with her needlework.

Cleemo has worked with wood all his life. He enjoys the feel and touch of wood, savors its graining and the hard and soft spots he finds as he works. He finds pleasure in polishing with oils and stains when his cutting and scraping is done at last. He loves to let his mind disclose to him, from an unformed lump of beech or walnut or oak, the captured bird within that he will slowly, over weeks of patient work, release from captivity to freedom. Cleemo specializes in birds, rarely attempting animals or other creatures.

As he carves, his thoughts take him far beyond Gyminge, even though he has never been out of the country. Like many unmarried people, he enjoys being alone with his thoughts. A call from one of the children brings him back with a shock from unfamiliar places where his mind has taken him... as though they were dreams in the night. He will shake his head with surprise at the dinner bell and realize that, without knowing it, he has been carving a blackbird's beak on a robin.

Cleemo enjoys the visits from Ambro to learn the art of carving. He's a good pupil, but he will have to learn a lot more patience if he is to succeed. Ambro has bought a goodly number of his birds and sometimes brings an order from his mother for a special bird carving.

He's not blind though. He notices without saying anything how the young man's eyes follow his niece as she goes in and out from the house. He notices too how Cymbeline reacts when Ambro arrives. She blushes, and her hands shoot up to smooth her hair. He doesn't want Cymbeline to get hurt. She is, after all, only a woodcarver's niece, and Ambro is the son of the earl of Up-Horton. He doesn't want them to get too fond of each other. One day, the young man will be betrothed to some cousin of high status, and that will be the end of that. He supposes that he really should begin to look out for someone to take Cymbeline as a wife, but he can't bear to think of the cottage without her. It would be as though the house were wreathed in darkness. She is its sunshine. These days, she's shining brighter than ever.

One afternoon, when Cymbeline has gone out for a walk, Barney tells him that yesterday, while up high in the elm tree; he saw Cymbeline and Ambro walking together in the woods. They were laughing and joking, holding hands and swinging them to and fro as they strolled.

Cleemo needs to say something. When she returns alone, Cleemo asks her whether she has seen Ambro recently. He hasn't been for his carving lesson for a few days. His question seems to unloose a flood of excitement within Cymbeline. She has nothing to hide. Barney, hearing the question from the next room, slips in quietly to listen and sits down on his low stool beside the fireplace.

"Oh, Uncle Cleemo. I have just come from seeing Ambro, but these days he can't come for his lesson. The king expects an attack on Gyminge by the Wizard of Wozzle and his men any day. The earl has been called to Count Fyrdwald's manor to plan our defense. While he's been away, Taymar and Ambro each have half of the border to patrol. They have to keep constant watch and stay alert at all times. Ambro has been busy.

"The earl will return soon. Ambro will see him as soon as he is rested. And, and … Oh, Uncle Cleemo. I am so, so happy! Ambro has told me that he loves me and wishes to marry me. He's going to tell his father and seek his permission. I do love him so. I love you and Barney more than anything, but somehow, this is different, so different. It's like, like a bird inside of me, fluttering its wings and trying to get out. It's as though I am suddenly filled with a thousand butterflies and they're all singing sunbeam songs.

"Oh, Uncle, what do you think the earl will say? Do you think he will give his permission? He's a kind man, and surely he'll be able to see how much Ambro loves me."

TUWHIT

Day after day ever since the earl left for the Dark Forest to meet with the king, Ambro and Taymar leave their home and their mother to go about the duties their father gave them. They leave early in the morning and sometimes don't get back until dark. On those days, Ambro doesn't have time to visit Cymbeline. Yesterday, he missed seeing her. He hopes today to call at the wood-carver's cottage after he checks the various patrols to the west.

Taymar is out patrolling the positions of all the border guards along his eastern section below the hill. He whistles a call to his owl friend, Tuwhit, who is never far away.

The owl, when young, had been found in a demolished barn and had been brought to the earl's young son to have as a pet. The fledgling was larger than Taymar himself, but the boy fed the hungry bird and cared for it until it could fly. The owl showed no inclination to fly away when it was possible. Tuwhit has also shown no desire, now that he is fully grown, to mate with another barn owl but is only happy when in company with Taymar. They are so close to each other that sometimes it seems they know each other's thoughts before they are spoken. Because the Gyminge birds are full Beyonder size, Taymar has grown up almost as though he has wings of his own. There is rarely any need for him, or Ambro for that matter, to walk long distances. All he has to do is whistle the special call and Tuwhit, wherever he is, hears and heads towards it. The owl responds to Ambro's latest call and comes gliding down, pinions outstretched, poised for a quick landing.

Tuwhit is not only valuable as a flying taxi, but he is also wise. He is loyal to Taymar above all other creatures. As the boy has grown and his mind has stretched with curiosity, Tuwhit has been there to talk to and to ask questions requiring answers. If the bird hasn't known the answer, he has attempted to find out.

It is time for such a question and answer session now as Taymar cuddles down among the neck feathers in the perch he has made his own. The bird is flying eastwards barely above the trees. Taymar is close to Tuwhit's ear to speak and be heard while his eyes can see over the bird's head to what lies beyond.

"Tuwhit, do you really think the Wozzleites will invade us?"

"Yes. There is no doubt."

"When do you think it will happen?"

"Soon. Within a week," answers the owl.

"How can we find out?"

"Go there."

Taymar presses with more questions. "Where? To Wozzle? How can we go there?"

"We must find a way to get in," replies Tuwhit patiently.

"How do we do that?"

"We have to get through the curtain or above it or below it or find a gap in it."

Taymar is puzzled. "How shall we do that?"

"Probably not through the curtain. I've already been flying around it. I flew around it again only this morning, but I can't find any leaks or tears in it anywhere."

"What about above it?" suggests Taymar.

"I have flown as high as I can, but haven't been able to reach the top. The curtain seems to continue upwards without stopping. I couldn't find any sign that it ever comes to a stop except that the clouds seem to float over it. I don't know whether an eagle could do better or not."

"That leaves below it. What about that?"

Tuwhit turns his head back to look at his friend and chuckles throatily. "I'm a bird, not a rabbit."

"Well said, Tuwhit. Let's ask a rabbit."

As they fly along, Tuwhit's sharp eyes search the land below him. Suddenly, he spots one of the wee creatures directly below.

"Hold on!" He folds his wings and goes into a steep dive. Close to the ground, he spreads his wings and his claws snatch hold. The rabbit, a small young one, caught napping before it can move to escape, is suddenly aloft. Tuwhit is not trying to hurt the animal, just transport it to a place for some questioning. He does all his hunting for food south of the Gyminge border at Gibbins Brook. This tiny Gyminge rabbit is way smaller than rabbits in the Beyond and would hardly be worthwhile as food for a large owl. He makes a clumsy landing, hopping on one claw while holding his terrified captive in the other. Taymar jumps off and relieves him of it. He strokes the trembling bunny gently and talks to it in soft words until its shaking subsides.

As they land, a boy jumps out of a sycamore tree on the edge of the woods and runs towards them. "Hello, Taymar. What'cha doin'?"

Taymar smiles a greeting and beckons the lad over. He knows the boy well. He is the woodcarver's nephew, Barney. He has a perpetual grin on his face, especially when he is in his mess-about clothes, perched in a tree, pretending to be somebody else.

Barney is *all* boy. His nose is sprinkled with freckles. He's untidy. He's a fidget. He has hands that are dirty more often than clean. With his catapult, which Beyonders call a slingshot, he can hit an acorn at twenty paces. He climbs trees, swings on branches, and catches fish and lets them go. He is a friend to all the animals and birds in the forest and knows where the rabbit warrens go as though he is a rabbit himself. He avoids soap and enjoys mud. He doesn't bother to fasten the straps on his shoes. He wears short, leather trousers, and his knee-length stockings droop around his ankles. His various caps are worn back to front. For years, he has been about ten years old. He has a quick, alert mind and invents new games to play by himself. He would enjoy having a friend his own age.

He takes a close look, recognizes the rabbit in Taymar's hands, and shouts a welcome when a whisper would have done. "HI, BROLLY! You've strayed a long way from home! What'cha doin''ere?"

The little rabbit relaxes. This is one person she knows.

"Don't be frightened, little one." Taymar's voice is quiet and soothing. Gently, he strokes the brown fur. "So, your name is Brolly, is it?"

The rabbit's voice is high pitched and frightened. She shakes her head. "Brolly isn't my real name," she answers. "I don't like the rain and always run to hide. Brolly is what my brothers and sisters call me."

"Well then I'll call you Brolly too. I'm Taymar, and the owl here, he's Tuwhit. You seem to know Barney already. We want to be your friends, and we'd like to ask your help because we are in trouble. If you can't help us, that's alright. We'll take you home whenever you like."

The shaking of the little rabbit lessens. "Please take me home right away, right now." Her voice is high, and her eyes are frightened with panic.

Taymar signals to Tuwhit and at the same time nods an invitation to Barney to come with them. The boy is always looking for an opportunity for a sky ride. Holding the rabbit carefully in his cradled hands, Taymar climbs on the owl's back and says, "Do you remember where you picked her up, Tuwhit? I'll ask her to guide you when you get near if you aren't sure."

Barney knows the drill about bird riding. He has been here before. He has made many fun expeditions on Tuwhit's back, sometimes with Taymar or Ambro and sometimes by himself. He settles down among the neck feathers and stretches out a hand to stroke the rabbit. He wonders whether Taymar knows about Ambro and his sister but chooses to say nothing.

As the owl lifts into the air, Taymar asks, "Brolly, will you answer a question for me as we take you home?"

Brolly nods. The rabbit is more comfortable now that she is going home. These strangers who have captured her seem to be friends after all.

"How do you get up and down Hampton Hill now that there's a barrier in the way?"

Brolly understands the question and is ready to talk. In fact, she talks a mile a minute until Tuwhit, without her help, glides in to a perfect landing on the edge of the path. It is Barney who is guiding him, not the talkative rabbit.

The rabbits are angry. They don't know what is happening, but the Gyminge birds have told them that the wall has been built by the new ruler in Wozzle: the wizard. The baby rabbits can no longer use the slides they have used for centuries. Going to and fro has become so much more difficult. Someone should do something about it. The rabbits have no quarrel with the Wizard of Wozzle or with any of Wozzle's people. They don't even know what stops them going to and fro. There is nothing they can see. Every single one of the old paths has been blocked. If it wasn't for the deep tunnel they have built to go below the barrier, they wouldn't even be able to visit their family members on the Wozzle side.

It's just such a big nuisance.

The Rabbits

Get Busy

Taymar whistles with delight. *So there is a way into Wozzle after all,* he thinks. *The tunnel will be too small for me to wriggle through or for Barney to wriggle through, even though he's smaller. Perhaps, though, the tunnel can be enlarged. Anyway, even if we ourselves can't get through, here is a way to find out what is happening in Wozzle and how far the wizard's plans to invade Gyminge have progressed. The rabbits will surely know what is going on.*

He asks Brolly if she can call her parents and the elders of the warren. She has no need to do so. As soon as the passengers are on the ground, hosts of rabbits are running, hopping, and bouncing as they hurry to greet the young relative they feared was lost forever.

Tuwhit flutters away and perches high out of sight. He will give them space to talk with the boys. As Tuwhit well knows, rabbits are fearful of owls. In Gyminge, however, they need not worry. They are perfectly safe, for owls find plenty of food available elsewhere and are not interested in titchy rabbits as their meals.

Taymar looks around and waits as Barney greets various rabbits, and then he addresses all of them. First, he introduces himself and Barney to the whole group and assures them that they have nothing to fear from Tuwhit.

"You all know about the wizard who has conquered Wozzle. We who live in Gyminge expect he plans an attack upon us as well. If he succeeds, life for all of us, even for you, will never be the same again."

The rabbits listen with close attention. Their ears are perked up to catch every word the young man utters. Heads nod in agreement.

Taymar continues. "We are preparing to fight. It will help us to know when the Wozzleites plan to invade and where they will attack. All the ground paths and the bird paths to Wozzle are closed. Can you help us?"

An elderly rabbit speaks up. "I was there this morning. I went to visit my brother who has colic. He told me that goblins are everywhere along the border. They are from other parts of Wozzle, not from near here. They're all over the slopes of the hill, right up to the very top. I saw many soldiers myself, and I overheard them talking. The big news for them is that the wizard himself will be visiting them this afternoon for a final inspection. There's going to be a big inspection parade. They were checking their weapons, polishing their buttons and their boots. You can't imagine the hustle and bustle."

Taymar has been listening carefully. Now he appeals to the rabbits. "Is there any way that my friend and I could get over to Wozzle so that we can see and hear what happens at the wizard's inspection? He's sure to be sharing his plans with the men who are taking part. This would be a good chance to find out what we need to know."

The rabbits look at each other doubtfully. None of them think it will be possible to get Taymar and Barney into Wozzle. Their tunnels are far too small to allow either of their visitors to wriggle through. If they were birds, they might be able to get there by flying over the top of the curtain.

Taymar explains, "My friend, the owl does not think that is possible. He has already tried to do that, but he couldn't find the top of the curtain." Taymar waits, looking around slowly, as the rabbits consider what they might do. They want to help, but they need to figure out how.

Bandaged Paw, the elderly rabbit, doesn't really have a bandage on his foot. He was born with one white front paw and was given this name by his father. He does some calculations in his mind as he sizes up Taymar. He shares his thoughts with the rabbit next to him, who nods his head. Soon, there are clusters of rabbits in excited discussion. They reach general agreement and are ready to share their ideas with Taymar and Barney. Several join in the discussion.

Bandaged Paw begins. "It has taken two rabbits working in shifts almost two days to dig the tunnel deep enough to go below the curtain and then, once below it, to climb back up the other side. If you, Taymar wriggle through a tunnel on your hands and knees, you will need a tunnel five times as wide and five times as high as our usual tunnel. We won't be able to work from both ends because that is sure to attract attention. The digging will have to be done from this end, and we'll put guards and lookouts at the Wozzle end. We also don't have two days, but only about four hours to dig. However, we now know exactly the line and depth to dig. It will be better if we take a different line than our own tunnel. We can make it much shorter.

"We reckon that with a hundred rabbits working flat-out and another dozen or so organizing them properly to get the dirt out, we could be ready in about four hours. This would probably be in time for the wizard's inspection. We can get hold of the rabbits we need. There's no problem there. There are enough of us, and everyone will pitch in and help. It will take perhaps twenty minutes to get them all here. Do you have other work to do for the next four and a half hours while we get digging? Wait! Before you go, we'd better measure your shoulders."

As soon as Taymar nods his thanks, the ground begins shaking with rabbit messages being thumped out and carried along the tunnel networks to distant members of the rabbit families. It's time for Taymar to go. Matters are in good, safe, and experienced paws. A whistle from Taymar and Tuwhit glides down from his hidden perch to a small hillock away from the rabbits. He doesn't want to scare them.

They're already busy organizing. The cluster of rabbits becomes an army. From all directions, they are pouring out of the burrows and the undergrowth. Only a few have pickaxes and shovels. The majority are planning to use their paws. Quite a number have woven wicker baskets for carrying out the dirt.

Taymar would have liked to stay and watch how rabbits organize for an endeavor of this size, but he must be on his way. There are the patrols still to be checked. Barney and Taymar promise to be back in just four hours and a bit as they take off on Tuwhit's back. They're not far into the journey before Tuwhit swings in to land on a wide limb of the oak tree that had been struck years before by lightning. This is a favorite resting place for him. There's room for the two Twith to jump off, scramble around to face Tuwhit, and help satisfy the bird's curiosity as the boys share the food that Taymar brought with him.

Both Barney and Tuwhit want to go into Wozzle with Taymar. Although Barney will be able to go, Tuwhit realizes that there's no way he can scramble through a tunnel that will barely allow Taymar to crawl through. He accepts that he must stay and wait at the tunnel entrance as long as nightfall if necessary. If by early nightfall the two have not returned and there is no news, the owl will find Ambro and tell him all that has happened. He will also go on to inform Uncle Cleemo that Barney is with Taymar before returning to continue waiting.

Barney is delighted with the way his day is turning out. *You see, people do need boys after all. I'm smaller. I can wriggle through the tunnel even if Taymar can't. Maybe I should go first. I have my catapult and a pocket full of stones.* He wonders whether he should take a practice shot or two but decides he might need the ammunition for some real fighting. Instead, he just twangs the leather and lets his imagination do the rest.

Taymar tells them both, "This venture is not to get into any kind of fight. We don't want to be discovered. No one must even know we have been there. The wizard must believe that all his plans are secret. We will only venture as far into Wozzle as it is safe for us to go and then we'll retreat. Perhaps later we can go back a second or even a third time. It's not beyond the bounds of possibility that we can attempt a rescue of King Leo at Lyminge Castle, but this first journey must be kept secret and cloaked in silence. Meanwhile, I need to resume the patrols to check the border and alert the men."

INTO THE TUNNEL

Even Tuwhit, who is not easily surprised, is amazed. He *thinks* this is the place where they separated from the rabbits four hours ago, but so much has changed that he isn't one hundred percent sure. They must have had even more rabbits than they expected and as many outside as inside the tunnel. The rabbits haven't just dumped the earth from the tunnel into piles. They've used it for landscaping and making paths. Some of the paths they've made have not yet been trodden. The fresh paw marks of the smoothers along the embankments and the paths themselves are clear. The rabbits have even leveled an area as a sports field and running track.

Bandaged Paw greets the trio as they land. He tells them that they have needed two directors of operations, both an inside director to oversee work in the tunnel and an outside director. The town planner has seized the opportunity to become the outside director. Taymar and Barney express surprise when they discover that the town planner is Bandaged Paw's own son. The proud father, greatly pleased with their reaction, coughs slightly and mentions that he had also been the town planner in his youth. It must run in the family.

Taymar and Barney are introduced to the outside director and congratulate him on his fine work. He is quite distinguished-looking, smartly dressed in a vest, a bow tie, and a trilby hat. He remarks, "We've all been working against a tight time schedule.

I realized that time is of the essence." He blows a whistle, three sharp, short blasts.

Out of the huge tunnel entrance, rabbits come running in a continuous stream. It is as though inside is a huge machine turning out rabbits from a never-ending supply of raw material. There are big ones, small ones, mostly middle-sized ones, brown ones, grey ones, and one or two black ones. Some have miners' lamps banded around their foreheads. Some have shovels and picks over their shoulders. All have brown dirt on their fur and whiskers and paws.

Now come the organizers. They are also running, although not as fast. They're the older ones, less able to actually work, but they can supervise. As they emerge, they join the outside rabbits in a great circle around Taymar, Barney, Bandaged Paw, and his son. The crowd continues to swell.

At last, the flow of rabbits diminishes. After a distinct pause, there emerges from the tunnel the final rabbit. He is the only one wearing a bright yellow hardhat, which he has acquired from some distant, unknown source. He too wears a vest but no bow tie. He's the inside director, a construction rabbit, and he looks down on town planners and their fancy dress. In one pocket of his vest, secured by a fine gold chain, is a large, gold watch. The circle opens to allow him to join those gathered in the center. He salutes them with a pleased smile on his dusty face. Removing his pocket watch, he flips the lid open and looks at it . . . twice.

The inside director clears his throat and begins. "Gentlemen."

Barney does not recognize himself as being included in this formal greeting, so the inside director repeats himself, looking directly at the boy. "Gentlemen, I have the honor to report the completion of the assigned task in three hours, fifty-seven minutes, and twenty-one seconds. Hip, Hip, Hooray! Hip, Hip, Hooray! Hip, Hip, Hooray!" He swings his yellow hat around his head as he leads the cheering.

The outside director removes his trilby and swings it likewise. Barney missed the opportunity to join in the first time around, but then, reaching behind his neck, grabs the bill of his grubby red cap and waves it around his head also.

Everyone is cheering. Finally, it settles down, and there is silence. The inside director bows towards Taymar. He steps two paces sideways and, with a wide, low swing of his hat, motions Taymar towards the tunnel that awaits him.

Taymar recognizes the immense effort that the rabbits have put into preparing this mammoth tunnel to help the Twith in their struggle against the wizard. He can't go without a word or two of thanks. He isn't accustomed to making speeches, but he has heard his father make dozens.

He clears his throat and begins shakily, "We are amazed at your achievement. We are grateful for your help and proud of your friendship. With a spirit like the one you have shown today, surely the wizard will be defeated. If that happens, you will have played an important part. We never imagined that such an effort in such a short amount of time was really possible. When time is not so pressing, we want to find out how you managed to accomplish this task in record time. To old and young, big and small, male and female, we will always be grateful. We will remember all our lives what the rabbits of Hampton Hill have achieved this day.

"There is very much more that deserves to be said, but you should all recognize that the time you have saved by your extensive effort must not now be wasted. You have created the path for us. Thank you for it. Now Barney and I need to be on our way along it."

High in the tree, Tuwhit watches. *I don't like to see Taymar go without me. Two are better than one, and Barney… well… Barney is only a boy, though a good one. A bird is better than a boy. Boys can't fly. It's going to be a long wait until dusk. Perhaps I should go now and tell Cleemo that Barney is with Taymar so that he and Cymbeline will not worry about the boy's absence. I'll wait, though, until they should be through the tunnel and then quickly nip off to see Cleemo.*

Barney would have liked to go first, but in actual fact it is Brolly, the little rabbit, who runs forward. The rabbits have decided that she shall have the honor of leading the Twith through the great tunnel. She has lost all fear and is pleased to have been chosen to lead. On her forehead is a borrowed miner's lamp, and lamps are also handed to Taymar and Barney. Taymar motions for Barney to go ahead of him, turns to wave a final farewell to the rabbits, looks up to include Tuwhit in the wave, and drops to the ground to begin his wriggle through the darkness into Wozzle.

They've not gone far when it is almost pitch black. The tunnel has turned slightly to avoid the roots of a tree. Taymar's body prevents even a trickle of light from behind entering beyond him. They're still far from the Wozzle end. The candlewick in the lamp struggles to maintain a tiny flame.

Ahead, Taymar can hear the movements of Barney, who is progressing without difficulty. If the rabbits have made a mistake on the size of the tunnel, Barney should still be able to wriggle through.

Occasionally, Taymar's shoulders are touching both sides at once. His head brushes the roof constantly as he inches forward on his elbows. It's not possible to crawl. The noises Barney and he make sound twice as loud as normal.

Rabbit guards have been left at the other end to bring warning if needed. Taymar concentrates on remaining inwardly cool and relaxed about the risks of getting jammed or the tunnel roof caving in. There are other places he'd rather be than wriggling through a tight tunnel in almost total darkness.

The way through seems to be taking a long time, thinks Taymar. *Surely by now we should have reached the bottom of the slope to begin slipping under the curtain. Why is the slope still going steadily downwards? Maybe it's just my imagination, but the tunnel seems to be getting smaller. And the dirt is starting to feel wet.* The earth really is getting damp. It's fortunate there is little loose soil in the tunnel. The rabbits have cleaned up well. Occasionally, soil dislodged by his head and shoulders falls and then finds its way beneath him. It might have been easier if he had removed his shoes and used his toes to help push forward. He's beginning to feel tired. It seems they've been going for hours. Fortunately, he doesn't have to worry about Barney, who is smaller and should be finding the going easier.

The slope is beginning to change. The ground is still moist, but surely the tunnel is now level. He wonders whether he'll be able to feel the Wozzle curtain with his back as he eases along. A fearful thought crosses his mind, *What if the wizard somehow created an alarm that will alert him to any movement at the bottom edge of the curtain or even below it? It's probably something he could do. Hopefully, he hasn't thought of it though. Anyway, it is too late now to worry about that.* Ahead of him, Barney is steadily moving forward. There has been no hesitation in his movements, and in fact his pace seems to be speeding up.

There surely is another change of gradient. After a long while going down and then on the level, they're going upwards at last. Suddenly, way ahead, the darkness is replaced by a bright light. It must be that Barney has arrived and tumbled out of the tunnel into daylight. Taymar sees ahead something small silhouetted on one side of the tunnel mouth. He wonders if it is Barney looking back down to see him. He stops to listen. There's nothing to hear. Taymar thinks, *If it is Barney, he is wisely saying nothing. It could be a Wozzle soldier though, looking and waiting. But then, surely a rabbit would be scooting down the tunnel to warn me. Well, whatever, there's no way I can turn around now.*

He is surprised at how tired he is. He has to go on, whatever lies ahead. It would be good to have his knife in his hand as he emerges into daylight in case it is a foe waiting for him. But there's no way he can untangle his knife from his clothing until he is able to stand up.

He continues elbowing himself forward. He has a cut from a stone on his left elbow. He hopes the dirt he's been pushing into it is clean. Now the circle of light reaches him. He can make out the sides of the tunnel, even the grass around the edges at its mouth. One last heave or two, and he tumbles over the edge into fresh, fresh air, glorious daylight and the land of Wozzle. Someone grabs him before he can speak and claps a hand across his mouth.

THE PONY

While Taymar, Barney, and Tuwhit become involved with a tunnel under the curtain, Ambro is on his patrol westwards towards Stowting. These days, he is in a dream. He can't get Cymbeline out of his mind, nor does he want to. To be sure, the situation on the border, their border, is very serious and maybe all that is left is a week of freedom before the fighting begins. That feeling of approaching battle is nevertheless pushed back behind thoughts of the girl for whom he will risk, even give, his very life. He's been unable to keep his feelings totally bottled up. He's hinted to his mother what he feels. She knows the girl. She has just smiled, hugged him tightly, and kissed him without further words. She knows and understands. *What a dear mother,* he thinks, *and oh! How I do love my dearest Cymbeline.*

He sings as he walks and runs, making up lines of badly rhyming lyrics to fit the tunes that come into his head. He builds on the nursery rhymes from his childhood. He plans, on his way back home, to drop in on Cleemo and Cymbeline. She'll be there, waiting for him. It seems weeks since he last saw her. If he's composed a suitable song in time, he will sing it to her as they take a short walk.

He's been using the track marked by his patrols. They've found the position of the curtain merely by throwing stones or firing arrows at it. Between fifty and a hundred paces from it, they've worn a patrol path to keep an eye on everything that is happening at the border line. He's visited several patrol points already and has been impressed with the alertness of his men. In each case, he's been challenged before he observed the challenger. He's praised them, listened to their reports, encouraged their vigilance, taken messages for their families, and moved on to the next patrol point.

He has come as far as the river which, after flowing through Lyminge Forest, turns south as it enters Gyminge. On its journey towards the bog at Gibbins Brook, it discharges into Gyminge Lake. Picking his way across the stepping stones, something ahead attracts his attention. It causes him to remain below the level of the bank, crouching down where he's arrived on the other side of the river. Slowly, he raises his head.

It is a pony that has caused his surprise. It has now turned away from him as it grazes on the long summer grass and the buttercups. It's a small pony. It's not a young animal, but a small, full grown, brown and white pony with a long tail that swishes at the grasses behind it.

Ambro knows that the animal is not from Gyminge, at least not from north of the Dark Forest. He surely knows most of the horses and certainly all the ponies that live in his father's domain.

The pony lifts its head, wheels around and looks towards him curiously. Ambro quickly ducks his head and is sure that the animal has heard no noise, but it's probably caught a glimpse of something moving. However, it makes no move. The pony is merely enjoying its meal and taking a break from eating. It has no harness or reins. Ambro has a quick instant of wishful thinking, *Maybe the pony is a wild one. I could break it and train it. What a wonderful gift that would make for my sweetheart.*

The white markings on a brown body give it a white patch on the forehead, a white-tipped nose, and full, white stockings on its hind legs. It has a thick mane perfect for a good hold when riding bareback. Its coat is rough, not smooth. A lock of hair tipped over its eyes causes Ambro to wonder how much the animal can see. Its legs are not wet or muddied. It has not recently come across the river; that's for sure.

Ambro thinks hard to explain how the pony happens to be where it is. It must be from Wozzle. There's no other place it can be from. Somehow, it must have strayed over the border. Perhaps it found a tear in the curtain. The grass is always greener on the other side, and the riverside meadow where the pony is standing is full of lush, sweet grasses and stems. All sorts of questions race through his mind. *Did it bolt from stables, or was it mounted when it broke free? If so, what's happened to its rider? Could a Wozzleite soldier have been thrown? There's no harness, so most likely it didn't even have a rider. Then again, it could have been a boy out on his pet pony. If he got thrown, he's probably lying on the ground somewhere in Wozzle. I wonder if an alarm has been raised? Could a search for the pony be under way? Perhaps it was startled by something, threw its rider, and then actually bolted at the curtain and broke through it. Maybe the curtain isn't as strong as we have been thinking. Well, the little guy seems placid enough now.*

Ambro slowly rises to full height and, after a pause, clambers up the bank to stand on the edge of the meadow. The pony stops eating and raises its head to look at him. It's not panicking, but it's beginning to be uneasy. Ambro could represent danger. The pony slowly turns and moves away, a few paces up the slope of the meadow towards the borderline. It's not yet time to gallop away, but it is time to be cautious. The pony begins to graze again, keeping a wary eye on the stranger by the river.

Ambro can almost feel the pony's thoughts and takes a cautious step or two forward.

The pony stops grazing and moves a few steps backwards. It's going to keep the distance between them. Ambro tries the clicking noises with his tongue that he makes to the animals in his father's stable. The horses there all recognize that the sounds mean carrots and affection, and they respond with their own whiffing noises to let their visitor know they are there and waiting. This pony, however, does not respond to Ambro's noises. As Ambro very slowly walks towards the animal, it backs away, turns around, and moves up the slope closer to the woods at the end of the long meadow. So far, it's moving only fast enough to keep the distance between them.

When Ambro stops, the pony also stops. It's as though there's a game going on. Ambro takes a long look around him. He'll go no farther than the end of the meadow. He won't venture into the woods. The border is somewhere quite close, and there's no point in getting into unnecessary danger. He would like to know exactly where the Wozzle curtain is and whether there's a tear in it. The pony has obviously not yet reached it or he would have bolted through the opening or been brought up short if there isn't one.

Ambro bends down and pulls up a strong handful of long grasses and buttercups. He calls out loud enough for the pony to hear. "Here you are. Come on. I'm your friend. I'm not going to hurt you. Come on. This grass is really good. It's better grass than where you are. Come on."

The pony doesn't move, though Ambro is slowly narrowing the distance between them. He's now only about twenty paces away. The pony takes fright at his nearness. It begins to move rapidly up the hill towards the woods. Obviously, the animal has come from Wozzle and is now looking to return to safety. As the meadow merges into the woods, the animal stops. The trees somehow mean security to it, but it's not yet ready to abandon the lush grazing completely. Although the pony is facing the woods, ready to bolt, its head is turned towards Ambro.

Ambro is making soothing noises, talking in gentle tones. "Good boy. That's right. Don't be frightened. Everything's alright. There. Doesn't that grass taste good? Have some more. That's right, old fellow. We're friends, aren't we?" Ambro pats the pony's flanks, rubs its neck, and scratches its back.

Slowly, the frightened alertness of the pony eases.

"Where are you from then? What's your name?" The animal does not answer, but it stands still, easing its watchfulness and relaxing. Ambro now has grasped hold of the pony's mane.

Suddenly, a noise catches Ambro's ear. He wheels around, tightening his hold on the mane. The pony too is alert and frightened and looks down the meadow towards the Dark Forest. Running up the slope towards them, spears and swords raised, are five goblin soldiers. They're wearing the grey uniform of the Wozzle army. As they're spotted, they begin shouting.

What's happening? Ambro wonders, *How can they possibly be in Gyminge without my even knowing? Has the invasion already begun?* The pony, startled, spins away from the Dark Forest and towards the woods beyond Hampton Hill. Ambro grips tightly the pony's mane and pulls its head around. As the pony turns, Ambro leaps onto its back. He is well used to riding bareback. Ambro isn't about to head into Lyminge Forest where he'd need help to escape. Digging his knees into the animal's flanks and giving it a slap on the rump with his spare hand, he heads straight towards the attacking soldiers.

Ambro laces the fingers of his left hand through the pony's mane. With his right hand, he reaches across his body to the scabbard on his left side. He grasps the hilt of his short broadsword, and as it comes clear, he lets out the family war cry loud enough to waken the dead. He's not going to give up without a fight.

A Fight in the

Meadow

The little pony, short-legged and by no means a war horse, responds to its rider's urging. The pony tries to behave like a full-size horse engaged in battle. Its nostrils are flared back. It gulps in great breaths of air. Its hooves are beating out a tattoo though the ground is soft. The downhill slope benefits them. Ambro swings his sword around his head. He's never before sung his war cry in anger, but now the little valley echoes with the sound. As he approaches the uniformed goblins, he increases speed and nudges the pony towards the middle spearman.

The middle spearman will become known as Lofty. Although he's wearing a Wozzle army uniform, Lofty hasn't always been a soldier. Neither has he always been a goblin. That he is a goblin like the others is due to the wizard. Under King Leo, he has been a bun baker—not a bread baker, but a bun baker. There's nothing wrong with being a bun baker or, for that matter, a bread baker. Both are needed. Many excellent people, usually women it must be said, have been bun bakers. A successful bun baker needs many qualities not usually found in, say, for instance, bread bakers. It's like comparing a china cup with an earthenware basin.

A bread baker deals with a simple, great lump of dough. There are limited ingredients, a flat tray or a pan, and a hot oven. Presto! Not so a bun baker. Multiple ingredients are needed in finely tuned proportions. They require elegant shaping. The timing of the exposure to oven heat must be exact to gain royal acceptance for appearance as well as taste, texture, and consistency.

The important thing is that while bun baking is a highly skilled vocation, it develops no other qualities beyond the kitchen that might assist in fighting battles, except perhaps strong arm muscles. This inexperienced spearman, running up a meadow slope on a hot summer's day, has no way to cope with a pony-mounted brigade of one charging towards him at breakneck speed. The oncoming horseman is screaming great oaths at the top of his voice, swinging a sword around his head, and is bent on a head-on collision or even worse. That madman can get hurt or hurt somebody else if he isn't careful. Bun baking has not, Lofty realizes, developed qualities such as courage, audacity, initiative, leadership, or skill using a spear that a military man might need. Perhaps if someone wanted a man to bake buns for an army and put him in uniform, Lofty might even then have failed to impress because of his untidiness of dress.

It's fortunate for Ambro that he chooses to steer the pony towards the center man of the five. Lofty is in the center and ahead of the others, not because of his courage or leadership skills, but because the other four men feel he can do less damage in the middle than on the flanks. They know that he's a man without courage but with a deep attachment to and affection for life. He loves it so much that he's only prepared to risk it when there are two men either side of him, making sure he does so. They are all more comfortable when they are running alongside a center man who is slightly ahead of them.

The middle spearman is taller than his companions. It might be easy to think that the taller a man is, the braver he is or that courage is measured out as so much per inch of height. It is not so. Lofty is also fatter than his companions. This comes from sampling everything he cooks before presenting it to the court or to whomever. Ever since King Leo was overthrown by the wizard, Lofty is now required to eat what he cooks before it can be served to the wizard. That's when he isn't being a soldier, of course. It's tempting to think that the heavier a man is, the braver he will be, as though courage is measured out per ounce of weight. Again, this is not so. Among any group of men, undoubtedly the finest fighters will be some of the smallest. Compare, for instance, a Yorkshire terrier with a St. Bernard or a mongoose with a hippopotamus.

It is tempting also to think that bun bakers are, by virtue of their arm muscles, especially well equipped to become pole-vaulters. Without doubt, arm muscles help. Years spent at the kneading board, pounding dough into shape, will certainly help a pole-vaulter gain height. However, Lofty has never tried to pole-vault in his life before today. If he had trained as a pole-vaulter, he would most certainly have insisted on level ground. Or, if he could have managed it without being discovered, even a slight slope downhill. He would never have chosen to make that superb exhibition of himself as "Wozzle Army Pole-Vaulter Laureate" in a meadow, thick with grass and tilting uphill, while an enemy charges downhill full bore at him.

What really happens is this. Lofty is terrified of outdistancing his fellows on either side of him. He wants, if anything, to be a pace or two behind when the collision with the charging madman occurs. If he had kept on looking ahead, the misadventure might never have happened, but his quick glance to the left shows him the horrifying truth. He, of all people, is ahead of his fellows. They're not being left behind by his exceptional pace. They're *deliberately* running more slowly than he. He doesn't have time to check the situation on his right side, but if he had, he would have seen that it is exactly the same. *He,* the middleman, is the point of the advancing arrowhead of the five-goblin cavalry.

At this stage, Lofty trips. He becomes distracted by the treachery of his friends on either side of him, and he trips. Undoubtedly, his speed affects the consequences. The point of his spear, instead of being directed at the pony or its rider, hits the ground. As it impales an unsuspecting buttercup, it becomes a hinge in the moist earth. The keyword here is *hinge.* The dictionary explains that a hinge is a joint on which a gate, door, or lid swings. What follows is a rotating motion over a quarter of a circle. It starts at nine o'clock and ends at high noon.

Several events unfold within split seconds. One moment, Ambro is heading at high speed towards the center of a rank of five goblin soldiers advancing towards him with murderous intent. The next moment, instead of the collision that cannot be avoided, the tallest and broadest foeman has elevated himself in a graceful arc more than twice his height into the air and, suspended like a juggler's twirling plate, is rotating on the end of his spear.

Because the spear is impaled into the ground, the point offers no danger to anyone, except, possibly, a worm that is sleeping just beneath the surface. But this is unlikely, and anyway, the fate of a worm at this particular point is of no concern to either Lofty or Ambro. The other end of the spear is rounded and blunt, so fortunately, it does not cause Lofty lasting harm as it comes to rest just above his belly button. But because Lofty is of considerable weight, the spear is no longer straight but is now severely bent. The "safe" end of the spear supports Lofty, and Lofty is slowly spinning like a juggler's plate on a pole in an anticlockwise direction. But Lofty is not perfectly balanced, and in addition to getting dizzy, he fears that when he falls, he will surely never see the light of day again.

Ambro does not halt his attack. Wielded by a practiced arm, his swinging broadsword swipes the bent, loaded spear at its midpoint. The other four spearmen, surprised by the sudden disappearance of their leading rider and needing a little time to understand why, fling themselves out of the way of the galloping warhorse that, for a moment, has forgotten it is only a small pony. If Ambro had happened to strike the spear at the inside of the arc, rather than the outside, the result might have been less dramatic. It is like cutting the string of a stretched bow ready to fire. *Doing!*

It is not Lofty's day.

CAPTURED

Ambro is through to the other side of the wall of goblin soldiers. He pats the little pony, which is wheezing and puffing after its charge downhill. Ambro wants to get back home before the enemy regroups. He takes a quick look behind him.

Three goblins are bending over Lofty. Half of his shattered spear is still upright beside him. The other half seems to be sticking up from his body which is flat on the ground. One soldier is disappearing into the woods, probably on his way to get more help. Either that or he is fleeing to report that they are outnumbered.

Ambro digs his heels into the pony's sides. It breaks into a trot. He smiles to himself. *What a story I'll have to tell Taymar when I get home.* They head down the hill, and then, suddenly and unexpectedly, the animal can go no further. They bounce back as though they have hit a trampoline sideways on.

The pony neighs with fright and alarm. It rears up on its hind legs. In a flash, Ambro is off his mount and slashing with his sword at the unseen obstacle. He lunges with his sword, but it just bounces back. Ambro glances back up the field. The group of soldiers is paying no attention to him. He tries stabbing the invisible curtain with his dagger—no impression. He and Taymar had previously tried cutting and penetrating the curtain but had failed. Even fire hadn't worked. The truth sinks in with dismay. He is trapped, trapped behind the curtain on the Wozzle side. He can't even think how it has happened. His mind is full of likely causes. It makes no difference, though. He turns back to the pony.

The little pony is in a state of shock. Ambro holds tight to the mane. He doesn't want to lose a ride he might need. There might well be long distances to travel. The pony's eyes are twitching and flickering nervously. It stamps a hoof on the ground as though that might help. It neighs as though raising a cry for sympathy. Ambro, still holding the mane, pats the pony's flanks and speaks quiet words to it. The pony might well represent his only chance of escape. If help has been sent for by the Wozzle patrol, soldiers will soon arrive. It's time to be moving, but he's not sure where.

He tries to think what might have happened. *Somehow the pony has penetrated the curtain to get into Gyminge. It hasn't come from the east, the way I did, or it would have had to cross the river to get to the meadow. It must have come downhill farther to the west. If there is a tear in the curtain, it might still be there. But if so, why hasn't my patrol beyond the meadow discovered it and come to warn me? There's been no sign of them. The wizard must have repaired the curtain, so wherever the pony had slipped through no longer exists.*

But how could the pony retrace its wandering steps back into Wozzle? We didn't have to go through any barrier. How can it be that there was no curtain to keep us from leaving Gyminge, but now we can't return because there is a curtain in place? Has the wizard deliberately moved the curtain into Gyminge to entrap me? Can it be that even now, somewhere, he is watching what is happening? He could be gleefully ordering a larger group of soldiers to bring me in, bound in ropes.

Ambro is suddenly anxious to be away from this place. The pony seems to want to go to the east. Ambro wonders, *Why doesn't the pony speak? Normally, the animals and birds talk freely to me. The pony understands what I say. I'm sure of that. But its neighing and nuzzling make no helpful conversation.*

"Okay, buster. You seem to want to go east, back through the woods. I would like to explore to the west to see if that's the way you came, so let's compromise and follow the curtain eastwards. I'll try not to drive you into the curtain again. Let's get going before we have the Wozzle army on our tails."

Ambro sheaths his sword and dagger, remounts, and, with his knees and heels, heads the pony towards Hampton Hill. He'll keep as near to the curtain as possible. As they enter the first batch of trees, he stops the pony. There's a worn track of recent origin, probably a patrol track that roughly parallels the one on the Gyminge side. He thinks, *If we keep to this path, the curtain should continue to be about fifty paces or so to the right. But—and this is a big but—at any time, we might meet the Wozzle goblin patrols who cover their border line.*

Briefly, he considers, *Perhaps we should rest up until after dark. We might have a better chance to escape if we are accosted by a patrol.* Looking back he decides, *We better press on. I'll have to take my chances as they come.*

Emerging from the woods and strung out down the meadow to the three soldiers and Lofty are a whole line of goblins. Some are even nearer, beyond Lofty. Ambro sees they are running in pursuit of him. *There's no time to waste. Fortunately, none of them are yet mounted; although there may be others with horses still on their way in the woods. I need to be moving.* He nudges the pony and it breaks into a trot.

Hours have passed. They are no longer following the patrol path, which lies between them and the curtain. Ambro has decided that's far too risky. He's spotted almost a dozen patrols so far. Instead, he's traveling the old, well-worn cross-country lane that goes along the flank of the hill. It's sheltered from the exposure of the cold winds at the top and avoids much of the woods lower down. Along the way, he has met country folk and exchanged cheerful greetings with them, as though he has as much right as they to be where he is. Ambro is quietly relieved to observe that not all the people are goblins. He finds that Wozzle is extremely eerie without birds. He has seen only once a curious raven that flew nearby but no other birds. The raven, he notices, is not the size to which he's been accustomed. It's much, much smaller. Most of the people he has met have turned their faces away from him as though they don't wish to be observed, as though somehow he will report them and get them into trouble.

The little pony, Ambro calls it Buster as he talks while they journey, has kept going strongly. He trots along faster than Ambro could comfortably walk. Occasionally, they'll stop for the animal to graze, and then Ambro will walk at a brisk pace for a while before he remounts. The pony's pace is quickening rather than tiring as the afternoon draws on. It's as though the animal is perhaps scenting home or at least is now in familiar surroundings. Ambro, as he rides on, catches glimpses of the distant sea that fills the great bay. It's a particularly clear summer's day; and beyond the sea, he sees distant white cliffs that, before the sea cut through, were joined to the chalk hills he walks upon.

Ambro begins sorting out in his mind what he needs to do. *I must somehow try to survive in the woods and avoid being captured until Wozzle begins its invasion. That might come in a week or so. Perhaps I can live off the secret charity of local residents who long for the good old days. It's a pity the blackberries aren't ready. As soon as the curtain is lifted by the wizard for his own forces, I will also slip through and scurry towards home.*

He turns a corner by a cottage and, caught by surprise, pulls the pony to a sharp halt. He turns into the shade of an oak tree beside a field gate. Approaching them along the country lane and barely fifty paces away is a body of goblin soldiers, some thirty or forty. About ten, front and rear, are riding horses. All are armed. Ambro realizes, *To turn and gallop the pony back the way we came offers little chance of escape. I'll have to brazen this one out.* He faces the pony towards the road. As the soldiers begin passing by, he raises a hand, waves, and yells out, "Hurrah for the army. Hurrah for the wizard! Hurrah for Wozzle!"

As he does so, unbalanced in his control, the pony rears high on its hind legs. Ambro is caught by surprise and cannot save himself. He slips off backwards and cracks his head a whacker against the field gate. At the same moment, while his head is full of whirling stars and shooting flames and pain, the pony that has thrown him is no longer there. In its place is an old man with a large nose, slightly bent in the back, clad all in black, and wearing a high, black hat. He is triumphant with the success of his strategy, and his right eye is twitching furiously.

OH NO! Ambro thinks with horror. *It must be him! It can be no other! It's the Wizard of Wozzle!*

The wizard, for it is indeed he, gives orders: "Take him, men. Tie him securely. He's an important prisoner and very danger-ous. Bring him with you to the inspection parade. I'm tired of carrying him. You there, dismount and give me your horse."

The Hideaway

Further to the east, at the mouth of the transit tunnel between Wozzle and Gyminge, it is Barney's hand that is over Taymar's mouth. Taymar is alert, aware who it is, and does not move. He remains lying there, still on his stomach. There must be something nearby that is dangerous. He'll wait until Barney indicates that it's safe to move. He hears voices, two men talking. Not a muscle moves. He tries to make out what's being said but cannot do so. The men are not moving away. If anything, the voices get louder but no more distinct. There are two men wearing the standard grey uniform of the Wozzle army coming towards them.

Barney removes his hand from Taymar's mouth. The tunnel opening has fortunately emerged into a bed of nettles and a tangle of bramble bushes. It's scratchy and difficult crawling out of the tunnel, but at least no one is liable to come very close.

However, Barney wonders how to distract the goblin soldiers. He doesn't need to do anything. The rabbit guards at the entrance know the dangers and have rehearsed what to do if surprised. They are experts at the art of distracting danger away from their warrens. One pops out and sits on a bank beside the bracken. It preens itself, smoothing its fur, examining its claws as though they might be in need of a manicure. Another pops up beside him.

The soldiers see them, halt in their tracks, and pretend to be trees. They're thinking of rabbit stew after the inspection. Another rabbit darts right across their path and into the nettles.

One of the soldiers grabs for it and misses. Off balance, he grabs at his friend who is just then easing a foot forward and is also off balance. Together, they fall into the nettles and blame each other while the rabbits regroup for another diversion.

This gives Barney an opportunity to bring Taymar up beside him so they can both look out. Barney, now that both his hands are free, loads his catapult and pulls it back, ready to fire. Taymar can now follow the noisy conversation. The two goblins are quarrelling.

Taymar is tempted to take them captive; remove one of their uniforms by force; and, in disguise, join in the inspection parade as a Wozzle soldier. However, the wizard must not be aware of the presence of Gyminge spies on the Wozzle side, so he discards this idea as being too risky.

The soldiers settle their argument, deciding they have come far enough. The inspection is only half an hour away; they had better get back and rejoin their unit. They won't climb back up the hill but will make their way around to where the parade is already forming up. They're easy for Taymar and Barney to follow. They are paying no attention to anything that is happening behind them. No one expects any danger on the Wozzle side. Two of the four guard rabbits are coming with Taymar and Barney. The other two remain at the tunnel mouth. Brolly is on her way to report to Bandaged Paw and the others. Then she'll come back to wait until the Twith are ready to return.

The inspection parade is planned to be in the great hollow within Hampton Hill. Taymar and Barney are both pleased to see where the soldiers are leading them. The breast of Hampton Hill tucks in on one side to form a natural hollow where thousands of men can be accommodated on the slopes. It's a location well suited for an address by the wizard to his men. They should be able to hear him clearly. The hollow is less well suited to an inspection of the troops, so maybe that part won't take very much time.

Barney is anxious that the wizard will be within range of his catapult in case some action is needed and would like to be as close to him as possible. The guard rabbits have an ideal place for getting close without being detected. Their two guests should be able to see and hear everything from under a fallen log at the edge of the wood, not far from the lower path that follows the foot of the hill. The log is a huge oak torn up by the hurricane of a few decades ago. Its roots still hold the dirt of the day it fell. While the parade is gathering, the Twith have time to explore. The log is hollow but only accessible from the broken limb pinned underneath it, not from either end. Although it's dark inside, the log could provide a certain and sure hiding place, for no one could possibly know about it.

Taymar has left his lamp behind at the tunnel. Barney's lamp is still strapped around his head and still lit, so he leads the way. Brambles and nettles have grown up, undisturbed, around the tree. Taymar carefully slashes a path to give a clear view while ensuring he's not seen or heard by the soldiers beginning to assemble on the slopes. Eventually, he's satisfied that he will be able to see everything that is likely to be important, except for the area immediately uphill from him. He clambers up through the branches and twigs to the hole that he must wriggle through. After the tunnel, that part is easy. He's in a huge hall chamber within the great tree. It could hold sixty Twith if necessary. There is evidence that rabbits, mice, shrews, and occasionally bigger creatures have made use of this cavern as shelter. But it does not smell and is nice and dry, filled with rotting, powdery oak. Barney has perched his candle lamp on a ledge, and the light is steady and adequate.

One of the lookout rabbits has returned. He has news to report. Taymar and Barney must be careful that they are not seen. A company of goblin soldiers is taking position on the tree itself. Some of them are clearing nettles and brambles for a path from higher up the hill. It's probably not really a defense position. They're not expecting any surprise attack. But it will give them a good viewpoint that's unlikely to be visited by the wizard during the inspection. There's method in their madness. The Twith should still be safe. They should be able to hear and see everything, but they might have to wait until the parade is dismissed or until after dark to make their way back to the tunnel.

A second rabbit scrambles into the log and interrupts the conversation. He has another news flash. There's a wagon on the path coming from Lyminge approaching the inspection site. It's drawn by two horses, and it's carrying a very strange load: a huge, bottle made of greenish-colored glass. It's bedded on thick straw and secured by ropes.

Taymar and Barney's faces whiten. They've heard of the glass bottles manufactured in Lyminge. They have been designed by the wizard especially for holding Twith. The whole country is aware of them. The wizard keeps his captives in them, and he has a large collection. Anyone who meets the wizard's displeasure is likely to find himself sealed up inside a bottle.

Taymar and Barney ease down the entranceway until they can easily see the parade ground and approaching traffic without being seen themselves. They make no noise and do not exchange words. They hear the rumbling of cart wheels and then see the first escort of horsemen pass by only a short distance away. Their upright lances have pennants flying. This is an inspection parade they are attending, so their uniforms are starched and pressed, and their armor is bright and shining. Now the wagon comes into view. These are not ordinary wagon drivers. They are soldiers, both of them, with stripes of rank upon their arms. The sergeant driver holds the reins of both horses, a matched pair of blacks groomed to perfection. They're not really cart horses as much as carriage horses. Now Taymar sees for himself that the rabbit's report is true. Upright on the flatbed wagon, cushioned on thick straw and secured by ropes to each corner of the wagon bed, is a captivity bottle. It's as tall as Taymar. The rear escort, again two black stallions immaculate in their appearance, follows after the wagon.

What can be the meaning of this? Does the Wizard plan to put someone who has displeased him, some poor villager, into a bottle as entertainment for his parade?

THE INSPECTION

The hollow alongside Hampton Hill forms a great semicircular arena, and above it, all along the rim of the bank, army tents and pavilions have been erected. In the center of these, with a view towards the sea, is the great pavilion, the field command tent, where the army has arranged a ceremonial banquet for its commander-in-chief. The weather is good; the sun warm but not too hot. Flags are flying in the mild breeze. The events promise well.

Below the curved, sloping sides of the hollow is the newly leveled area where the inspection parade will take place. For more than an hour, the hollow and the parade ground have been filling with goblin soldiers. There are generals, colonels, majors, captains, lieutenants, sergeant majors, and sergeants, plus scores of corporals and hundreds of soldiers.

The army band has been practicing for weeks. Even though the youngest bugler can only manage three tunes, and one of them is "Three Blind Mice," he has been included to increase the strength of the band because of his marching skills. He is more certain than some of the others not to turn left when the command is shouted to turn right. Under threat of having kitchen slop duty for six months if he makes a mistake, his strict instructions are to "Oompa, Oompa, Oompa" from start to finish and not to let any other note escape his instrument.

The wizard has sent Rasputin as his messenger to alert the troops that he will be arriving shortly. He and ten of his men will be on horseback, escorting an important prisoner. The newly captured intruder from Gyminge is a spy and is about to be tried and punished by a battlefield court. This villain has been generating bad feelings, which harm the otherwise normally friendly relations between the neighboring countries of Wozzle and Gyminge. This cannot be tolerated. Friendship is everything.

The wizard has approved the parade program. There will be a full parade of all troops, followed immediately by an inspection. Then a demonstration of drill will place the troops in their listening positions for an address by the commander-in-chief himself. The final and ultimate event will be the ceremonial bottling of the prisoner. The officers have requested that their commander-in-chief join them in a banquet in the field command tent following the conclusion of the program. Tomorrow, the wizard will be ordering a general holiday to celebrate the plans he will be disclosing for the future use of the army. He will also discuss the possible onset of battle, should any foreigner be unwise enough to attack Wozzle.

Rasputin is informed by the reception committee that the bottle the wizard ordered to be brought down from Lyminge has arrived safely. The charcoal fire for melting the candle wax has been conveniently located nearby and has already been lighted. There are reserve supplies of candle wax if they should be needed.

The band strikes up as soon as the lookout posted in the ash tree spots the approaching cavalcade. From each of the assembled army units, shouted commands of officers and noncommissioned officers echo to and fro across the parade ground. Soldiers snap to attention. Some shoulder their pikes, others level their spears, and a few draw their swords. Those with war axes seize them with both hands, and those with bows set arrows to the strings. All these actions are done in unison and with precision. A hundred feet, a thousand feet, hit the ground as one.

Taymar, lying on his stomach with Barney beside him beneath the oak tree, recognizes that here is a possible opportunity presenting itself. Asking Barney to maintain the watch, he climbs back inside the hollow oak, beckoning the two guard rabbits to follow. The two rabbits listen carefully. They must act on their own. They repeat their instructions to confirm that they know what to do. They will send one of the other tunnel guards and Brolly back to take their place. There's no time to waste. They slip down to the ground, lollop into the woods, and are gone. Taymar rejoins Barney and tells him what he is planning.

The wizard is met on the edge of the parade ground by the mounted honor guard that falls in immediately behind him. The prized prisoner, paraded on horseback behind the wizard, is roped, blindfolded, and gagged. With horsemen on either side and before and behind, he is led and stationed in front of the podium where the wizard will be giving his speech to the troops. A huge amount of rope has been used to entirely wrap the prisoner. Hardly a finger can wriggle. Foot soldiers assist him to dismount. A soldier on either side holds a tethering rope in case he might somehow try to escape. A few paces from him is the green bottle. The bottle wagon is stationed to the rear of the podium, its horses already harnessed. The wagon will leave the parade ground with the bottled prisoner to return to Lyminge as part of the concluding ceremonies.

The wizard inspects his troops, remaining on horseback. On these occasions, the raven sits on his right shoulder, looking all around, lest some missile be thrown or shot at his master. "Oompa, Oompa, Oompa" goes the little bugler for the two hundredth time. He is wondering about possible variations on the last Oompa.

The horsemen, the archers, the spearmen, the axmen—all are inspected. The wizard is in a good mood. The day has gone well. If only some of these men had a tiny fraction of the common sense that he has, they too could be generals. As he moves around, those ahead of him are called to, "A-TEN-SHUN!" In turn, they all present arms. After he has passed by, they drop back to stand at ease.

Taymar sees the wizard for the first time. He has heard a great deal about him, none of it good. The parade has come as close as it will to the secret observers. The wizard, small and stooped at the shoulders, rides a horse well. He wears a black cloak and a tall, tapering, black hat with a floppy brim that falls over his eyebrows. His right eye is twitching. No hair is visible, but Taymar notices with interest that the wizard's ears are unusually large. He is clean shaven. His long, prominent nose and broad mouth give him a distinctive look. Taymar will remember that face.

The wizard acknowledges the cheers with a wave of his long, bony fingers. His eyes, spaced wide apart, project the man's personality and inner power. Even as Taymar watches intently, he is trying to think of a way to rescue the wizard's prisoner before he is locked into the dungeons at Lyminge Castle. *Poor man. His heart must be full of fear.* Taymar wonders what he has done to incur the wizard's wrath.

At last, the inspection is finished. The wizard pronounces himself vastly satisfied with the army's turnout and appearance. He permits the parade colonel to start the ceremonial drill. He rides to the podium, dismounts onto the steps provided, and sits at his ease to watch the proceedings. He thinks about his prisoner. A thorough search of the man has revealed a letter he carries. It is from some maiden, Cymbeline, a love letter of sorts. It confirms that the prisoner is none other than the younger son of the earl of Up-Horton, Earl Gareth himself. What a prize! The young fool has not had the slightest idea that his trusty little pony was the redoubtable Wizard of Wozzle. The wizard is pleased with himself. For him, their encounter was like playing tiddlywinks with a three-year old, like stealing cake from a blind man. He permits himself a congratulatory smile.

The soldiers stationed on the oak tree are enjoying themselves. They have avoided the inspection. All they have to do is sit tight. However, their joy is short-lived. They do not avoid the drill after all. The parade colonel calls them to attention, marches them down to the center of the parade ground, and has them demonstrate drill maneuvers in double quick time. They belong to the engineers, and he is in the signals himself. He marches them back into the hollow with the others and mentally pats himself on the back for spoiling their day.

As the drill comes to an end, the hillside begins to fill with men released from the parade ground. They are, turn by turn, being given permission to sit by special order of their commander-in-chief. Row upon row, they ascend in semicircular arcs up the hill. The generals are in armchairs, the colonels on seats, and the captains on benches. The lieutenants and lower forms of life sit on the grass. When the parade colonel has completed the drill and the seating, he briskly marches up to the wizard, halts abruptly, and stands at attention, his arms and legs as straight as his back.

"Beg to report, SIR! The army is ready for your address, SIR!"

The wizard nods. He waits until the colonel has seated himself. Slowly, he rises. He looks out and up at the sea of faces subject to his command. They are completely silent, waiting. Now begins the next step of his plan for unchallenged dominion. The world lies before him. He takes a deep breath.

Under the oak tree, Taymar and Barney are watching carefully. They have been hearing easily the parade ground commands. There's going to be no difficulty hearing the wizard. Barney whispers to Taymar that he thinks he can break the bottle with a sling stone. Taymar tells him to wait for awhile, but probably this is what they will need to do. A possible plan is forming in his mind. First though, they need to hear the wizard's plans revealed.

Addressing

the Troops

"Friends, although I speak to you as your commander-in-chief, I consider each of you, each of you, from my generals down to the youngest bugler among you, as my friends." The youngest bugler has been driving the wizard crazy. There have been no less than five hundred and seventy-two "Oompa, Oompa, Oompas." And every single one of them has been off key, sounding like a chicken trying to solo among a choir of nightingales. "Ever since you honored me by electing me as your leader"—this comes as a surprise to everyone present—"I have met and tried to deserve your trust.

"We have been through difficult times together. We have struggled to overcome poverty. We have succeeded. Where are the poor among us? We have struggled to overcome illness and bad health. We have succeeded. Where are the sick among us?" The wizard's audience is not aware that the sick and the poor have all mysteriously disappeared.

"We are peace loving and have tried at all times to be good neighbors to our friends in Gyminge. What have we done to merit their attack upon us? The armed forces of Gyminge are massing upon our borders. You have seen their preparations for war. You have seen the way they have attempted time and time again to create an excuse to invade our borders." There is surprise among the crowd as they look around and find every person shrugging his shoulders. No one has seen any such thing.

"I, as your leader, have defended our country up to this time. I appreciate your confidence in me. Now, however, it is up to you. Yesterday, so I have discovered, the enemy in Gyminge set the date for its attack upon us. It is less than one week away. They have found a way to penetrate the barrier around our country that I have developed to protect us. We are no longer safe. Any moment now, they will be upon us. Your wives and your children—what will happen to them? Your mothers and fathers who reared you, your aged grandparents—how and where can they flee?" The wizard pauses to dab tears from his eyes as he speaks with a voice breaking with emotion.

"Wozzle depends on you and you alone. Our health, our welfare, our future hopes and dreams, our livelihoods, our peace, our prosperity, even our jobs—all of it rests upon your shoulders. I know you will not, cannot fail us. Your brave hearts will yet vanquish the Gyminge invaders. The people, your people, my people, our people rely on you.

"Imagine your land controlled by King Rufus. Imagine the laws of Gyminge governing you. Can death be worse? Imagine the oppressor's yoke upon your shoulders. Slavery. Slavery? Never! His men shall never have your maidens, your wives, and your children. It cannot be. It shall not be. We will make any sacrifice, yes, *any* sacrifice, so that it shall not be."

The men are on their feet now, waving and shouting, cursing and cheering. The hollow is filled with a vast eruption of sound. The wizard has his audience going. He enjoys the sensation of approval.

"Do we need to sit back like lambs in the fold, waiting to be slaughtered? No, no, no. They will find that we are lions, not lambs. Do we need to wait for them to attack us? No, no, no. Let them beware lest their victim prove to be more than a match for them. With the secret equipment I have designed, they will be helpless, powerless. There's a weapon you haven't yet seen and Gyminge has not dreamed of. If they don't change their ways, we shall use it fearlessly and effectively. If we choose to move against them, there will be hardly more than one day, I assure you, before we are at the walls of Gyminge Castle."

There is another outburst of cheering and shouting. Maybe, with the skill and wisdom of their commander-in-chief, they will not have to fight at all.

"I haven't been on holiday while our enemy has been planning to strike. I have been tireless in preparing the defense of our beloved country. While you have slept, I have been on duty. I bring the first of our captives for you to see. There will be many more, I assure you. This wretch thought he could find a way to lead his troops into our beloved land. Did he think we were sleeping? He was not expecting my vigilance. We will show him how the people of Wozzle treat unwelcome guests. This is the son of the commander who opposes us, sent to spy out our land before they attack." He commands the guards, "Unbind the prisoner save for his gag and his feet."

Everyone watching turns attention from the wizard to his prisoner. The soldiers unravel the ropes, twisting him around until he is giddy and he almost falls. The soldiers push him upright. As his blindfold is removed, he blinks and looks around. Without fear, he observes the wizard enjoying his moment of triumph. Stretching his arms a little from his sides and arching his back, his feet shuffle within their ropes. He sees the green bottle beside him, smells the fire behind, and knows the fate intended for him: being sealed in a bottle for the wizard's pleasure, perhaps forever. Ambro shivers at the thoughts crossing his mind. *I hope that Cymbeline never comes to know what has happened to me. I wonder if I will ever see my family again. Apart from my dearest love, I will miss Taymar most of all, and I know Taymar will miss me, too.*

Taymar himself is barely a hundred and fifty paces away. Only Barney hears the gasp of horror and dismay as Taymar recognizes his brother. Taymar's mind works rapidly. Time for despair and wondering how it has all come to pass will have to wait for later. More urgent now is how the rescue of Ambro can be arranged. His eyes search the skyline above the hollow. There is nothing at all to be seen there. How he wishes Tuwhit could have found a way over the curtain.

He climbs back up into the hollow of the log taking a twig to light from Barney's lamp candle. From the twig he lights a larger twig and then a branch he recovered from the ground where they had been lying. His only weapon, apart from his dagger and Barney's catapult, is fire. He must use everything he has. As he rejoins Barney he hears a rustle and noise behind him. Brolly and the replacement guard rabbit have arrived. Taymar welcomes them back. He has a job for them both, but first he'll let Barney know what he should do.

"Barney, listen carefully. Everything depends on you. Get your stones out. We might need all of them. Don't fire until I tell you. First, get the wizard. Aim for his nose, and don't miss. Then fire at the bottle. After you have smashed that, turn your attention to the wagon. First, hit the driver. Try for his rein hand.

And then go after the near horse. Smack him on his rump. After that, choose your own targets among the wagon escort. Save at least one stone for later. I'll be after Ambro."

Taymar has produced his dagger, which is unsheathed in his right hand. He would have liked his broadsword but wouldn't have been able to wriggle it through the tunnel, so it has been left behind with Bandaged Paw. The dagger will have to do. After a moment's thought, he slips the dagger back into its sheath. He will need both hands free to start with. They should at least have the advantage of surprise.

The bottle is now the center of everyone's attention. Six soldiers have been appointed to place Ambro inside as smoothly and quickly as possible. They are experienced men. They have done the job hundreds of times in Lyminge. Ambro's hands are retied behind his back. He is seized and lifted towards the bottle, which has been carefully placed on its side. The tight ropes still binding Ambro's feet are replaced with a loop of rope that can be loosened and removed easily. The prisoner's feet are inserted into the bottle. The foot rope is released and withdrawn.

Ambro can see only the boots of the soldiers pushing him into the bottle. Next, his hands are released as he slides further into the bottle; and now both feet and hands are free. The rest of his body slides in, and finally, the gag is removed. There is very little spare space in the bottle. Ambro can hardly move.

The wooden plug to seal the bottle is now inserted and kicked tight by the sergeant of the bottling party. Although he has done this scores of times, it always surprises him how quiet observers become when they see a bottling for the first time.

The bottle is tilted upright. Ambro adjusts his balance to stand as well as he is able. He's not very steady and leans against the side of the bottle. His feet have been bound for a long time. As the blood begins to flow again in his legs and arms, his limbs are screaming with pain. No matter. The wizard shall not see him flinch. He stamps his feet up and down to increase the circulation, and the pain begins to ease just a little.

Ambro smells smoking candle wax as a full ladle is poured on top of the bottle plug. There is more wax if it is needed, but the sergeant shakes his head with satisfaction. That plug won't come out in a month of Sundays. The sergeant turns to the wizard. "Beg report, SIR! The bottling process is complete. The top is securely sealed, SIR!"

The wizard gives permission to the sergeant to load the bottle onto the wagon as soon as the seal is cool enough. Taymar, silently witnessing the bottling, notes with a sigh of relief that things are finally beginning to get underway on the hilltop. He continues twirling his flaming brand around to keep it burning steadily and whispers instructions to the rabbits. Brolly darts out of the oak tree on her errand.

FIRE

The two black stallions draw the bottle wagon forward. It halts beside the bottle. Two goblin soldiers tilt the bottle against the side of the wagon and then lift and push it forward to the center of the wagon bed. Ambro tumbles around inside the bottle as it is tilted, shoved, and rolled. At last, the bottle is lifted upright, cushioned on straw within its frame, and its neck secured from movement by ropes tied to the four corners of the wagon. The bottle is on its way back to Lyminge from whence it has come— only now it contains a prisoner instead of being empty.

The loading sergeant inspects the ropes. They are strong and tight. He marches around in front of the wizard. "Permission to depart for Lyminge, SIR!" The wizard and the sergeant are old acquaintances, but in front of the troops, the sergeant is professional in addressing the wizard. The wizard nods permission.

If the sergeant had dared to approach the wizard from the rear rather than from the front, he might well have seen a tiny female rabbit setting the wizard's cloak alight with the candle from her miner's lamp. However, his relationship with the wizard does not permit this kind of familiarity, and besides, this is a ceremonial occasion. All things must be done in good order. Flames burst out from the smoldering cloak of the wizard and run up his back to clutch at his hat. Brolly darts away unseen. Barney has climbed on top the fallen oak. He takes careful aim at the wizard's nose, fires his catapult, and hits the target exactly. The wizard's nose is of generous proportions. It has been so since birth. Even so, a fraction of an inch higher or lower and Barney would have missed entirely. The wizard suddenly swings around anticlockwise as a mighty force is applied without warning to the tip of his nose.

A simple understanding of levers helps here. Assume the spine acts as a fulcrum, the point of rest on which a lever moves. The farther from the spinal cord a sharp and heavy blow is applied, the more its effect is felt. There will probably only be a small amount of permanent damage, but for the moment, the effect is, to say the least, gratifying. The wizard disappears over the edge of the podium in a confusion of pain and flames.

The generals, who are nearest and lodged in armchairs, have no chance of going to the aid of the flaming wizard before the younger officers behind them who are hungry for promotion. It doesn't matter how many men are needed to pick up a man in flames; there are more than enough to do the job.

The two guard rabbits Taymar had sent off earlier have picked up his miner's lamp at the tunnel mouth and made their way to the crest of the hollow. Running along the backside of the pavilions and tents, they have put the tiny flame to good use. Their natural fear of fire has disappeared in the importance of their assigned task. The rising northeasterly wind has been the cream on the cake. By now, tents are setting fire to other tents.

Taymar bellows out from beside the oak tree at the top of his voice, "FIRE! FIRE! THE CAMP IS ON FIRE!" The side of the oak, twisted and deformed, funnels, distorts, and enlarges the sound and makes it difficult to determine its origin.

The soldiers do not know where the alarm has come from. They cannot see Taymar. All they know is that a voice as of a mighty rushing wind is bellowing at them, "FIRE! FIRE! THE

CAMP IS ON FIRE!" The religious ones among them—there are not many—utter a swift prayer in passing. A quick glimpse behind them up the hill to the tents confirms the truth of the call.

The decorated strawberry ice cream cake, planned as the centerpiece of the latter part of the ceremonial banquet, is used to put out the fire in the lower portion of the chief cook's clothes. He hurriedly stuffs the cold cake inside his belt and waistband. Once he realizes what he has done, he decides to take immediate, compassionate leave. His wife is expecting triplets, and he can pretend that she has sent a sudden call for help. He leaves quickly before he meets up with the ice cream cook, who has spent all day on the shiny, red and white creation.

The assembled troops on parade are caught in confusion, helped along by the youngest bugler. The tune at which he is best, the one where his skills shine like a full moon in a dark sky, is not the early morning wake-up call, "Reveille," or even, "Three Blind Mice," but "The Retreat." This soulful melody he can play without ever hitting a wrong note. Even the high notes sound like pearls on the necklace of a queen, as his only admirer, his mother, once told him. His rendering is superlative and as loud as he can make it. It adds to the fear already aroused in the troops by the wizard's own address.

"The Gymingers are attacking!"

"They're all around us!"

The cry is taken up along the rows of soldiers scrambling to get up the hill to their tents to rescue their belongings. They abandon those intentions in favor of a more direct anxiety: to avoid the enemy. There is little value in possessions when lives are at stake! Their actions suit their words: "RUN FOR YOUR LIVES!"

Down below, on the parade ground, the generals have been slow off the mark, but the cries of alarm from the hillside work a remarkable transformation. The generals are not only outclimbing and outpacing colonels and majors; they are passing lieutenants and lance corporals almost as though all of them were standing still.

Several other things are also happening simultaneously.

The mounted horsemen of the wagon escort fall in before and behind the bottle wagon. Brolly begins lighting fire to the straw hanging over the far side of the wagon. Wherever she can start a fire, she is to start one. The straw blazes away with a great rush upwards and sets alight the unused kindling. The spare candle wax catches ablaze, adding fuel to the fire greedily consuming the straw. As the wagon begins its trundling ride towards Lyminge, it approaches the fallen oak. Barney aims his second stone at the shoulder of the bottle. There is an almighty crash of breaking glass. It does not merely break; it shatters into a multitude of pieces. Ambro, unhurt by the glass smashing around him, tries to keep his balance but cannot. He drops to his knees and begins crawling forward struggling through the flames towards the coachman's seat. Taymar has climbed atop the fallen tree. He takes a flying leap onto the wagon bed as it passes by. With the wagon blazing like an inferno, Barney realizes there will be no need for him to fire a stone at the driver or spook the horses. The blazing fire will create more havoc than he can. He makes his way back to the tunnel and will wait for Taymar and Ambro there.

As the mounted escort rides behind the wagon, they have no idea that their horses have had a fear of fires since their great grandsires were scared as foals by a lightning strike. All ten horses rear up on their hind legs. They neigh, they prance, they bolt in all directions. Naturally, most of them bolt in the way they are facing—towards Lyminge. They overtake the front escort and leave them standing. Some have lost their riders.

Horses are less stupid than they look. Some horses are even observed to be intelligent. However that might be, every horse knows that its sole purpose for living is that it shall win races. Ingrained in the deep instincts of horses of all shapes and sizes is the desire to come in first in any race they are part of. The horses in the forward escort have been preening themselves. They are in the leading group of animals, the A class (for advanced) and not in the B class (for behind). Imagine their chagrin when the whole of the rear escort dashes past them, going like the clappers. They flash past so quickly that it is impossible to actually count and determine whether all ten have gone by, but it is a safe bet that they have. The front escort does not have the benefit of blazing straw on a wagon to stimulate them, but the mere challenge of the race is enough. The leading horses waste no time rearing and bucking. They are not initially off to a racing start, but they are soon into their stride. By the time they round Hampton Hill, they are catching up fast.

There is still more happening.

The bottle wagon driver is terrified to find that he is driving a flaming chariot. Never in his wildest dreams has he imagined this. He fervently wishes there were a lake to jump into, but there is none. The second wagon driver, thankful he has not had to take over the reins, has long since departed, about ten seconds ago to be precise. He decides he will go back to teaching those unruly ruffians that had driven him out of the schoolmaster profession years ago. He had thought there could be nothing worse than modern-day boys, but he has discovered that there is something *much* worse.

The sergeant driver is carried along by two fine, black stallions racing out of control with a bottle wagon on fire, bouncing and clattering behind them. To make matters worse, leaping onto the seat beside him is a screaming madman with a flaming torch in one hand and a dagger in the other. He flings the reins at the madman and takes an immense leap at a riderless horse from the rear escort that had started off in the wrong direction and is now trying to catch up with the others. The driver leaves the flaming cart behind as Taymar, with his brother now beside him, pulls hard at the reins and both struggle to keep their balance. They are around the bend of Hampton Hill and heading down the straight by the time the horses can be brought under control. The burning wagon is pulled to a reluctant halt. The horses, flecked with sweat and wild-eyed, are stroked and calmed. Their heaving chests slow down to steady breathing.

The two brothers hug for a moment. There are a few cuts and bruises and burns, but neither is seriously injured. They exchange few words. The stories will come later. Their hearts are full of gratitude for each other, and that is enough for now. Since it's too far to walk back, they unhitch the horses and ride them back down to the transit tunnel where they find Barney and Brolly waiting for them. The horses are patted on their rumps to send them on their way home, but they head off towards Scotland, hoping to distance themselves as far as possible from the mayhem surrounding them. They will not, however, make it that far.

The boys say farewell and give high praise to the rabbits that have been guarding the tunnel entrance. They advise their friends to stay alert! Brolly starts the journey back first, and then Barney. Ambro slides headfirst down into the tunnel and as his feet disappear from sight, Taymar follows. They are on their way home.

THE WIZARD'S
ATTACK PLAN

It is now several days since the wizard's inspection of his troops. The declared holiday has been canceled. The colonel in charge of the parade has been demoted to corporal in charge of the field laundry. The two bottle wagon drivers have been set to work polishing the silver in the officers' mess. After that, it will be the horse brasses. Punishments have reverberated down through all levels of rank. The squad of engineers who failed to discover the ambush from the fallen oak tree is now weeding Lyminge Forest.

The wizard has called, with little notice, a meeting for mid-afternoon in the repaired command tent on Hampton Hill. He is late and seems a little out of breath when he arrives. Although his nose is severely swollen and slightly to one side, he smiles to himself. Even Rasputin appears to be smirking as though enjoying a secret joke. The wizard stands beside an easel which holds a map fastened to the board. The raven perches on top.

The generals, five of them, sit uncomfortably beside two traitor seers from Gyminge, Zaydek and Haymun. Career soldiers have little respect for spies and spying. Those are tactics and methods that cut across the skills acquired by military training. The generals far prefer drills and discipline, uniforms and spit and polish, parades and salutes, weapons inspections and barrack inspections. Spies might be necessary to gain certain objectives, but they should be discarded as quickly as possible. It's not only that the generals don't like Zaydek and Haymun, but they don't trust them either. The generals may be smarter than the wizard thinks.

The wizard has decided on immediate attack of Gyminge. There will be no further delay. He informs his audience that he has chosen to be a cuckoo while their invasion is under way so that his commands can be heard across the battlefield. No voice carries as clearly as the cuckoo's, and he has tried it out this morning on a trip into Gyminge with Rasputin. All went well. They found that most of the wild birds there have left. A few are still flying around that he would like to see gone, particularly the barn owl that lives in Up-Horton. They know him and have kept well clear. They had been about to circle the big lake by the castle, but they saw a flock of geese overhead. Those birds were just too big to tangle with, so they had left quickly and will return at dusk to check the situation at the castle itself.

Now the wizard begins outlining his strategy for attacking Gyminge. He wants their complete attention as he is about to explain how the invasion will succeed beyond the wildest dreams of anyone save himself. He emphasizes that planning, his planning, is the key.

"The attack will begin at late dusk this evening."

The generals start nervously. The wizard might be ready, but they are not.

"The signal will be two cuckoo calls in quick succession, "Cuckoo, Cuckoo." Got that? Any questions so far?"

There are none.

"There will be a mock attack down Hampton Hill, making as much noise as possible, but no soldiers, not one, will cross the border. The curtain will remain in place. Fires will be started in the woods on Hampton Hill, on the Wozzle side. The Gymingers are gathering their forces to repel an attack there, so let's give them some excitement but no action. There will be only a small force of Wozzle soldiers, the useless ones: the cooks, the officers' servants, the orderlies, the office workers, the sick and injured, the laundrymen, the bandsmen… Oh. I better put that boy bugler in jail for the night. We daren't have him playing the wrong tune at the wrong time. And, oh yes, the two bottle wagon drivers will complete all the troops needed. They must take along anything they can find to bang for making as much noise as possible. They must shout and yell. This is a key assignment. Everything will depend on this. Is everything clear so far?"

Heads nod. It is.

Actually, everything will not depend on this. In fact hardly anything will depend on this. The wizard, however, prides himself on his skills in man management. It is what makes an average leader into an outstanding one. The wizard makes his first assignment. "General Overwait, you will command this distraction force." He happens to be the fattest and least mobile of the five. This will put him in a place where he can do the least damage.

General Overwait, who sees this appointment as a reward for his outstanding abilities, feels that this is well within his competence to organize from the comfort of the command tent itself. He tries to prevent a smile of relief and delight crossing his face. Instead, he offers a smart salute. "YES, SIR!" and proceeds to lose interest in all that follows.

The wizard goes on. "Our real attack will be along the river, on the west side of it." The wizard points out the line of the river on the map fixed to his board. About two hundred paces either side of the river, along its journey through the Dark Forest, trees have been cut away long ago to permit settlements. Fields have been cleared and farms established. Water has been available from the river, and the land is rich for growing crops.

"Our men will make absolutely no attempt to exchange arrows or spears with any of the enemy who appear on the opposite bank. They can safely be ignored." The wizard permits himself a smile. The generals are perplexed, but they will have to wait awhile before he enlightens them.

"Let us be absolutely clear about our objectives." He likes the sound of that remark. A leader is talking. He repeats his remark. "Let us be absolutely clear about our objectives. Our immediate objectives are three.

"First is to cause all of the wild birds to leave. We don't want them interfering or causing us trouble later. Second is to capture Gyminge Castle. This will, without doubt, involve fierce fighting, and we shall need the best of our forces there. Third, we are also determined to prevent the removal of Gyminge treasures to the Beyond. These are not only the royal jewels and other treasures, but most particularly this refers to the Twith Lore." He turns to the two Gyminge turncoats. They are both clothed in the long, white gowns worn by acknowledged seers.

"Gentlemen, give us your advice where the Lore will be found."

Zaydek, the senior of the two, gaunt and thin faced, quiets his plump companion, Haymun, with a raised hand and replies. "Sir, Dayko is the high seer, and he keeps the Lore. He has a house several hundred paces west of the castle. It is across the footbridge, over the brook, and then up the hill to the top. I have never seen any guards around the house. One other seer, very junior, stays with him to see to his needs, but the place is quite undefended. There should be no difficulty in preventing the removal of any valuables, but we must be quick. Dayko might choose to destroy the Lore rather than let it go out of his hands."

The wizard nods. "It's up to you, gentlemen, to prevent that happening. General Esscort, give your best officer and twenty of your best men to our friends from Gyminge. The principal objective is to lay hold of the Lore. Be sure your men do not fail in helping our friends accomplish that."

The wizard's eye twitches furiously. The general and the two seers all think the twitching is a personal warning towards themselves, with a threat of dire consequences if they fail to secure the Lore. They are right about the consequences anyway.

The wizard has not finished.

The Bubble

"Gentlemen, we shall, as soon as it is possible, extend the curtain around Wozzle to include Gyminge as well. We shall combine the two kingdoms under my leadership, and we shall rule from Gyminge Castle rather than from Lyminge. General Battershell, you will be in charge of the attack on the castle. Do as little damage as you can, when you capture it. I have plans for its extension. Why am I so certain that you will succeed in your mission to save our beloved country? Go out to the front, and look out over Gyminge. Survey the territory that will soon be ours. Go along, all of you."

The five generals and two seers rise. Once beyond the pavilion, they are stopped short. They find that they can go no farther. There is something in front of them unseen, and they cannot advance. Remaining inside the pavilion, the wizard stands still, arms folded, smiling. "Go along, gentlemen. Go farther. Find a way out." General Esscort, the youngest of the generals, sees that there is no way forward. He turns sharply and runs to the back of the tent. The unseen barrier is there also. He pushes out his left arm and runs, touching the barrier, the whole way around the pavilion until he is back where he started. They are trapped within their own private curtain.

The wizard and Rasputin have not moved. "Come back in, gentlemen; take your seats once more. Let me explain our secret weapon: the bubble. In order to ensure our rapid progress across the country to take the castle, I have perfected the bubble. It's a mere matter of using the unique skills I possess. The method requires that I fly in a circle around any particular area that I wish to enclose. By uttering a few special words chosen and designed by myself, a small curtain is at once in place, which begins closing itself at the top to form a bubble. The bubble is not very high—it doesn't need to be—only about as tall as an oak tree.

"The men within the bubble are protected against arrows shot high or against weapons and stones thrown against them from outside." The audience of seven breaks into clapping. The ingenuity astounds them—a war without casualties.

The wizard allows the clapping to continue for a while before raising his hand. "This is not all. Those inside, as you yourselves have found, cannot move outside its limits. The bubble does not move, and those entrapped within cannot pick it up and run with it. It is thus particularly well suited to locking up defenders so that they cannot move. There will be no way for them to respond to an attack upon them." As if answering their unspoken thoughts, the wizard announces, "Oh, yes. There can be more than one. We will have multiple bubbles in position wherever they are needed."

There is more enthusiastic clapping from the generals. They are working out the possibilities and mentally choosing where bubbles should be placed. The wizard again allows the clapping to persist.

"If I were to create the bubbles now, that would merely alert the enemy to the surprise we have for them. We mustn't do that, must we?

"To launch our attack, I shall first remove a portion of our defensive curtain to allow our troops to enter Gyminge. Then

I shall give the signal to advance. Even as I sound the attack call—two distinct cuckoo calls—I shall be flying around the encampment where the river enters the Dark Forest. Our enemies know that this is the weakest point in their whole defense. Men are concentrated there already to guard it and block it. I shall enclose all those men, leaving only enough space to the west side of the river for our troops to walk past them as though … as though they are going to a picnic.

"I shall then fly along the center of the river until it leaves the forest. By swinging east and returning, I shall bubble up all the defenders on the side of the river opposite your men. No arrows they fire or spears they throw will do anything more than bounce off the inside of the bubble and be flung right back at themselves. They will not be able to threaten our advance in any way. Those bubbles, and a third that I shall place over Count Fyrdwald's manor itself, will ensure free passage from our border to the lake at Gyminge Castle."

The wizard now assigns duties to his other two generals. Pointing to the shortest of the five men in uniform he says, "You, General Naughtsowtal, will be in charge of clearing up the opposition north of the Dark Forest. Your troops will advance down Hampton Hill and along the west side of the river as far as the Dark Forest, secure it, and then progress westwards. Do not halt your advance. Surround, but do not, at this moment, attack Earl Gareth's estate at Up-Horton. All their men will be out along the border. Save our escaped prisoner alive when you lay hold on him, and his parents and brother too. I have a special interest in them, you know. I doubt you will need any of my bubbles to help you. What do you say, General?"

General Naughtsowtal agrees, acknowledging the assignment the wizard has given him. With a bubble preventing enemy reinforcements coming from the south, he will be well able to manage.

The wizard turns to the final general. "That leaves you, General Chesterton. Your task should not be too difficult. You will clean up and capture the Dark Forest itself. I will have had time before you get there to put the bubble around Count Fyrdwald's manor and the roads that feed to it. This will slow down his communications and the way he uses his forces. Can you manage the rest yourself? I'll be busy at Gyminge Lake."

General Chesterton considers himself the most fortunate of the three attacking generals. With three bubbles locking up Fyrdwald and the bulk of his defenders, there should be no difficulty on his part to secure the forest. Out of curiosity, he asks, "What is your intention, sir, with the enemies who are trapped beneath the bubbles?"

The wizard laughs, relaxed and at ease with himself and his plans. "Well, General, I imagine they will go hungry for a few days. I doubt if it will hurt them. Let's let them stay there while we secure the rest of the country. When everything is quiet, we can start some discussions with them. They'll be more agreeable when their stomachs are a little empty. What do you think?"

The wizard has on his easel the list of the troops that are available. These he shares out among his five generals, starting with the cavalry. "Have your officers begin their individual planning immediately. They are to have their troops in position and ready to move an hour before sunset. Are there any questions?" The generals may have questions but they would not dare to ask them. "Fine, then. I'm going to go have a rest. It will be a long night." Unnoticed, the wizard has already removed with a spell the bubble that had encased them.

JOCK AND CRUSTY

Far, far to the north of Wozzle lie the crags of Ben Armine and the forest in northern Scotland that bears its name. There, a great golden eagle swings lazily in the soft air. The sky is bright blue, the midsummer air pleasant as cumulus clouds build distant castles. The bird is simply enjoying its gift of flight. Resting on an updraft, it only needs to barely move the tips of its wing feathers as it rises higher.

On the eagle's back sits a Scot. One o' the wee folk to be sure; the bird could not carry a Beyonder, but unmistakably a Scot. On his bright ginger hair, he wears a tam pulled rakishly over his left eye. Those eyes, steely blue, leave no doubt as to his self-confidence and assurance. He is broad across the chest and of sturdy build. His white ruffed shirt is tucked neatly into a colorful kilt. The tartan is his family plaid, predominately red with some patches of green running through crossed by black and yellow lines. Over his shirt, he wears a plain, brown vest. Knee-length stockings and shoes with flaps falling over the top complete his attire. In one of his stockings is a sheathed knife called a dirk. It is made of bronze and is very sharp. He speaks with a brogue so thick you could cut it with a knife. Jock has no trouble understanding the eagle's yelping "Kaa" of sound, but the eagle has some difficulty with Jock's Highland dialect. Jock tries to remember to speak to the eagle in the British language of his grandparents, but sometimes forgets and lapses into the lyrical speech of his parents.

"And wha's th' gossip ye 'ave, Crusty, me lad? Any news o' yur sister or yur cousins?"

Crusty continues to soar. There is plenty of time to answer. They have all day. The weather is perfect and the view glorious.

Jock is a mountain climber. He has been a climber as long as he can remember. He loves the solitude of the high rocks and ridges. His home is among them, and he looks for no other. The eagle and the man have been together since even before Crusty was a helpless, downy fledgling seeing for the first time the light of day. As Jock had been wandering along mountain crags he had never climbed before, he had one day, long days ago, spotted a Beyonder making for an eagle's eyrie. Jock was outraged and thought, *Not on my territory!* He made sure he got to the nest first.

The Beyonder had been observing the nest for some time and had waited until the mother left her long vigil of incubation to forage food for herself. It had been a hard and dangerous climb for the young man. The eyrie was just within reach. As his groping hand reached up to investigate and, if possible, grab one of the two eggs, Jock stabbed the outstretched hand with the point of his dirk—enough to draw blood, but not enough to wound seriously. When the bandaged hand received the same treatment a second time, a little harder, the intruder wisely withdrew.

From that time until the eggs hatched, Jock appointed himself as guardian. He told the hen eagle that he would ensure that no one interfered with her clutch. Throughout the five remaining weeks, he was never far away from the white eggs blotched with brown.

The great, tawny, buff brown bird, almost from the moment he learned to fly, seemed always to have his guardian on his back. As he matured to independence, their friendship grew stronger. They were rarely far from each other. Crusty's sister eventually followed her mother farther north. Crusty alone decided to stay in familiar territory.

There is yet no answer to Jock's question. While Crusty is deciphering Jock's dialect, he swings in towards the massive structure of twigs perched on the west side of the high crag between two large rocks that is his home. His yellow legs clutch the flattened stone.

Jock makes himself comfortable in his usual place in the cleft that cushions his back. His arms are folded behind his head, his feet crossed at the ankles. He sits facing the bird. They can both see the vast, green brown sweep of hills and glens and the sun reflecting from the lakes far below them. How they love this land. There is no place anywhere they know of that is more lovely than right here. At last, Crusty is ready to reply. "I was down on the lake this morning doing a little fishing. A new Greylag goose had just come in from down south. She spends part of the year here and part on a lake in the far south of England, near the far sea. A whole colony of geese migrated from here some years ago. The bird doesn't know if she will be able to go back again. Most of the others from the colony have decided that it's best to follow her back here, and she's just the first of them to return.

"The goose had a lot of news to share. The Greylags live among your size people, Jock. There are many Little People there, she says. On the edge of their lake is a castle where King Rufus lives. He is a good man. All the birds like him. But an invader, a neighbor from the north, someone whom they say is a wizard with immense magical powers, is about to attack them. He might have already done so, but if not, he is certainly preparing to attack soon. He surrounds his land—I think she called it Wozzle—with a curtain that no one can see and through which the birds cannot pass. Most of the Wozzle birds left before he could do anything to them, and those that remained have just vanished. The Gyminge birds know that, and many of them are leaving as well. If the wizard should conquer Gyminge, something bad will most likely happen to them, too. That's why the geese are coming back up here."

"Gyminge! Gyminge?" Jock is excited, disturbed. Something is stirring in his memory. Recollections are pouring back. He has heard stories of Gyminge from other Little People of his youth.

"I remember… I remember stories 'bout Gyminge. Or was tha' Lyminge? Me brother, Munro, went there on one o''is journeys, long afore 'e decided ta go ta Cornwall. It was 'e tha' found our ancestors 'ad cum frum there. Our grandfather was cousin ta good King Leo's father. They're fine people, wise people. Aye. King Leo was king o' Wozzle. If th' goose is right, then th' Twith down there need 'elp, Crusty. They need 'elp, 'n' they need it right away. This is an emergency. Wha' are we doin' wastin' our days 'ere while our family needs all the 'elp it can get? To be sure, they may be in distant parts, but they're still family. Let's go down 'n' talk to th' goose 'n' make sure of wha' she's sayin'. It's 'bout time we got down ta doin' some good somewhere 'stead of just enjoyin' ourselves. Cum on."

On the lake between the moorland slopes, it's not hard to locate the new goose. She's busy preparing a nest near the water's edge while most of the others, long-time residents and already well housed, are in the water. She greets Crusty and is glad to meet Jock. She's happy to honk and tell all she knows. She herself has many friends among the Twith. Princess Alicia, the daughter of King Rufus and Queen Sheba of Gyminge, has a favorite beach that the geese also share. They know her well.

Everything is new to Jock, and he is full of questions. The Greylag is able to answer most of them. She gives them directions for the trip south, and she has warnings too. She explains about the Wozzle curtain and tells them to be careful to avoid that. She doesn't know for sure, but it could well surround both Wozzle and Gyminge by now. Jock is afraid that if it does, they will be too late to help. Whatever happens, he knows they must not get trapped inside it.

SOUTH TO GYMINGE

It will be a long flying day for Crusty. They have left Ben Armine as the first rays of dawn are creeping over the distant hills, throwing contrasting light and shadow into the valley. Soon, the high peaks of Scotland are left behind.

They stop in on their way south to visit a fellow climber friend of Jock's in Northumbria. He lives in the Cheviot Hills just beyond the Scottish border. The two men met in the Highlands. Jock was able to give some help to Jordy when he was in trouble on Craig Maggie. Jordy claims that Jock saved his life, though the Scot is silent about that incident. Since that time, however, they have done much climbing together and have visited each other's homes (with Crusty as a taxi). Over the years, they have shared their concerns over the misfortunes of the Twith Logue, who are steadily being driven westwards by the invading Beyonders.

Without hesitation, Jordy stops what he is doing. He's planning to make caraway seed buns, but, anyway, he's out of caraway seeds. What Jock tells him is much more interesting and challenging. His own people need help. *That's enough. The buns can wait,* he decides. He flings a few things into a knapsack, including a dagger, an axe, and a sheathed broadsword that sticks out of the top. He remembers a towel and leaves the cups in the sink to wash up when he gets back. Jamming his flat, tweed cap on his head, he exchanges his slippers for his climbing boots and asks, "What's holding you up, Jock?"

Jordy is taller than Jock, although not by much, and a little more sturdy. He is brown-eyed and dark-haired, going thin on top. He has a good sense of humor and is always ready to laugh. As most mountaineers and hill climbers are, he is self-reliant and full of initiative. Jordy is a good problem solver.

The Twith men make a good pair. They get on well together. They feel strongly about the same things. When they see injustice and brutality and wickedness, they are anxious to do something to put things to rights. The Englishman can talk nonstop once he gets started, and Jock is content to listen, form impressions, and remember.

Crusty lifts off easily with his two passengers and their luggage. He flies along the coastline, keeping it in sight for several hours. This line now recedes as they fly over sparse, uninhabited moorland. As the flight continues, the rhythm of Crusty's strong wings never falters. Long acquaintance with Jock has given the bird many of Jock's own ideals. The bird is never reluctant to share in expeditions to help others, and he is willing to accept the same risks as his small passengers. Life, even for a bird, has higher values and goals than looking after oneself.

Crusty glides down near a great river estuary thronged with small sailing ships manned by Beyonders. While the two passengers wait under a solitary oak in a meadow, Crusty fishes in the river. The sun is past its zenith, but the afternoon is still young. They would like to arrive before dark. There are long hours of daylight left, so they should be able to do so.

They journey on. The sun is warm. The land gets flatter and flatter, and all three notice the changes in trees, fields, and forests. There are many more Beyonders here. Homes and towns and villages are closer together. By early evening, they come upon another great estuary. The goose had told them to look out for this one. Crusty descends, searching for landmarks. The main landmark they are to look for is across the estuary, an area without birds not far from the coast that will soon lie directly ahead.

Crusty, flying high, observes the increasing flocks of birds. There are hundreds of birds in the flecked cirrus sky. He wonders how many are fleeing from the wizard. Crusty sees the great flock of Greylag geese heading north in their typical vee formation and merely waggles his wings in greeting. A migration at this time doesn't fit with the seasons, for it is only midsummer. That means they will be the Gyminge birds, and confirms that he is on course.

"There, over there, a little ta th' left, Crusty. Do nae go inta th' empty area. Stay where th' birds are." Ahead, in the distance, is the sea. Their destination is closer than that. They are nearing the end of their journey.

Crusty finds new strength for his broad, tiring wings. He veers a little to the left, heading for the center of the great, curving bay in the distance. The bird-empty area further to their left is smaller than he expected. He's accustomed to the great, open spaces of the Highlands. They are flying over a cluster of small towns and villages. Jock exclaims, "Look, Jordy! All those people down there are Beyonders. Th' Twith must be survivin' among them as best they cun. Ye can nae tell there are any Twith there a'tall. Wozzle 'n' Gyminge will be so small; it will be easy ta miss them altogether if we are nae careful."

Crusty flies low over a wood and follows a small stream that seems, after it leaves the wood, to feed into a small pond. There are a few birds flying around it, but only a few. He spots an owl in the distance and then an unusual pair of companions: a cuckoo flying alongside a raven.

Jordy and Jock lean over, looking down. They have a better idea of the size and scale to which the Twith Logue are accustomed. The tiny pond beyond the woods becomes to them the great Gyminge Lake. On its south side, there is no doubt of the castle. They shout to Crusty as though he has not yet seen it.

As the great bird glides in to land in the meadow alongside the castle, Jock and Jordy see, flying from the mast at the north round tower, the royal standard of the king of Gyminge. They have arrived, and at least for the present, King Rufus is still in control.

The people of Gyminge are unaccustomed to visitors arriving on the back of a golden eagle. While they are acquainted with bigger birds, such as swans, the eagle is a rare bird in their land. There are few birds of prey that nest or breed in this area. Apart from the owl, only the kestrel is common, and he is less than half the size of the great eagle that has now landed.

Tumbling off the eagle's back come two Twith never before seen. One of the two is wearing a woman's skirt rather than a man's breeches. They are speaking in English, but with unfamiliar dialects. The people cannot make out what they are saying, and neither can the guards from the castle gate. They both speak so fast that Jordy is no more intelligible than Jock. They could be people from the moon as far as the Gymingers are concerned.

Jock tells Crusty, "Wait right 'ere. I'll go ta th' castle with Jordy 'n' see wha' we should do next."

GYMINGE CASTLE

King Rufus has returned home only that noon from the castle in the Dark Forest, where he had been meeting with Earl Gareth and Count Fyrdwald. The tension of a possible war with Wozzle has been hard for him, and he is tired.

Queen Sheba has been missing both her husband and her daughter. The princess is down in Blindhouse Wood where she will be safe in case of attack. The days have been long and lonely for the queen. She has not liked to see the birds on the lake leaving. Somehow, their presence spelled a comforting security. She quiets the aching pain of her own heart when she sees how worn her husband looks. In all their married life, she has never seen him looking so sad and discouraged.

Her husband shares with her the events of the Dark Forest. The chances of Gyminge resisting an attack by Wozzle are very slim. There is no doubt of the bravery of their defenders, but against the vast array of forces from Wozzle, they are facing the end of the Gyminge they know and serve and love.

Especially, the king talks of his private conversations with Earl Gareth, and he asks the queen to go to the cottage in Blindhouse Wood to inform their daughter. The queen must tell Alicia all he has shared with her. She will need to be ready to leave within the hour. He will do his best to bring their daughter home as soon as the danger is over. If Gyminge should fall, she must remain where she is until help comes. If the queen feels led to remain with Alicia, this might be wise.

However, he will not try to persuade her to do so against her will. He knows that she does not want to be long separated from him. As they rise, he reaches out and gently squeezes her hand. He needs her touch.

King Rufus names the trusted menservants that alone must travel with the queen. They will need to take good horses and adequate provisions. She must tell no one where she is going, lest there are Wozzle spies where she least expects them. All preparations have been made in good time. The king accompanies his wife for the first mile or so and then reluctantly informs her he should return to the castle. It is important that he confer with the high seer. He needs to seek his counsel before nightfall. As the king parts from his beloved queen, he wonders when he will see her again.

King Rufus arrives back at the castle in time for the evening meal. Having finished eating, he dismisses his servants and is now alone, deep in thought. Standing, looking northwards across the lake out through the dining hall window, he heaves a deep sigh of sadness and near despair. It's almost eerie without the birds. He misses not only the geese, but the crows returning in their noisy flocks to the tall, distant trees across the lake. It seems rather odd to miss crows and their raucous chatter, but he does. Thoughts from the past flit across his mind. *It was in this very room as a boy that I heard of the death of my grandfather. People with us at the time had suddenly bent the knee before my father and called him "Sire" and "Your Majesty." And it was in this room that the family celebrated my betrothal to Lady Sheba. Later, it was also here that we held our marriage banquet. It was here, too, that we celebrated the birth of our precious little Alicia.* A roomful of memories crowd in upon him.

A sudden knock on the door interrupts his reverie. A servant has come with a message. "Sire, there are two Twith Logue from the north seeking to meet you. They are foreigners and one is clad very oddly. They arrived on a great golden eagle. I've never seen a bird like it."

The king is curious. He glances at the great hall clock. He is expecting Dayko within the hour, but there should be enough time to at least hear what these foreigners have to say. He wonders, *What could have brought them to Gyminge?* "Bring them in and bring refreshments for them also. They will have traveled a long way."

Jock and Jordy have never been inside a king's castle previously. They are not overawed, although their roving eyes quickly scan and scrutinize each room as they are brought from the gate to the king's dining hall. They both bow as they meet the king.

King Rufus might not be wearing his crown or royal robes, but he is a man of great presence. Clothed in a simple short tunic over leathern breeches, he is a big man—very tall by Twith standards—and broad shouldered to match. He has huge hands, and his arms are firmly muscled. This man is strong. His auburn hair is neatly trimmed and combed. Clean shaven, he has a sunburned, open-air face. His dark blue eyes are penetrating and seem to look right through a man. Blue eyes are not common among the Twith Logue, and the king notices immediately that Jock also has blue eyes.

He smiles a welcome and stretches out a hand in greeting. He has long ago learned to put no force into the grip of a handclasp; so he is surprised by the firmness of the grip of the two strangers, and he matches them. He seats them near the window so they can enjoy the view north as they talk. The servant, quietly and unobtrusively, places food and drink within reach.

The one with the strange clothing is first to speak. Scots tend to speak quite quickly and Jock himself rattles on more than most. His tongue tries to keep up with his brain. He has already realized that people in Gyminge are going to have trouble understanding him; although, on his part, he understands them just fine. He deliberately speaks very slowly and as distinctly as he can. The king is able to follow most of what he says; although, once or twice he signals to Jock to slow down a little and repeat himself.

Jock speaks respectfully to the king, "Sire, me name is Jock, 'n' this is me friend, Jordy. We live in th' fur north, 'n' me golden eagle, Crusty, 'as brought us 'ere. Livin' near us we 'ave Greylag geese which winter 'ere 'n' return ta nest on our coastline. Just yesterday, one o' them told us tha' ye are in a spot o' bother 'ere." Jock's face shows his concern. "We feel part o' th' same family, 'n' thought we should cum ta 'elp. Is there anythin' we cun do, anythin' a'tall?"

The king seems a bit hesitant and Jock quickly reassures him that they are trustworthy. "I think ye must know, Sire, tha' we would ne'er tell a lie or participate in deception o' any sort."

The king relaxes a bit and nods for Jock to continue.

"If ye need more o' us ta cum down 'n' 'elp, we cun go back 'n' gather our friends. We just did nae know how much time ye 'ave left afore yur enemy attacks." Jock bows towards the king. "We are at yur service, Sire, if ye cun use us. It might be tha' ye will want ta move yur men quickly frum one place ta another. I reckon Crusty could carry thirty o' us in a pinch."

Jock straightens and motions towards Jordy. "Jordy 'n' I are both 'andy swordsmen, 'n' Jordy is also good with th' axe. Ye could ne'er find a better man to be at yur side than 'e." Jock pauses and allows Jordy to speak for himself.

Jordy has observed how Jock slowed his speech. He tries to do likewise, and the king appears to understand him. "Sire, most of our experience is in the mountains, and we're accustomed to risking our lives. It may be that you'll not want to risk family men. We'll be willing to go in their steed. Neither Jock nor I have any kin waiting for us at home."

King Rufus likes these two men. Given time, he'll be able to understand them. They are offering their lives to help him defend his kingdom. Surely, certainly, he will need them and use them. He tells them so and also speaking slowly informs them, "I'm expecting a visitor now, but you are welcome to be my guests in the castle overnight. Then tomorrow at breakfast, I will discuss with you how you can best help." He calls for a servant to show them to the castle guest rooms in the west wing. He will not take a refusal. "Yes, of course you may go out to inform your friend, Crusty." A second servant enters silently and whispers to the king.

Dayko, the high seer, has arrived. The old man, clad in simple, loose, white clothing held at the waist by a wide, embroidered belt, shuffles past Jock and Jordy just as they are leaving. Taken aback at the sight of Jock, he stops and turns to look back at the retreating strangers. He looks at Jock long and hard, studying his clothing as though he has never seen a kilt before. A look of mystification crosses his face. It is as though he is recognizing some long-lost friend in the past. The worried look on his face gives way to a look of joy. He mutters to himself quietly, "It's all happening as I saw. Then there is hope after all. Yes. There *is* hope after all."

THE EARL RETURNS

Earl Gareth has said his good-byes to King Rufus and Count Fyrdwald. The long meeting in the Dark Forest is at last over, and he is returning home.

The earl, tired and drawn, has arrived at his estate castle just before noon. An earlier messenger had brought news of his planned return, and his wife and sons greet him together with the assembled servants in the great hall. He embraces his family warmly, but all notice how worn and weary the earl looks. Back in their own hall, the servants discuss this among themselves and decide that things cannot have gone well and the earl must have brought bad news.

Taymar and Ambro withhold the stories of their own adventures until their father is rested. After a brief meal, their father sends them back to their duties. He will talk with their mother, rest awhile, and meet with all the officers who can be spared from the defenses later in the afternoon. "I want you boys to keep watch at the border line until the officers return. Be cautious, and stay *alert*. Matters are very serious. I will tell both of you at suppertime everything I am free to share, and then I'll spend some time with each of you separately. Off you go then."

Taymar is excited. His father has told him that his mother and he have news for him that is very important. They will share it with him after supper this evening. Whatever it is, it is to remain a secret for some time to come, even from Ambro. He wonders to himself, *What kind of secret can it be that I can't even share it with Ambro? We don't keep secrets from each other. We always share everything.*

There is a high, wooden stockade fence recently erected around the estate belonging to the earl of Up-Horton. As Taymar strides outside, he spots Tuwhit perched in his usual place, high in the oak tree. He beckons the barn owl down and climbs on his back. Taymar asks his companion to follow once more the path of the usual afternoon patrol. They stop at each guard point. The men are alert, and patrols are still out. They are at the bottom of Hampton Hill and have only a short view, but there is nothing to report.

The owl waggles his wings over the tunnel entrance they have recently used. Several rabbits wave. There is no sign of activity from among the trees up the hill. They swing around at the end of their flight and turn back. All's quiet for the moment. There is a bird at each patrol point that will act as a messenger if there is news to send back to his father.

Taymar is on edge all afternoon, even while attending to his duties checking the guards. Tuwhit notices this and asks if Taymar is worried about something. His father is now back, so it can't be that. Taymar admits to his friend that he's curious about the news his father has promised to share with him later this evening. His father has told him that it is a secret he can share with no one. It must be very important, and he wonders what it can possibly be. Tuwhit raises his eyebrows and wonders too.

The afternoon drags on for both Taymar and Ambro ... they are each anxious to talk to their father. Evening does eventually come to Up-Horton. The early moon, moving towards fullness, bathes the landscape with long shadows as it rises. The defense headquarters, once a residential hall, has in recent months become accommodation for troops. It has been hastily fortified with a surrounding wall of pointed, vertical logs. The large, main room is lit with blazing rushes. The fire in the big, central hearth glows red with only little smoke and occasionally throws sparks.

Although there are usually others sharing the table with them, this evening, the four are dining alone. Each has dressed formally for the evening meal, as is their custom. Both boys wear open-neck shirts and unadorned, leather jerkins tied by a belt at the waist and full-length trousers narrow in the leg. They wait. In his own time, their father will tell them all he deems they should know. They notice how suddenly their father has aged. It's not only physical tiredness; somehow, a part of the spark that made him their enduring, unchanging hero appears to have left him.

The earl compliments his wife on the meal she has had the servants prepare and wipes his lips. He waits until the servants have cleared the table, stoked the fire, and pulled the great dining hall doors closed. He looks around at the three people most dear to him in the entire world. He wonders where they will all be in just a week's time.

"First of all, King Rufus sends warm greetings to all of you. He suggested that all three of you move to Gyminge Castle until the crisis is over. Of course, I told him that wasn't likely. I knew none of you would agree, and he understood. He just smiled and said that his own family felt the same way. The queen has said that she will remain with him, come what may. However, Princess Alicia is a different matter. The wizard would consider her a most desirable hostage and a valuable trophy. Despite her protests, she has been sent off into hiding into the countryside.

"The king is certain that Wozzle *will* attack. He explained to us the plans he has made for the defense of the country. The whole of Gyminge has been placed on alert, even though the attack will undoubtedly come from the north. The manufacture of an arsenal of weapons—pikes and staves, spears and javelins, swords, axes, shields, and bows and arrows—is proceeding as fast as possible. All smiths have been ordered to drop other work and even unskilled men have been sent to help. As soon as the first weapons are ready, they will be issued to all able-bodied men. They will then be trained in how to use them.

"The king feels that circumstances favor the Wozzle army. With the unscrupulous wizard as their leader, and considering his unquestioned skills, they might well prove victorious. They far outnumber Gyminge troops and have been preparing for this campaign for a long time. The wizard also holds the advantage of surprise. He will choose the timing of an attack to suit himself. It's not far to the full moon, which would be a good time for a surprise night attack.

"In addition, the wizard is better informed. News of our preparations for defense is undoubtedly getting back to him. If the rumors of his powers are true, there is nothing to stop him from changing into a sparrow and flying the length and breadth of the land, even right into Gyminge Castle itself. It has to be assumed that everything about the defense of Gyminge is known to him. However, because of the curtain around Wozzle, little more than rumor is available to King Rufus about what preparations and planning are being made by the wizard. The king has no knowledge of where the wizard might be massing his forces. It could be anywhere along the border."

The boys are somewhat better informed than their father,

but they keep silent until they have an opportunity to share their Wozzle experiences with him later in the evening.

The earl changes the direction of their thoughts. "The king told us that the evening before his meeting with us, he had sent for the old seer, Dayko, to seek his wisdom and counsel. The old man had arrived deeply worried, more distressed than the king had ever seen him. He warned the king that the future is clouded and unclear, but there is no mistaking that there will be war. He urged him to send both the queen and the princess to safety, not just into the countryside, but over the southern border in amongst the Beyonders. If the wizard surrounds Gyminge with a barrier similar to the one around Wozzle, there will be no hope of escape. The Twith culture and our great traditions will not be able to survive. Dayko recommended that the king send a small group of his best people into the Beyond, taking with them the most valuable Twith treasures, in case the worst does happen.

"The king trusts that every man, woman, and child will do what is required when called upon. He is convinced that every person will fight with great courage, but Dayko warned the king to exercise caution about this. Dayko has been concerned for somewhile about the decay in Twith standards of behavior. He fears the long period of prosperity may not have been good for us. He cautioned the king to be careful about sharing secrets. He has a sense there might be spies within Gyminge, although he hasn't yet been able to identify them. He suspects there may be traitors in some of the most trusted positions; he even has doubts about a few of the seers in the king's own inner circle."

This news comes as a shock to the earl's three listeners. Taymar thinks, *Traitors in Gyminge? How can there be traitors in*

Gyminge? Who would be a traitor? The king is loved by his people. They would give their lives for him. Is it really possible there are people who would deceive the king? He asks his father, "Do you think there could be any of our neighbors who would lie to us? Doesn't the Lore say that deceit will be followed by defeat?"

His father does not reply immediately. He is busy running his acquaintances through his mind. *There is not a single one who cannot be trusted completely. Yet Dayko, if anyone, would know. He has a touch on the pulse of the land and its people, and can see into the heavens. I cannot think of anyone who might prove to be a traitor though.* He shakes his head slowly. "No, my son, I can think of absolutely no one who would either deceive us or be a traitor to our king. Yet who knows what lies in the depths of a man's heart? There could be hurts he harbors or strong ambitions he feeds upon. It is hard to imagine there might be men we know who envy the king and would replace him with themselves if they could. It's not beyond the realm of possibility though. And, yes, you are right. Lies and deceit will ultimately lead to our defeat. And defeat for all of us, not just those who lie and deceive. Our whole existence depends on always telling the truth."

Plans for Taymar

The earl of Up-Horton now changes the subject. He has shared as much as he wishes at present. After he has talked separately to the two boys, he will visit some of the forward positions before going to bed. He will resume command of the northern area from his sons at daybreak tomorrow.

Ambro leaves for a last check of some of his positions. He agrees to be back in about an hour for his visit with his father and mother. By then, Taymar will have left to check his own patrols, and Ambro will have his time to talk with his father and tell him about Cymbeline.

Taymar waits. He stacks logs on the fire, and sparks fly. They are alone, the three of them. The earl looks at his wife and smiles at her. Taymar begins the conversation. His father needs to know. "Sire, while you were away, I went over into Wozzle. I want to tell you the news of the situation there." In as few words as possible, he tells his father and mother all that has happened. The wizard has spoken of some secret new weapon that would enable his troops to get right to Gyminge Castle within twenty-four hours, but he has not revealed or even hinted what it is. His mother hears more details than the boys had told her earlier.

The earl listens intently, approvingly. "Well done, my son. I would have expected no less from you than you did. This will help us considerably. Do you think it will be some while before the wizard can repair the damage you caused and be ready to start again? We shall need every day."

"Father, he might change his plans. That I cannot say. He is undoubtedly a very powerful man, and he has a large army, though we shall give a good account of ourselves."

"I shall reflect at length on what you have told me, my son, after I have listened to Ambro also. Meanwhile, I must report my own journey, as it will affect you. First, your mother and I enjoin secrecy upon you. Less than half a dozen know what I am about to share with you. You will guard your words carefully, even with your closest friends and with Ambro. Is that understood?" Taymar nods.

"Your mother and I are proud of you, Taymar. We've watched you grow through the years. You have responded well to your tutors. You have acquired by hard work the various skills you need. You are disciplined and a man of integrity. Your word is your bond. You take reproof well, and you are just and fair in reproving others. You think clearly. You act by what is right rather than by what is convenient and less costly. Although you are young, you are already a leader of men, which you have just demonstrated brilliantly by your actions in Wozzle and in the rescue of your brother.

"I would have been happy to have you succeed me as earl of Up-Horton, not only happy, but proud. However, I must tell you that it will be your brother Ambro and not you who will succeed me."

Taymar hides the sudden dismay sweeping across his heart. He tries to hold his smile unchanged. He has always expected that one day, hopefully long distant, he would, as the oldest son, succeed his father. His father had shared that expectation. Fearful thoughts cross his mind. *What has happened? What have I done to incur my father's displeasure? Where have I failed?* His father is smiling. There's no sign of reproof on his face. Taymar looks at his mother. She too is smiling. They surely can't be enjoying his disappointment.

He blurts out, "Ambro will make a wonderful successor to you, Father, but I hope it will be a long while before that happens. You're still young. The country needs your wisdom and your bravery, and we need you in our family. You know that mother and we boys depend on you."

"My dear son, the times are uncertain. I expect to be here for a long while yet if we survive the attack from Wozzle. However, for a very good reason, I don't expect you to be here with us. There are other plans for you." His father is suddenly no longer smiling as though amused at an inner secret. "Give me your right hand, Taymar."

Surprised, Taymar stretches out his right hand, palm upwards, across the small table towards his father. It is a strong, broad hand—no scholar's hand this, no musician's hand, not the hand of a scribe or even of a booklover. This is a hand tested and trained for struggle, disciplined by repeated exercise with bow and spear and staff. Except for the deep scar across the palm, it is a hand like his father's: with thick, short fingers and a strong thumb.

The earl takes hold of his son's right hand and turns it downwards. On the finger next to the little finger, he pushes a ring he has been holding hidden in his hand. The ring, although a man's ring, is only just big enough to slip on Taymar's finger. The earl says nothing.

Once the ring is positioned, Taymar raises his hand to more closely examine it. The gold band is broad, mounted with an engraved shield. Saying nothing, he brings the ring yet closer to study the engraving more carefully. With a start, he recognizes the distinctive design he has known from his youth, but it's not the crest of his own family. It has a crouching lion and a black, rearing stallion, a castellated crown and the kingdom motto. It is the royal crest. Taymar is confused. *Why has father placed a royal ring on my finger? What does this mean?* His mother and father are watching him intently. Both are smiling.

The earl passes his son a small pouch of unused, soft leather tied by a long, thin leather strap. He has had the pouch made by the saddler since he arrived home. "This ring, my son, must never fall into other hands but yours. It bears the king's authority. Before you return to your patrol tonight, Taymar, you must put that ring into the pouch, tie it tightly, and wear the pouch around your neck constantly until it is safe and right to wear the ring openly. It is possible that it might be a very long while. Listen carefully.

"After the three of us had finished our meeting, King Rufus and I talked privately for a long while, Taymar. He shares Dayko's concerns and uneasiness. He feels that the time of his reign will soon end and that the magic of the wizard is about to overwhelm us. Even if our people prove more valiant than those of Wozzle, who in the past have been our good neighbors, we have no answer to the power of the wizard's magic.

"King Rufus is taking to heart Dayko's counsel to him. He asked me whom he should send ahead to the land of the Beyonders, someone who is loyal, brave, and cool-headed, yet wise and mature; someone who can rally all those of us who might escape and at the same time be patient enough to wait until the right time to return. He must be a leader whom others follow readily, but he must also be willing to be led. Circumstances will not always favor open leadership. This man must be someone whose love for his own land is enduring and far stronger than any attachment he might form in the Beyond. He must value his own life less than that of his friends. He must be resourceful and able to act quickly and firmly. Most importantly, he must be able to leave immediately, before Wozzle attacks, lest we are surrounded by a curtain and escape becomes impossible.

"I thought of all the people I know. The search in my mind was easy and short. I answered the king that there was only one person I knew who was suited to the task, and I named him to the king. The king smiled and said that Fyrdwald had given him the same answer. He was pleased that our choice was the same. I named you, Taymar, my beloved son." The earl's eyes fill with tears. He knows that he is about to lose his son, perhaps forever, but there is pride in the tears also.

The countess rises, weeping, and comes around to Taymar's side of the table. As she puts her arms around her son, she bursts into deep sobbing. Taymar rises and holds her close until her sobs subside. "Dear son, the time has come when our way of life is ending. Your father and I will stay together, and with Ambro, we will fight while we can. We shall not yield easily, but the future of Gyminge rests in your hands, not ours. Of course, you know that not a single day will pass while you are away from us that we shall not be proud of you and desiring you were with us. Perhaps it's for this that you were born. Without this assurance, I could not bear to lose you, not even for a moment."

Taymar finds the thought of leaving immediately for the unknown Beyond almost overwhelming. The venture to Wozzle had been the first time he has been out of the country since the overthrow of King Leo. Until then, his whole life had been spent among his own people. However, the thought does not even occur to him to question this new direction for his life. Much as he might like to refuse to go and choose instead to stay and fight, possibly die, with his family and friends, he knows he cannot. He battles back the tears ready to surface and seeks to comfort his mother. This is a time to be strong. Weeping is for later.

The earl rises and, coming around the table, gently leads his wife back to her seat. He has not yet finished with the king's assignment for Taymar. "The advantage that Wozzle has over us is the wizard's magic. The king knows of a great western king, a Beyonder who lives far off in the land of Cornwall. He is King Druthan. He knows of us and has good thoughts towards us. In his kingdom, even the use of good magic is not allowed, although he is well versed in it himself. King Rufus has written a letter asking for you to be permitted to learn good magic, wherever that schooling might take place. It might be with King Druthan himself, or he might send you off somewhere even more distant. But if he permits this, you will most surely be able to answer the magic of the wizard when you encounter it in conflict. Here is the letter that you are to take with you."

The earl has still more to talk about and tell, but Taymar breaks in.

"Father, when is it that the king thinks I should leave?"

"Without delay, my son. We must expect attack no later than the full moon, and it is essential that you be away before then. You will travel on Tuwhit. We know that you and he are close friends, and you can benefit from his counsel and help. I will relieve you of your duties at dawn tomorrow. By midmorning, you can be on your way. There will be no time for farewells to your friends. In any case, it is better that the wizard, if he should indeed prove victorious, not know that you have gone out to the Beyonders to make preparation for a return.

"This is only part of the king's plans for you, Taymar. There is yet more."

Princess Alicia

The earl continues. "King Rufus and I spent time together, Taymar, just the two of us. He sought my counsel. He is determined to lead the defense of our country and, if it proves necessary, to die for it. He knows that Queen Sheba will not be parted from him in life or in death. They are resolved on their action, and I did not try to persuade him otherwise. There are great causes from which a man should not try to escape and in which his wife must be permitted her part." He smiles towards his wife, who is dabbing her eyes with her handkerchief.

"If the worst should happen, then what will be done about Princess Alicia? This is of deep concern to the king. She must not be left to the mercies of the wizard. She is presently hidden in a woodcutter's cottage halfway through the south forest, way off the beaten track. She will only be safe there for a while before the wizard's troops hunt her down. Something must be done to help protect her, but what should that action be?

"I gave the king two pieces of counsel, my son. The first was that he should persuade the wizard of the death of the princess by causing some of her bloodied clothes to be found floating in Gyminge Lake. There is talk of a serpent in the lake. This might lead the wizard to stop searching so diligently for her.

"The second counsel was that you should escort her to the Beyond and keep her with you until it is safe for you both to return. Tuwhit can easily carry the two of you and her old nurse as well."

Taymar is startled. Occasionally, he has seen the young princess, auburn-haired like her father and graced with the beauty of her mother's lovely features. It must be at least five years since he saw her last, at her father's coronation. She had been in attendance with them. She must have been about eleven then. A few weeks previously, not long after King Rufus had ascended to the throne but before the coronation, the earl's family had been invited to stay at the castle. While the parents discussed state and family business, the princess had given the two boys a tour. She had shown them her secret hiding places, where she eluded her tutors. She didn't like schooling, especially when she was the only pupil. They had had fun together, but that was long ago, and things are far different now.

"The king asked me whether my son would take good care of her. I answered 'Sire, he would give his life for her.' He asked me again the same question, as though he needed reassurance. I gave him the same answer, but this did not seem enough for the king."

Taymar breaks in. "Oh, Father, you spoke well for me. Surely I would give my life to defend the princess. If she needs a knight, I will be one to her. Only over my dead body might anyone approach her with violent intent. I am sure she would find no more faithful guardian anywhere in Gyminge than I would prove to be."

"I know, my son. I had no hesitation in saying that she could have no better protector than you. The king then asked me a question that caught me by surprise. He said 'Gareth, my daughter will need more than protection. Will he love her? My child has grown up being loved. She could not bear a loveless life. To protect her will not be enough. She needs to be loved,

loved not only as a princess but loved as a woman. If we are conquered, who will there be to love her, save your son? Could he find it in his heart to love her?'

"I did not answer but asked him to speak further. Taymar, the king is desperately concerned for the protection and for the future of his daughter. The king stretched his hand towards mine and grasped it firmly. 'Gareth, old friend, 'he said, 'I know Taymar. Ever since I became king, I have had him in mind as the possible future husband of my daughter. I have watched him grow through reports from others besides yourself. You can be proud of your son. He is a credit to you and the countess. It is our responsibility as parents to choose the partners for our children. If you will agree that our children shall be betrothed, then you will relieve the mind of a troubled father and king, and I shall have no fear or doubt in trusting my lovely daughter into Taymar's charge. She is now no longer a girl but a maiden fit and ready for marriage. I can think of no better husband for her than Taymar, and I shall be proud to count him as the son I never had if you will agree.'"

Taymar has known since childhood that one day, his parents will choose a wife for him. It is the custom of the country, and it is a custom that works well. Husbands and wives learn to love each other after marriage rather than before marriage. Such marriages endure. He has sometimes wondered which of his acquaintances his own wife might be; although it's possible it could be someone he has never met before. He has several distant cousins of suitable age and has assumed that probably one of those would be chosen. In any case, he knows his parents will make what they consider the best choice for him.

Never in his wildest dreams has the thought of the most desirable young woman in the country crossed his mind. He tries to imagine how she might now look. She had been a pretty girl. He can assure the king that he will love the princess, but an anxious thought crosses his mind, *Will she love me?*

Taymar's eyes sparkle with excited surprise. "What did you answer, father?"

"I replied that I could answer for my wife as surely as I could for myself."

The countess smiles and nods.

"I told the king that we would be deeply honored by such a betrothal and that I would advise you of it as soon as I returned home. I was sure you would also be honored and pleased. We would await the king's pleasure before any announcement. Until then, it will be a closely guarded secret."

Now it is Taymar who nods his head. The conversation has gone from overwhelming to mindboggling. Not only is he to leave home tomorrow morning, perhaps never to return, but he is betrothed to the crown princess. Now he understands why he will not succeed his father as earl of Up-Horton.

"Did I answer well, my son?" The earl rises from his chair and comes around the table. He gently restrains Taymar in his place as his wife joins him, their free hands one over the other on their son's shoulder.

Taymar turns his head and looks up, first at his mother and then at the earl. "Yes, Father. Oh, yes, you did."

"The ring I just gave you, Taymar, came from the hand of King Rufus. He removed it from his own finger. It bears the seal of his authority. I, in return, gave him my signet ring. He will send it to Alicia without delay with an explanation that she is now betrothed to you and is available to no other suitor while you live. The king said that the princess remembers you and Ambro and sometimes talks about your time at the castle even though you have not met since childhood. You will confirm yourself to her by showing her the king's ring. My own ring will be far too large for the hand of the princess, but she will keep it until you exchange rings of your own choosing.

"These two rings are the signs of your betrothal. The king will no more go back on his word than I would mine. The exchange of rings means that the king is granting you the same authority that he himself possesses. If Wozzle should vanquish him, then you exercise his authority completely. You are accepted as his son, and no true citizen of Gyminge would ever dispute that. As far as your mother and I are concerned, as far as the king and the queen are concerned, your betrothal has occurred, although the national celebrations of such a great event must await happier times. The king will tell only one or two of his closest counselors and, of course, Dayko. Should the king be unable to do so, these men will confirm the betrothal to the people."

Taymar is still looking up at them, trying to absorb all that he has just heard. Suddenly, his ears catch a familiar sound from outdoors. A look of concern, almost of fear, crosses his face as he rises and runs to the door, flinging it open.

There, in front of him, is Tuwhit. The entrance doors are barely big enough to allow the full-sized owl to wriggle through into the great hall. Tuwhit is out of breath and gulping for air. Taymar rushes forward to support him, crying out, "What is it, friend? Do you bring good news or bad?"

"Bad news. I've come from Ambro. The invasion has begun. Wozzle men are pouring across the border at the river. Our men are falling back. There are just not enough of them to hold their positions. The birds are flying out while there is still time for them to flee."

ALARM

Earl Gareth reacts on the run. He grabs the hand rope of the bell and rings furiously. The great notes boom and echo. Servants come running.

"Bring my armor, quickly, my sword, my shield." To the hall steward, he orders, "Saddle my horse, and bring it here. My guards shall meet me at the gate at once, mounted, with spears. No delay. Hurry.

"Taymar, be off at once. Wait for nothing. On the way, tell Fyrdwald. Alert the king. Waste no time. Farewell, my son. Farewell. Don't forget all that we have tried to teach you."

They share a long, strong embrace.

The doors swing wide open as a gust of wind blows through the great hall. They have been left half open since Tuwhit's entry. There is shouting outside in the courtyard. Orders are being given and received. The earl's garrison runs to its stations. The tall gates are now closing. They will be reopened for the earl as he leaves to go to the front for the fighting. After that, they will be barred. Then it will be only the picket gate that can be used—or over the top. A trumpet blows. In the far distance is the noise of men shouting.

The countess stuffs nuts and fruit into a satchel for Taymar. Her thoughts are sad, *Will I ever see him again?* She would like to weep, but the time is not now. She holds back her tears and hugs her son tightly. How dearly she loves him. Now her thoughts turn to her other son. Thoughts that stab sharp with pain chase through her mind. *Where is Ambro? He must be at the river. Does he still live?* "Go now, my dear son. Serve the king with all your heart and all your strength. Perhaps we shall yet meet again. Pick up the woodcarver's family as you go. Oh, and take this."

From her neck, the countess removes a fine, gold pendant necklace with a large, glowing ruby mounted in its own flowered setting. She thrusts it into her son's hand. Without explaining, she pleads, "Will you give this to Cymbeline, as a remembrance?"

The tears will not be held back, but they must be, just a little while longer.

"Go, Taymar. Go. Trust always in the truth, the Lore, and the Twith. One day, you will be back. May we be here for you. Until then, remember us as we shall remember you."

Her resolve breaks. She buries her head in her son's shoulders, sobbing bitterly, uncontrollably, even as she pushes him away. She must not allow grief to overwhelm her. "Go, my beloved boy. Go while there is time. I will say farewell to Ambro for you. Please go."

Taymar sees beyond his grieving mother. He takes one last look around the great hall, the gallery, the banners, the long table, the fire. With longing in his heart, he wonders, *Will I ever see any of this again?* His father's great axe crossed with the long spear decorates the wall. The earl removes them both. The spear he retains for his own weapon, but the axe he hands to Taymar. "You will need this. May it serve you as it has served my father and me. May it never fail you." One last time, he hugs his son. "Be on your way, Taymar. Everything depends upon you now."

The owl is waiting at the door beside the earl's saddled horse. Taymar nestles down into Tuwhit's neck feathers.

His father springs to the saddle, and into the darkness, he yells, "The gates. Open the gates!"

Galloping across the courtyard, other mounted men move out of the darkness and shadows to fall in behind him. As the gates swing open one last time, the great owl is seen flying across the rising moon and then is lost in darkness. As though in farewell, a distant cuckoo gives its call … twice.

Tuwhit flies southwards across the arable fields, wooded copses, and grazing meadows towards the Dark Forest. Cleemo's cottage is just on the near edge. There's no time for Tuwhit to explain to Taymar what has already happened on the border. There'll be time for that later. Over towards Hampton Hill, there appears to be smoke and flame above the woods. Noises of men shouting split the night air, fading away in the distance as the owl continues his flight.

Taymar tries to make sense of this new world, so different from just two hours previously: an invasion by Wozzle, secrets about Alicia, his new responsibilities that he cannot even share with Tuwhit, and leaving for the Beyond—Cornwall. Severe doubts crowd his thoughts. *Will I ever see my father and mother or Ambro again?*

Tuwhit lands in Cleemo's garden at the edge of the Dark Forest. The trees are silent of the usual bird sounds. Only a cuckoo can be heard in the far distance. The sound mystifies Taymar. *It is night. Why is the cuckoo calling?* Tuwhit announces their arrival as Taymar jumps to the ground. He leaves his satchel and axe with Tuwhit and runs to the cottage door. Barney is there to fling it open for him.

Taymar bursts into the room. Cleemo and Cymbeline are sitting by the cooking fire, one busily carving and the other engaged in her needlework. No time for long explanations. "Wozzle has invaded. We must leave right now. All three of you. You have one minute to be ready. Barney, bring your catapult and stones. We shall need them. Cleemo, bring your woodcarving tools. Quickly, grab what you can. We're leaving right now. Take some clothes, warm ones. Cymbeline, throw some food into a bag. Where's your coat, Barney? Leave your slippers, Cleemo, and put on good shoes. Hurry. We have to be on our way."

Barney moves fast. Cleemo and Cymbeline rise and rush into action—no hesitations, no questions. Some bags have already been prepared and stand ready by the door. Cymbeline scoots upstairs and gathers a few precious extras. They might never come back, but at least they have their lives. She folds carefully the drawing of Ambro she has been working on and tucks it into her bag. If the three had been given any time, they might have argued or paused to better select what to bring. They have not been given enough time for much of anything.

Taymar spreads the embers from under the fire and douses them with the jug of drinking water on the table. Returning to Tuwhit, he hopes he won't have long to wait. He doesn't. The three soon emerge carrying what they can. Cleemo carefully locks the door behind them.

"Where, where is … ?" Cymbeline calls the question back before she completes it, decides against it, and replaces it with another. "Your family, are they all safe?"

"My father is out fighting along the border towards Hampton Hill, my mother is at home. I haven't seen Ambro since we had supper together earlier this evening. He should have been nearby though, for he was to see my father after I had finished, but there was no time."

Cymbeline's eyes fill with tears. Taymar thinks it is because she is leaving, perhaps for the last time, the home she has worked so hard to make beautiful. As Taymar makes sure the other three passengers are comfortably settled on the back of Tuwhit, he remembers the gift his mother had given him for Cymbeline. He fetches it from his pocket and hands it to her. "Here Cymbeline, this is for you. My mother asked me to give it to you, for a remembrance. Do you have good hold of it?"

Barney Walks on Air

As Tuwhit launches into the night air, Cymbeline, recognizing that she has been given a necklace, slips it around her neck and lets the central stone fall beneath her clothes. She doesn't want to risk its loss and will wait to examine it until they land and things are quieter.

Taymar searches behind him. There are fires in the woods at the border and sounds of fighting there and at the river. The wizard must have launched a two-pronged attack. There is no sign or sound of any activity ahead of them. Taymar asks Tuwhit to head towards Fyrdwald's manor. The count needs to be told the invasion by Wozzle has begun. They fly over the canopy of treetops that makes up the Dark Forest. Taymar can't see any reflections in the river from the last few streaks of light in the low, western sky, but maybe they are not high enough. The rising moon appearing over the horizon to their left is nearly full.

The manor sits on a low hill in a commanding position. Taymar sees its silhouette against the sky, a black outline of towers and walls and, in the center, the high keep with the flag hanging quietly from its pole. That strikes Taymar as strange. *There's only a little wind this still summer's night, but I would have thought to see the flag fluttering. At least a little bit.* As they approach, lights in the courtyard and manor rooms come into sight. The noises they hear seem strangely muffled. There's already activity in the courtyard. No one appears to be moving out, although the gates are open. Taymar finds that odd, indeed.

Taymar is anxious to quickly give his message and be on his way. Tuwhit descends to land in the manor courtyard. But he never does. Instead, he bounces and tumbles uncontrollably. He is surprised. *What unseen something have I collided with way up here in the air?* His wings and feathers are in all directions. He tumbles over himself, head over tail. His passengers grab for and hold on to him and to each other like grim death.

Barney slips, yells, and is gone. Taymar releases his axe and with the hand now free tries to grab him but fails. The axe also falls. So does much of the baggage Cleemo and his family have brought.

Tuwhit struggles to regain control. He sees Barney tumbling past him, but cannot grab him. He is just beyond reach. There's not enough height for him to pursue the boy down and catch him before he lands. First, he must get himself back into balance; otherwise, he'll lose his three other passengers also. He gives a great double downbeat with his wings. They're not yet working together, but that almost does it. He beats again. He's on an even balance once more. He twists his tail feathers. Nothing like this has ever happened to him, not even in the hurricane. Now there is shouting from his back.

"Barney! Barney?"

Barney is walking on air. Tuwhit can't explain it and doesn't try. All he knows from a glimpse downwards as he twists in the air is that his fallen passenger has not crashed into a courtyard heap but is walking on air. Without hesitation, Tuwhit swings around low to pick up Barney. Any questions and answers will have to wait. His claws touch and skid along some sort of surface. He doesn't know what it is, but there's definitely something in the way. He can see nothing except the courtyard way below and people running about, some looking up and waving. He swings around again for a second attempt at retrieving Barney.

Barney is keeping his head. He doesn't understand what is happening, but he is walking on something. He is sure of that at least. He holds out his arms, trying to balance himself, all the while stumbling around, slipping, sliding, and bouncing, as he tries to gather up everything else that has fallen.

Taymar hooks his legs around Cleemo, who grips Tuwhit's back feathers with his legs and arms and even his teeth. Cymbeline, legs hooked around feathers, clutches her uncle. With both arms, Taymar reaches out to Barney, hoping to achieve a midair rescue.

Barney, still bouncing and swaying, avoids him. He must first retrieve Taymar's axe, his own catapult, and Cymbeline's bag stuffed with clothes. He yells at Taymar, "Here. Grab this." Taymar snags the bag and catapult and passes them back to Cymbeline. He misses the axe but the second time round gets that and Cleemo's bag too.

Tuwhit banks sharply and brushes against the unsteady boy who seems to be bouncing on nothing. Though the boy's arms are full, Taymar is able to grab Barney under the armpits. Barney jumps, almost somersaults, back into the cushion of the owl's feathers. Taymar tumbles over backwards into Cleemo, and all four passengers roll around on the owl's back. Tuwhit gains a little height and tries to stay level as his passengers regain their balance.

Taymar yells, "It's the wizard's curtain, Tuwhit. He's brought it inland. It's a new trick of his. Somehow, he's closed it in over the top so it makes a bubble instead of a curtain, and Barney's been walking on the top of it. Circle slowly at this height until we are settled. Then test with your claws to see if there is a way down. If we can't find one, let's try to find out how big the bubble is before we move on. But we must hurry. Maybe the wizard has done the same to Gyminge Castle."

The general alarm sounding in Fyrdwald's manor carries up to them as they circle. There is no way down through the top of the bubble. Even if they found a way, it would be unwise to descend, lest they too become trapped inside and would be unable to continue. Tuwhit takes a wider sweep. His tip feathers touch the bubble at treetop height. He can't approach the manor and the clearing in which it stands. He's kept back above the trees of the forest. The various roads and paths can no longer join together. The wizard has blocked with his maneuver the passage of troops and people from one side of the Dark Forest to the other.

"Head for the castle, Tuwhit. Be ready for the same there. Hurry!"

Tuwhit now flies as fast as he is able. He flies higher in case there are other Wozzle bubbles beneath or ahead of him. The weight of his small passengers makes little difference. They soon sight Gyminge Castle by the lake.

Suddenly, Tuwhit screams, "Whoo! Whoo! Whoo!" and banks sharply to the left. He surges down towards the water, screaming loudly as he goes. The sky is almost empty of birds, almost but not quite. Tuwhit's keen eyes, accustomed to foraging in the dark of night, have spotted a pair of birds lazily circling the castle ahead. He identifies the birds: one raven and one cuckoo, an unlikely pair. He already knows about the wizard's raven. He follows his instincts and reacts immediately. This is danger, danger to the castle and the king, danger to Gyminge, maybe even danger to themselves.

Tuwhit heads straight towards the two birds, and his screams alert them. Recognizing danger, they abandon their circling path and the bubble being created to flee from the screeching owl that is heading straight towards them. Standing upright on Tuwhit's back is Taymar with his axe ready to swipe. He and Barney recognize the raven as the one they had seen at the inspection parade in Wozzle. Barney is already within range to get off a good shot with his catapult. His first stone catches the raven on his beak and almost knocks him into the water. The raven's lower beak shatters, and the bird freefalls. Before the boy can reload and fire at the cuckoo, it quickly darts to the left and heads south. That bird has suddenly found energy enough to migrate to the Mediterranean without stopping and flashes off with the speed of a swallow on the last day of summer.

The wizard's curtain is left incomplete. The owl touches a part of it, recognizes it for what it is, and follows it around to the east side of the lake where it had begun and where it ends. The castle and the area around it have not yet been curtained. Tuwhit drops over the castle wall into the courtyard. As his passengers clamber off, he turns his head towards Taymar.

"We were in the nick of time, Taymar. Call me when you want me. I'll check where the bubble is in place and patrol above the castle to make sure those birds don't come back again. Why doesn't Barney stay with me? We can perhaps use his catapult again."

As soon as Tuwhit and Barney have taken off and gained height, they follow the curtain in an anticlockwise direction to see where over the lake it ends. Suddenly, they are joined, to their surprise, by a great golden eagle, a stranger, flying alongside them.

Crusty calls out, "What's going on? Who are the people you just brought? I brought some too. Has the attack begun? I saw you chase those two birds away. Maybe I can help. My name's Crusty."

TAYMAR AND THE KING

Taymar wastes no time. He orders the sergeant of the guard to take care of Cleemo and Cymbeline. He is accustomed to giving orders, and this is no time for long explanations. He runs across the courtyard towards the king's chambers. He has been here before and knows the way. He shouts to the guard at the inner gate, "NEWS FOR THE KING," and runs on across the garden to the main entrance. He pulls the bell rope. A servant answers the door.

"Arouse the king. I bring news. The invasion has begun. I am Earl Gareth's son."

The servant does not hesitate. It's almost as though the news has been expected. He asks Taymar to pause in the entrance hall. Running up a long flight of steps, he disappears into a corridor on a higher floor.

The king, wearing clothes roughly pulled on round himself and tidying them as he hurries down the steps, greets the young man with a hug. Taymar has no need to further introduce himself. The king knows him.

King Rufus has aged since Taymar last saw him. He is still straight and strong, and his auburn hair is not yet tinged with grey; but there are more lines to his face, and his step has less spring in it. He has also had little sleep recently.

The king greets Taymar warmly and instructs his servant to go tell the captain of the guard to sound the alarm. The senior officers quartered in and around the castle should gather immediately in the great hall. He will meet with them as soon as he has acquainted himself with the news that Taymar has brought. The servant should also find the two strangers who arrived yesterday and request that they attend the king without delay. The high seer is also to be notified.

When the servant has departed and can no longer overhear, the king is able to speak freely. "Before your news, my son, allow your father to greet you. I could wish the days were happier for you and for my daughter, but they might yet return if we can weather this present storm. More greetings later, but for now know that the queen is with Princess Alicia at a hideaway in Blindhouse Wood. The queen will have told her of your betrothal. Come with me to the inner room. Tell me your news as we go."

Taymar tells King Rufus everything. He uses words sparingly but begins with the adventure in Wozzle itself. He recalls as much as he can of the wizard's speech to his troops. "The attack proper began this evening, at late dusk. Wozzle appears to be attacking at both the river and Hampton Hill. My owl brought the message from the border and reported many soldiers attacking at the river. My father instructed me to leave immediately, and as I flew off on my owl, he headed towards Hampton Hill. The last we knew, Ambro was still out by the river. I brought with me three of my friends."

The king asks, "Does your owl intend to flee with the other birds? If so, could I have a word with him before he leaves?" Taymar tells the king, "No, Tuwhit does not intend to leave. He would be happy to answer any questions you have."

Into the room come two Twith who are strangers to Taymar. One wears a woman's skirt instead of breeches. The king does not break into Taymar's story to introduce them but motions them to sit and listen. Taymar continues.

"We tried to warn Count Fyrdwald but weren't able to do so. However, the alarm was sounding at his manor as we left." He describes the Wozzle bubble as far as he is able. "It encircles Count Fyrdwald's manor and the cleared area around it. Now the roads through the forest are no longer accessible to the manor.

"As we arrived a few minutes ago, we encountered two birds crossing the lake. I've seen the raven before when I was in Wozzle. He is the wizard's assistant. The other bird, a cuckoo flew off to the south as Tuwhit approached. It was almost certainly the wizard himself. He was in the process of erecting a bubble, or at least a curtain, around your castle. It is only partially completed as his mischief was interrupted by our arrival. My owl is now patrolling the area."

The king thinks hard. Many considerations press in upon him: his wife and his daughter, the power and strength of the enemy now striking at his kingdom, the preservation of their Lore, leadership qualities that will be necessary, possible casualties, the future itself. He reaches his decision. It's a hard one, but both he and Dayko have seen it coming.

"Taymar, these are my orders for you. Leave immediately on the owl. Go at once. Take others with you if you wish, but do not delay to collect them. Take them only if they are already here and ready to travel. We may no longer have hours but only minutes. We must manage with what we have. You say the wizard flew south, so he may even now be weaving a curtain along the line of our border. You must be over the border before you get locked in by a curtain. Did your father give you my letter to King Druthan of Trevose?"

Taymar nods his head and pats his vest pocket. "I have it right here, Sire."

"Good. Go to Cornwall, find him, and make yourself known to him. He will help you. When you can, as frequently as you are able, return to the place where the river from Gyminge enters the Beyond at the bog. That is the one place we all know and can find. Anyone else who is able to escape will head directly there. It will become the rendezvous for any Twith who are free. One day, you will all return to Gyminge."

Taymar is uneasy. He is not anxious to go. All he knows is Gyminge. "But, but…" He wants to ask about Princess Alicia.

The king puts his arm around the boy's shoulders. "Taymar, my son, go now. I, as your king, ask you, beg you, command you. I know you are concerned for the queen and the princess but they shall have to be left behind. Time is too short. We will do what we can, and we shall also try to escape. Our friends," he indicates Jock and Jordy, "are here to help us. They have an eagle that can help patrol the castle skies. Perhaps they too can escape with others, but you must go now. You are the hope of the Twith. Do not even delay to get the Lore. We must find some other way to save that, or we must hide it. On your way, my son."

The great hall of the royal castle has been filling with men. News of the Wozzle invasion has spread like wildfire. There's no panic but an acceptance that everyone will fight to the finish.

Taymar bows to the two strangers who have not said a word, only listened. The one with the skirt excuses himself from the king to accompany Taymar. As they hurry across the garden,

Jock introduces himself. He speaks slowly and deliberately. "Me name is Jock. Me friend, Jordy, 'n' I 'ave cum frum th' north ta 'elp th' king. We've cum on me eagle. I know we must nae allow ourselves ta be locked in by th' wizard, so I'll give me eagle instructions ta replace yur owl in patrollin' th' castle skies. I'll return ta th' king as soon as I give Crusty 'is instructions."

Taymar whistles into the night sky to call Tuwhit. His heart is heavy. The land of his birth is likely to fall to an overwhelming enemy. All that is familiar in his past is likely to vanish like smoke into darkness.

"Jock, I am pleased to meet you and grateful that you have come to help us. If things go against us, I trust that you and others will escape. Bring with you, if you can, Princess Alicia. I bear a responsibility from the king for her care. If there had been time, I would have taken her myself, but you have heard the king's command. I have no choice. I will take my three companions and be on my way."

There is a fluttering in the skies. Down into the castle courtyard come Tuwhit and with him his new, feathered friend who has recognized Jock standing there.

The arrangements are explained, but there is a surprising disagreement—disagreement not from the birds but from Barney. "How can Crusty carry out his patrol without my help and guidance? He's a stranger. He doesn't know anything about Gyminge. He needs someone to show him around. Suppose he comes upon some of the enemy? My catapult is an essential weapon. I'm staying. Cymbeline, you and Uncle Cleemo can and should go, but I'm staying here."

Cymbeline and Cleemo decide they are not going to leave without Barney. They will follow later. For now, they will join

Barney on Crusty's back, and when the eagle leaves Gyminge, they will leave with him. Cymbeline speaks for both of them. "We've decided. We're not going anywhere without Barney. And who knows? Perhaps the wizard will not succeed in his plans. Then we won't have to leave at all. We hope to see you soon Taymar. Good-bye, and have a safe journey." In Cymbeline's heart are thoughts not only of Taymar but of Ambro and hopes for reunion with him. It is her heart that is holding her back.

Tuwhit, with Taymar alone nestled down for a long flight westwards, follows the line the cuckoo had taken and heads south into the night sky towards the border and on into the Beyond.

The Wizard

Surveys Progress

The wizard, still disguised as a cuckoo, turns around as he reaches the boundary of Gyminge and finds a tree to rest in. He is breathing heavily after his race away from the owl. His right eye is twitching furiously.

The battle is going well. The troops are pushing down the west bank of the river and should soon be approaching the lake. He has emphasized to General Battershell that he should divide his forces and go around the lake from both directions. That way he will trap the castle defenders. The wizard thinks, *I will need to make sure the general actually does what he has been told. As a good leader, I need to remain with my troops; otherwise, some fool will disobey quite clear instructions and attempt to act on his own. Come to think of it, where is Rasputin? We should stick together. He needs to follow orders, too.*

The bubbles placed around the east side of the river and the manor in the Dark Forest have been gloriously successful. The wizard is pleased with himself. *What hope do the Gymingers have against such a superb master of battle tactics as myself? They've never had an enemy as cool and calculating as I am. I'm a real fighting machine, that's what I am!* He considers whether the time is ripe to encircle Gyminge with a curtain to join up with the Wozzle curtain. He decides against it. That can wait awhile. There are probably some birds still left. Better to leave them a way to depart, lest within the curtain they continue to cause trouble.

There is no sign that the owl has pursued him. Time now to check the progress of his troops along the river. He no sooner takes off and gains height than he sees, approaching him at a low level, a familiar bird. It's that blasted owl. He curses, but his curses have no effect. He's being chased again! Immediately, he closes his wings and drops like a stone. Opening his wings a few feet above the ground, he darts into a thicket, where he hides. The owl flies low above him but does not hesitate in its flight. The wizard thinks, *Well, good! He's not after me; he's heading for the Gibbins Brook Bog in the Beyond. That's fine; I'm well rid of the creature. May it fall exhausted into the sea.*

After a short pause, once again, the wizard takes flight north towards the lake. Now that the owl has gone he should be able to complete the bubble around the castle. He flies low over the lake. He wonders again, *Where is Rasputin?* He calls out, "Cuckoo? Cuckoo?"

That turns out to be a *big* mistake. Something hits and bruises his wing. He swings away and tilts himself to look upwards. One of the largest birds he has ever seen is swooping down upon him. If the wizard raced like one swallow before, now he races like two swallows. Inches above the water, he scoots for his life, heading towards the castle. Missiles hit the water ahead of him. Not far from the castle, he sees a small, open window, too small for the pursuing bird to follow him through. In he flies, any old port in a storm.

It's a bedroom, a large bedroom. Its door is closed. There are two empty, single beds in it, both recently occupied. The bedding is thrown back as though the residents have left in a hurry. The wizard is not going to go out into the peril of the night sky any more. It is too dangerous. He needs to change himself into something safer than a cuckoo, and he needs to do so quickly, before the residents of the bedroom return.

He decides that a mouse is a safer option, but before he makes the change from a cuckoo to a mouse, a helpful thought comes to him. *I wonder whether the castle has cats?* He decides that probably all castles have cats because of the rats. Out goes the mouse idea. He'll try being a cat himself. Before he makes this change, he has a second fortunate thought. *The natural enemy of a cat is a dog.* Dogs are unreasonable about cats. Something happens to a dog when he sees or even smells a cat. Its hackles rise. Its back crouches. Its legs go stiff. It opens its jaws wide, anticipating the meal. All dogs may not have castles, but it is certain that all castles have dogs. Out goes the cat idea. He doesn't really like cats anyway. He remembers the kitchen cat at Trevose castle. He'll try the dog thing instead. He decides that will surely be safer than a cat.

Now he must figure out what kind of dog he should be. A third helpful thought strikes him in quick succession to the earlier two. He is thinking brilliantly at this point in the invasion. *Dogs fight each other. They need have no reason; they fight each other naturally. Just as lovebirds love each other, dogs fight each other. When that happens, the bigger one usually wins and the faster one escapes.* There is a pause in the wizard's thinking while he wonders whether to go for size or speed. He decides for size, a Great Dane over a Greyhound. He recognizes he better not delay any longer. The two people who so recently vacated their beds might come back at any moment. If he should be caught in the midst of changing, it might be hard to excuse himself. There's no time to waste.

He listens carefully for noises. He hears shouting but no footsteps. Quick as a flash, he changes from a cuckoo back to himself, the wizard. He tries the door and finds that it's latched but not locked. He lifts the latch and leaves the door ajar. Now he changes himself into a Great Dane. He has always rather fancied Great Danes. He flexes himself, standing proud on his long legs. His coat is light brown, his jowls dark, and his ears upright and alert. This is better than being a cuckoo. He nuzzles the door open. In a moment, he is out of the bedroom and down the corridor. Two men run towards him, one of which is wearing a woman's skirt. The Great Dane darts up a narrow staircase out of their way. Though they see him, they do not pause but run into the room he just left. He hears them shouting out of the window. Now he runs on up the staircase and onto the parapet of the defense wall of the castle. He looks over the edge through one of the crenellations down to the lake below. Hovering a few feet away is the huge bird. On its back are a man, a boy, and a girl. They are talking to the two men at the open window. The one in the skirt is saying, "Nae, we did nae see any bird in th' room. Th' door was open, so it must 'ave flown on through. We'll alert th' king tha' th' wizard is in th' castle."

The wizard decides on a quick exploration. Dawn is near, and the moon has lost its glory to the tinge of light in the eastern sky. The castle gates, great doors inside a raised portcullis, are open, and there is continual traffic going through them. It shouldn't be hard to escape when it becomes necessary. After a tour of the walls, right around the perimeter, he runs down the steps into the courtyard. No one has interfered with him or paid any attention to him. There are several other dogs in the courtyard, but none like him. None of them, separately or together, is interested in a fight when they see his size. None are suspicious of the Great Dane as he lopes through the gate and trots off clockwise around the lake following the shoreline road that circles back to the castle. There's no sign yet of the approach of the Wozzle forces. No one pays any attention to the Great Dane running around among the king's soldiers, sniffing and smelling. And no one notices that the dog has a twitchy right eye. The dog crosses the small, wooden footbridge and runs up the hill towards the high seer's house. He finds the small clearing in the woods nearby where Gyminge soldiers are already gathering.

Having seen what is necessary, the dog, with an easy run, continues his clockwise circuit of the lake. Somewhere, he is going to meet up with his own men. The plan for the attack on the castle is already formed in his mind.

Overhead, the eagle circles.

CRUSTY ON PATROL

A small, arched stone bridge carries the lake road over the river as it enters the lake on the north side. The king has decided to make his stand at Fowler's Bridge on the south side, where the stream leaves the lake on its way to Gibbins Brook. Troops from the castle are moving on the double towards Fowler's Bridge. The defense positions, including obstacle trenches and embankments of heaped earth, have been prepared well in advance. The king himself will be engaged in the defense of the bridge. Jock and Jordy will assist him, while Crusty maintains his patrol to protect the castle.

There are similar defenses at the other bridge. More soldiers are heading up the hill to hide near the house of the high seer. They will ambush the attacking troops from Wozzle by circling around behind them when the fighting is well under way.

Crusty has patrolled through the night without a break, never stopping to rest. Barney too has remained awake and alert, although Cleemo and Cymbeline have slept in fits and snatches. As dawn breaks at last, ending the long night, Crusty circles higher and higher. He remains centered over the castle, keeping a wary eye for either the raven or the cuckoo. This is Crusty's first experience of a wizard's magic and his apparent gift of vanishing into thin air or changing himself into a different creature. Barney has been explaining to Crusty how the wizard had changed himself into a pony.

Surprisingly, Barney's sight is almost as keen as the eagle's. Both the eagle and the boy are seeing an ever larger area as they soar higher and the light improves. Down below, there is plenty of activity. People, both soldiers and civilians, are walking and running about. Most are heading south towards the castle. But something catches Crusty's attention far in the distance along the river before it joins the lake. What Crusty sees approaching the lake is a huge body of people close together. The beat of his wings deepens. Crusty decides to investigate this crowd. It is perhaps Fyrdwald's defending army retreating. Even worse, and more likely, it is the army of the wizard that has broken through the Gyminge defenses in both the north and center of the country. In that case, the enemy is now advancing on Gyminge Castle, though it is likely to be several hours before they reach it. They begin to look more and more like goblins as the bird gets nearer.

Meanwhile, Barney sees something different. Just a little ahead of them on the road is a dog running at a steady pace *against* the flow of the traffic. He wonders to himself, *Why should that be? The dog doesn't seem to be lost as though looking for its master. It's running with purpose against the flow of people. It's on some kind of errand.* Barney recalls his glimpse through the castle battlements of an animal, a huge dog, as they talked with Jock and Jordy at the window of their room. This dog is also huge. Barney draws Crusty's attention to it.

Dipping his head, Crusty takes a long look. He too recalls seeing such a dog back at the castle. He calls back to his passengers, "Hold on. I think we're on to something. I'm going down." Cymbeline and Cleemo hold on tight. The girl forgets for a few moments the ache in her heart over missing Ambro.

Barney prepares and holds ready his catapult as they descend in a steep glide. The boy has plenty of ammunition. In the castle courtyard, while Taymar was busy with the king and Barney and Tuwhit were patrolling above, Cleemo and Cymbeline had been collecting round pebbles for Barney. They are well aware what size stones he needs and have collected a bag full of ammunition for him. His catapult is proving an important weapon.

As they draw nearer the crowded road, they notice a black bird flying beside the dog. The bird is a raven, and Barney recognizes it as his target from earlier on. The strange appearance of the bird's head is due to the fact that its beak has been broken, probably by a stone from Barney's catapult.

Crusty swoops low over the dog's back, latching his claws into the dog's hindquarters. Crusty is immensely strong, but he has never before attempted to lift a Great Dane by its hindquarters. However, since the dog is large only by Twith standards, to Crusty, he is of no weight at all. He plucks the dog into the air and, gaining height, swings over the deepest part of the lake.

At this point, the raven is not having a particularly good day. The wizard has been telling him off for earlier deserting his position when wounded. And although the eagle is not actually pursuing him just now, he still wishes he were a duck accustomed to swimming long distances underwater. Rasputin is not a duck, so he hopes that he can do a midair reverse turn faster than an eagle loaded with a Great Dane. He succeeds, turning around on a sixpence, the fastest full turn he will ever make. Rasputin flies off south with the supersonic speed of yet another migrating swallow.

The dog, twisting and struggling desperately, slips from Crusty's claws and falls. When he falls, he is high over the lake, so his landing is not only wet but hard as well. The dog is not positioned into a dive, and he lands on all fours. It hurts. The splash is immense.

The wizard is thinking faster than usual. Even at usual times, his thinking is pretty fast. *Things are going awry. This is not the way I planned it. Was a dog the best creature to be after all?* This is a question that crosses his mind as he sinks into ever deeper water, water that is rumored to be home to a dragon and carp of huge size and appetite. Several more questions crowd into his mind. *Do eagles eat Great Danes for breakfast? Do carp eat other fish? Presumably, dragons feed on anything.*

The dog never emerges from the lake into which it has plunged. The wizard discovers that there are toads in the water, so it must be safe for toads. No one will know there is an extra one. Now he wonders, *Is it going to be possible to make the change underwater?* He finds he can, and soon the Great Dane is lost forever. In its place is a new toad, one with a sore rump and a furiously twitching eye, swimming rapidly towards the far shore without coming up for air. It's beginning to look as though changing himself into most anything carries dangerous risks to health and safety.

Overhead, Crusty realizes that with the wizard and the raven still around, he must be vigilant in his patrol duties or the wizard will encircle Gyminge Castle with a bubble. He must not let himself be distracted by an attack from the distant Wozzle forces.

He resumes his patrol and touches down at the castle gate long enough for Cleemo and Cymbeline to disembark. They will report what has happened and what they have seen. He is grounded only for a moment and is off again, back into the air with Barney still on his back.

CRUSTY FORGETS

The blue morning sky overhead is cloudless, with mere traces of distant cirrus clouds far to the south. It promises to be warm. The castle armories are open. The stored weapons are being distributed. Outside the castle gate, there are hosts of defenders, most of them fully armed with bows and arrows, spears and javelins, staves and axes. Some are carrying supplies of throwing stones up onto the battlements. On the walls, others are stacking them in neat piles. The portcullis chain is again being greased. The king is busy checking positions of his men, instructing officers about their duties, and giving orders. He has an air of quiet confidence, but Jock and Jordy are well aware of his deep unease at the outcome of the fighting that lies ahead.

The two northerners avoid interfering in the king's activities as he prepares his defense. They have warned him that the wizard is probably in the castle or the area around about. The king responds that the wizard has probably changed from a bird into another creature. For sure, he won't be himself. The king hasn't noticed any strange animals himself. Since the wizard's right eye is reported to twitch, he should be easy to spot. The king instructs the castle steward to search. He will immediately notice any strangers and know which animals should be around and which not.

King Rufus has sent for Dayko. Gazing over towards the hill, he sees that the old man is on his way. Someone, probably the king's messenger, is helping him. When he arrives, they will retire briefly to the king's private chambers for discussions. He turns to his two companions. "Jock, I'd like for you to be present also while I meet with Dayko. And Jordy, will you please make your way to Fowler's Bridge and consider what might be done to improve the defenses there? Jock and I will be along as soon as our meeting with Dayko is over."

Jock has seen Crusty drop off two of his passengers, and he makes his way over to greet them. He knows that they refused to leave on the owl with Taymar. He has also seen them carefully selecting and gathering small stones, but they have not been formally introduced. The man, with his kindly face fringed by white hair, introduces himself and his companion.

"I am Cleemo, a woodcarver from up north beyond the Dark Forest. This is my niece, Cymbeline. The other one of us is Barney, up there riding on your friend, Crusty. We need to share our news. Shall we tell you and then you can pass it on where it needs to go?"

Jock agrees, and while he and Cleemo sit on a low wall out of the way of all the activity, Cymbeline busies herself collecting more pebbles for Barney. Each one that she collects is likely to soon be needed.

During their conversation, Cleemo finds that he would rather do the talking. For now, the little Scotsman is too difficult to understand. First, Cleemo explains how the wizard had changed himself into a dog and that Crusty had dropped him into the lake. The dog never surfaced, so perhaps he changed himself into a fish or something. The main news, however, is about a large body of men, perhaps thousands of them, approaching the lake from the north, along the west side of the river.

Jock looks around quickly. Dayko is still a hundred paces distant, about to cross the footbridge over the brook. He whistles shrilly and loudly. Crusty, hearing the call, cuts short his circling patrol, flies across the castle, and lands by the gate. Only moments have elapsed. "Crusty, take Barney 'n' 'is sister 'n' 'is uncle. Take Jordy too; 'e's off towards th' bridge. Quickly, get more news 'bout wha's happenin'. Who are th' men, wha' are their weapons, which way are they goin'? Do nae get involved in any fightin' a' this stage. Just get back with th' news as quickly as ye cun."

Dayko greets the king, and they walk together towards his chambers. The king nods for Jock to accompany them when he has finished with the eagle.

Jock wants to congratulate Crusty. "Well done 'bout th' dog. Keep yur eyes open. I might be with th' king when ye get back, so ask Jordy ta cum 'n' find me or th' king. Off ye go, then."

Crusty has no problem picking Jordy out amongst the crowd of citizens approaching the castle in their hundreds and the troops and stalwarts heading for the bridges. Crusty knows him a mile away with his flat tweed cap and the jaunty stride that is all his own. As soon as the bird lands, Jordy is up on his back, no questions asked. He'll find out soon enough. Again, Cleemo does the introductions. Jordy tells them that he has come down from the far north to help. Cleemo and the others seem to be having difficulty understanding, so Jordy repeats himself more slowly. He thinks that the beams on their faces mean they begin to grasp what he is saying.

Cleemo tells Jordy of their errand. They are to investigate what's happening where the river enters the lake. Crusty climbs ever higher as they talk. He watches out for a raven or a cuckoo or any strange creature that might need further attention. Visibility is good. The sky is clear. He glides in a shallow downwards curve. His passengers crane forward to see better. They locate the arched stone bridge over the river just where it enters the lake. This bridge is larger and longer than the one on the south side.

All along the left side of the river are thousands of goblin soldiers. The column seems to stretch almost back to the Dark Forest. The spears they hold flash in the gaining light. At the bridge itself, there is a bottleneck. They can't cross the bridge because of the Gyminge forces defending it. Yet, they are not bypassing it to proceed anticlockwise around the lake. Instead, they are using all their combined strength to clear the bridge of defenders. It will allow them to divide their forces and advance in both directions around the lake.

The king's men at the bridge are in dire straits. They are outnumbered at least one hundred to one. Jock might have told Crusty not to engage in fighting, but the bird conveniently forgets. This is the very situation where Crusty and Jordy thrive.

The eagle screams a mighty, "Kaa!" His claws are stretched out to grab unsuspecting goblins as they flow towards the bridge. Jordy yells a war cry he makes up on the spot and waves his axe around his head with little hope of making contact with something. Cleemo and Barney yell too. In the excitement, Cymbeline screams at the top of her voice.

Barney fires as though he is a clockwork machine with the spring wound to its limit and with no sign of running down.

Doink! Conk! "Take that!"

Bam! Thwack! "And that!"

Thump! Bang! "And that too!"

Cymbeline keeps her palm full of pebbles. Barney grabs them and fires. He aims too, not just firing at random into a large crowd but picking out the leaders.

Crusty swoops low across the heads of the goblin soldiers. Just like a plow cutting deep through soft and fallow ground, each claw cuts its own furrow. The goblins have never met such murderous intent in one creature. A swan defending its young is merely snoring compared with this screeching ball of fury. Most of the attacking army throw themselves to the earth, trying to bond themselves with it or even better, beneath it. Those near the lake think drowning might be a better alternative and plunge in.

The defenders of the bridge do not know what is happening, but they also kneel lest they be mistaken for the enemy. Crusty, however, is making no mistakes. He sweeps up and down the columns of invaders. By now, they're all flat on the ground, back as far as the eye can see. At least he's given the defenders a breather. He makes a swinging turn for one last run up the columns of prone men to be sure they stay that way. And to maintain their terror, there is always that screaming, "Kaa!" For good measure, he sweeps above the bobbing heads of the goblins in the lake that are anxious to avoid becoming either victims of Crusty or a meal for underwater creatures of unknown size and shape.

Crusty knows that he cannot be in two places at once. While he has been attacking the goblin invaders, the castle has been undefended against the wizard's bubble. Heading straight back to the castle, Crusty collides with the unfinished end of the curtain that Tuwhit had encountered earlier. Spinning dangerously off balance and coming too close to the water for comfort, he recovers himself, and screams "Kaa!" one final time. Gliding towards the courtyard for a landing, he drops off Jordy so he can report to the king. He must get back to his patrol duties. He feels much better now that he has played a part in disrupting the Wozzle attack.

THE RING AND
THE GOBLET

King Rufus and Dayko have made their way to the formal sitting room of the king's chambers. This is an upper room that opens out onto the castle walls to permit the king and queen to stroll and exercise. The doors are closed now so that none might overhear. The windows face the northern shore of the lake.

Dayko has a usual chair when he meets with the king. The king pulls up this chair to face him before he seats himself in his high place. The old man has been coming to the castle for such a long while that he can hardly remember when he has not been coming. He was counselor to the king's grandfather, appointed high seer by his father, and welcomed to continue by King Rufus.

In appearance, Dayko has thick, white hair and a long, white beard. These create a frame for a round, weather-beaten face made remarkable by two twinkling blue eyes undimmed by the years. Tall in stature, he still carries himself uprightly, though sometimes he limps a little and uses a stick for balance. Sandaled feet peep from beneath the one-piece, full-length, belted, white gown covering his thin, angular body. His hands are unusual, not the long, thin hands of an artist or a musician, but the broad thick hands of a man who loves and enjoys physical labor. By instinct, he is a farmer. With Gerald, his assistant, he cultivates the field at the back of his home and the gardens to the front. Often, he will bring to the queen or to the castle kitchen gifts from his garden.

Dayko has had the gift of seeing into the future since he was a boy. Occasionally, looking into a clear glass of water, he will see movements of people or things taking place that later on will indeed come to pass. At other times, staring into a pool or even deep into the sky, the same thing happens. These sightings are not to him abnormal or strange but merely part of a gift that he and a few others enjoy. Sometimes, it is enough to be at peace, close his eyes, and let pictures float across the screen of his mind. Working in the field, he will suddenly know the unknown as thoughts from elsewhere press in upon him. They are unconnected to anything he is thinking at the moment. He has created for himself an arena of awareness and expects to become aware of future vistas that few others are able to visit. He knows that his seeing and being aware are somehow related, closely related, to truth and truthfulness and integrity. These have been the keystones of his own path to becoming a seer. He fears the effects of deceit upon his land.

Dayko is a very old man, but Twith only show the age they wish to. Since the death of the present king's father, Dayko has allowed the years to carry him along and age him. It is no fault of King Rufus, but he has lost heart somehow. Little by little, the people have changed. These days, they are different. He finds himself hankering after the old days, when people were courteous and a Twith's word was his bond, when men and women guarded their words against untruthfulness and taught their children likewise. He's aware that some of the younger seers would like to see him gone. One or two of them would like his place and have hinted as much.

Dayko sees Jock enter, the strange-speaking man with the attire of a woman. The king introduces them. "Dayko, this is Jock. He's from Scotland. He has come south, with his friend and a large bird, an eagle, to help us in our struggle. Jock, this is Dayko, our high seer. He is my most trusted friend and advisor." The king adds a chair for Jock, forming a triangle.

The king wastes no time. "Gentlemen, there is little time left. I fear there might be only three or four hours at most, so we must use this time well. First, I'll ask Dayko to share what he sees for the future. Then later, I'll seek counsel from both of you." He opens his hands towards Dayko in an invitation to proceed.

Dayko is sparing with his words. This is not a time for long speeches. "We are about to see the end of the past. We now have to take the steps we need for the future. The future for the Twith is far distant, so far distant that we cannot imagine it. Because the owl and the eagle are part of that future, I bring you this, Jock. Mix this powder with water. Give it to both birds as soon as you can. It will give them the same hold on life that we Twith enjoy. Do not lose it or waste it. The larger one is for the eagle. Without it being used properly, we may never see the Twith future." Dayko brings from the pocket of his gown two small, brown, earthenware pots, each sealed with a wooden plug. He passes them over without explaining how Jock is ever going to meet the owl again.

"We have brought this calamity upon ourselves. Perhaps we might yet survive. We have Earl Gareth's son, Taymar, in the

Beyond. Before it is too late, we must get others there also, for it is they only who might one day return.

"You, Jock, I have seen before, before I saw you here earlier today. I saw that a man dressed as you are dressed and wearing the colors you wear will lead the return. I did not know that men wore such clothes until you came, but you have given me hope.

"The eagle must take you, and whoever else you can manage, as soon as possible. Do not delay for people to get ready. Only if they can leave at once shall you take them. Establish yourselves in the Beyond, where the stream leaves Gyminge and enters the bog. This is a place every Twith knows and one that we will be able to find in days to come. It's the one place that anyone who escapes can locate immediately.

"You must leave in good time, this day. Do not stay for the battle. Wozzle is far too strong for us to withstand them for long. Whatever help you can give now is of far less value than the hope of the future that rests with you.

"Wait to lead the return until the time is right. You will know very well when that time comes. It is far years from now. I am too old to go with you to help you. I will stay here with my friend, and we shall see the end of this through together. I will send my disciple, Gerald, with you. He's a good man, though still young, and you may trust him. I will send with him my seer's belt and the Lore and, with your permission, my king, the ring you still wear on your finger. I am aware that you have given to Taymar your royal ring which allows him to act on your behalf. But the ring of ascension which I myself placed on your finger is even more valuable as it identifies you as the king himself."

King Rufus holds out his hand for the two men to see. There are several rings he wears, but the dominant one by far is on the middle finger of his right hand. It is a gold ring made to fit a large finger, and it is heavy. It is not solid gold, but rather a gold filigree band wider in height at the front than the back and tilting out at the top because of its larger diameter there than at the other side. The open spaces of the filigree are filled with rubies artfully cut to shape. Combining the creative talents of the jeweler and the goldsmith, the ring is a harmonized blend of red and gold. There are almost three dozen rubies thus set. Surmounted by the smaller rubies like a crown to a head, the largest ruby is in the front center of the ring. This jewel is pear-shaped, larger at the bottom than at the top, and deeper red by far than any of the other rubies—as though there are hidden depths to it that the eye can only barely perceive. The entire ring glows with the look of live embers. It is strikingly beautiful, fit for a king.

Dayko continues, "When the Twith one day return, some other high seer will place the ring of ascension on the finger of perhaps a later king than my present Sire. The ring could be hidden here, but it will probably be safer in the Beyond, and it might well be needed to ensure the return. What does my Sire think?"

The king smiles sadly. He kisses the ring a last time and holds his hand out to Dayko. Slowly, Dayko eases the ring off the king's finger and then slips it into his pocket. These men are close friends, and there is absolute trust between them.

"I shall send also the goblet of consecration if I may take it from your cabinet, Sire. You have kept your promises. A new high seer must receive the same promises from some future king who will also need to be anointed with the oil of consecration." The king nods his assent.

Dayko walks over to the cabinet fixed to the wall opposite the fireplace. It is full of treasures not yet stored away for safety. It's now too late to do anything about that. The high seer removes a small, pewter goblet that has a long history but little worth of itself. It is not jeweled, but it has been used for the consecration of all the monarchs of Gyminge from the very first one. It is one of the historic treasures of the kingdom. Along with the goblet, Dayko takes also a small vial of oil, the oil of anointing.

Dayko's Farewell

In the cabinet also is a small, wooden chest that attracts Dayko's attention. It has a lock in the front from which a key protrudes. Five reinforcing straps of leather strengthen the curved, hinged lid. Within the lid is a secret compartment, and the box itself has a shallow upper tray divided into three sections. At the sides are leather handles. All corners and edges are reinforced with metal bands, and the exterior is decorated with strange artistic designs. The chest has belonged to the queen since her childhood and holds some of her most precious treasures.

Dayko asks, "Might I have your permission, Sire, to send the chest to the Beyond with Gerald? It is sizeable enough to carry all that needs to be sent." The king, knowing that the queen would give her approval, reaches into the cabinet, lifts gently the treasured chest, and places it into Dayko's outstretched hands. Dayko has more counsel yet to give, but he pauses. "Perhaps your highness also has instructions or advice for Jock before I continue."

King Rufus smiles and rises. At his signal, so do the other two men. The king draws his great broadsword. Addressing Jock, he says, "You may kneel." Jock kneels. The king touches Jock first on the right shoulder and then on the left with the flat blade of the sword. "I appoint you as leader of the Twith in the Beyond, to serve for an indefinite period of time. You are charged with my authority to act in my place at all times until you return to this land. Only my own ring used in my stead shall overrule any action of yours. Arise, Lord Jock."

Dayko is suddenly urgent in manner. Jock has been charged by the king with the care of the Twith future. He resumes his conversation with the king and Jock, now Lord Jock, and speaks with great earnestness. "Sire, today we shall suffer defeat, no matter how brave we all are. I have seen it. The forces against us are too strong by far. The world we know will end this day. A long darkness will descend upon our land. What are your thoughts for Princess Alicia and the queen? Will they be safe?"

A sudden chill washes through the king. "Do you know, Dayko? If you have seen, tell me. Tell me at once."

Sadly, the seer, shaking his head ever so slightly and giving no response, allows the king to continue.

"If I could, I would bring them both here so that they could leave for the Beyond on the eagle with Jock. They would stand a chance there. Yet I cannot go, and I also know they would not go though I command them to do so. They would stay with me no matter what happens. It is better they remain where they are. There is one small, very small, chance for them and for me. From this room, through and behind the fireplace, there is a secret door. Come with me. I'll show you. There. You reach up and behind this stone and pull, like this."

The king's actions suit his words. All is as he says. This is the secret of the castle that only the monarchs themselves have known and passed on privately to their own sons. A whole side of the inner part of the fireplace swings open and aside without making any noticeable noise. The pivot of stone bears and balances on oiled oak at top and bottom. Revealed before them is a small room where are gathered candles and a lamp, tinder and flint, clothes both for man and woman, shoes and boots, weapons, preserved foods, and drinking water. One or two bundles, wrapped and tied, are on a small table. There is a tiny spy hole back into the room when the door is closed. From where they stand by the fireplace, they see faintly a low, arched opening at the far side leading to a tunnel that descends into darkness. This room and tunnel are part of the original castle.

The king closes the door and pushes gently until it clicks into a locked position. As he leads them back to their seats, he pauses at the window to look across the lake. All is quiet there at present. There's no movement of armed men along the far shore.

"While my men fight, I shall fight as I am able. If, when all is done, it is possible to get back here and into that room, then, though they sack the castle and set it afire, I can survive. When things are quiet, I can traverse the tunnel at night to Madman's Cave in the quarry in Blindhouse Wood. People do not go there because a man who was mad once lived there. They are afraid, and we have one or two things hanging in the cave that make noises to keep them fearful. I can make my way then to where the queen and Alicia will still be. My fear is that the queen is already on her way back and thus might fall into the hands of enemies. But she is resolute and wise and will do her best to survive. She and our daughter are the only other persons except yourselves who know of this tunnel."

As the king pauses, Dayko continues. "When your highness allows me to leave, it will be farewell. I will return up the hill to my home and not expect to see you again. I have already dispersed the other seers to their homes, and they must take their chances. Only Gerald remains with me. Once back home, I will prepare the package for Gerald to take to the Beyond. We shall then wait for you to arrive, Jock. You must not delay for long. The wizard might even now be encompassing Gyminge with a curtain similar to that around Wozzle. I thank you Sire, my dear friend, for all your past kindness. I only wish that I could have served you more ably and wisely than I have."

He half rises, ready to go. Before the king can urge him to remain for safety within the castle, a servant knocks at the door. Jordy is with him. Quickly, resting his axe against the back of the chair, Jordy tells his story of the last patrol. Thousands upon thousands of goblins from Wozzle—axmen, bowmen, spearmen, stone throwers, even some cavalry lancers—are at the river bridge. Crusty has scattered them, but it is only for a short while.

Jordy is right. From the window, a long, unbroken line of foot soldiers can be seen running clockwise along the north shore, proceeding around the lake. They are led by cavalry at full gallop.

Crusty had planned to continue patrolling the castle, but he can see the Wozzle armies moving around the lake in both directions. He's not sure now whether he should continue his patrol to prevent a bubble being thrown over the castle or not. He suspects the northern river bridge has now fallen and thinks it might be better to go attack the Wozzle forces and try to stop them from advancing further.

THE CLOSING CIRCLE

Fowler's Bridge has not yet been crossed. The king plans to use the area beyond the bridge on the lake road as a defensive line to protect the castle on the landward side. The bridge and the whole river bank will be stoutly defended.

Most of the Gyminge forces that will later defend the castle itself are arranged by companies along this inner defense line. During previous weeks, they have been engaged in cleaning and deepening the streambed immediately in front of them. During the hot days of early summer, it had been a rather pleasant duty to splash around and occasionally splash each other as they moved baskets of mud and stones to increase the depth of water. As they work, the larger stones are set aside for later use in throwing down at the enemy from the castle parapets. The water is now the depth of a man's full height. If the enemy does approach them, they must first either cross the bridges or swim. Now the Gymingers are about to test how well their work will serve them.

The small, wooden footbridge that Dayko uses to return to his house will be destroyed by fire before the enemy gets close. Dayko, in returning home from the castle, walks as quickly as he is able. He has declined the help the king has offered. The soldiers on the footbridge ask if he will be coming back. He shakes his head with a long, deep sigh. They ask further whether they have permission to burn the bridge. Dayko knows that the Wozzle soldiers will attack him before the main assault develops on the castle. Once the bridge is gone, there will be no easy way for him to return to the castle and safety. He simply tells the soldiers to waste no time, and they move into action. All has been prepared. The smoke and flames soon rise skyward. The fire takes hold and springs from one end of the bridge to the other. The bridge has been in place for centuries. Within an hour, it is nothing but a memory of blaze and sparks. There is a crashing and splashing of timbers into the water.

Gerald, guarding the contents of the high seer's house and particularly the Lore, comes forward as far as the brow of the hill to meet his master. They turn and pause to look around as though it is for the last time together. The king's standard flies proudly still at the highest point of the castle. From the rise, they can see advancing from the west huge numbers of enemy soldiers stretching back around the lake far into the distance. The king's planned ambush, hidden in the copse, is going to make no impression on this vast, approaching army. Within a short time, the goblin army will be at Fowler's Bridge. To the east side, the enemy is farther away from the bridge but approaching fast. The circle is closing.

The eagle has abandoned patrolling. The castle must take its chance with a bubble. It is time for more aggressive measures. Crusty and Barney are fighting on both fronts. They have Cleemo and Cymbeline identifying visible targets and supplying stones for the catapult. As the Wozzle forces strive to join together at the castle gate, Crusty swings in a decreasing arc between the two sides, attacking first one side and then the other.

The cavalry troops, the prize units of the Wozzle army, are leading both advancing prongs of the encircling movement. The horses are terrified as Crusty approaches them low and head on. They rear on their hind legs and neigh in terror. They prance and dance and wheel in terrified circles. A stable fire is a picnic compared with an attack from a screaming bird, its wingspan the width of a company of cavalry, mere inches above their heads. Their riders, accomplished horsemen though they are, cannot hold their steeds in check or force the animals to advance. Barney is again the catapult machine, aiming to unseat the hapless horsemen. Making two or three screaming passes over the cavalry, Crusty claws reluctant riders from their saddles, discharging them into the lake. The cavalry units are put into full flight back towards and on past the lagging infantrymen. As they race away, Crusty wheels round to attack the other side of the pincer movement. He and his passengers scream with the excitement of battle.

Jock, Jordy, and the king pause at the castle gate. The king hesitates a moment before he mounts. He gives instructions to the guard commander at the gate. "Stand ready to drop the portcullis into position. You must wait, however, until all our men are safe inside." He emphasizes again, "No defenders shall be left to the mercies of the enemy outside a dropped portcullis. Once it is dropped, it will not be hard to deal with one or two Wozzle intruders if they do manage to slip inside."

A groom holds the royal horse. It has been fitted for battle with its own armor. A unicorn spear protrudes from its helmet. The king also is wearing his battle armor. The cuirass consists of a breastplate of bronze across his chest linked by broad, leather straps over his shoulders to a similar back plate. He is further protected by shoulder plates, overlapping metal plates on his forearms and thighs, a fauld across his abdomen, greaves for his shins, sabatons for his feet, and gauntlets for his hands. His bronze helmet has a moveable visor and is surmounted by a small crown. Although the crown clearly identifies him as the king, the monarchs of Gyminge have never feared being targets in battle. At the king's right side is his sheathed dagger for close-quarter fighting. At his left side is his sheathed great sword. Fixed to his left forearm is the shield bearing the rampant horse, crouching lion, and castellated crown of the king's standard.

Jock has his sword but has declined armor. Jordy has his axe and, like his friend, is without armor. The king gives Jock his clear orders. "You are not to join in the battle at the bridge. You must leave Gyminge before it is too late to get away. You and Jordy join the three already on Crusty, go collect the young seer Gerald, and be on your way. The nearest border is to the south. Follow the river—that's all you need to do. Waste no time. I hope I shall be around to welcome your return." His tone, however, indicates that he regards this as unlikely.

The king embraces the two men from the north that, in such a short time, he has grown to trust, admire, and love. He looks long at Dayko's house. The old man has emerged to wave him farewell and pauses to stand looking at the men prepared to defend Fowler's Bridge. The king needs to be with them. He springs to the saddle, waves back at Dayko, and is off at a gallop to join his men and face the enemy at Fowler's Bridge.

THE BATTLE AT

FOWLER'S BRIDGE

Wozzle troops steadily approach the castle gates from both sides of the lake in spite of Crusty's efforts to keep the two advancing forces pinned to the ground. The cavalry has dispersed to the rear and will play only a minor part in events to come. The infantrymen are fearful of Crusty, but the bird cannot give his full attention to either of the two prongs of goblin soldiers. As soon as he swings to attack the eastern troops, the western troops rush for the bridge, throwing themselves face down to the ground at the last minute when the bird returns. And so the enemy is slowly making progress in its attempt to capture the castle.

At the same time, the goblin archers are firing arrows, standing their ground in the bushes beside the lake road. With the great firing distance of their longbows, it is hard to miss the massive bird flying low overhead, and a few javelins are within range as well. Crusty spreads wide his feathers to act as a screen for protecting himself, but the bird begins to hurt from a hundred hits on his underside. There is nothing his passengers can do to protect him.

The king, mounted on horseback amid his defenders at Fowler's Bridge, realizes that the planned ambush near

Dayko's house will not, cannot succeed because of the huge number of Wozzle troops arrayed against them. There are too few of his own men in hiding, and if they do not rejoin him without delay, they will be cut off. There is no hope of reinforcements or relief from elsewhere.

The wizard watches the action with satisfaction. He has not changed from being a toad and is resting on a lily pad far enough from both the shore and the castle to be safe from violent action in either place. A good commander, he tells himself, needs to give clear, concise, well planned orders to his officers and then refrain from interfering as those orders are carried out. Certainly, he has considered what he might do to speed up the result of the battle, but with that obnoxious bird flying around, no other bird is safe in the skies and few other creatures on the ground. He doesn't know where Rasputin is, but he silently commends the bird for his absence. There will be plenty to keep him busy later. As for himself, no sense in being ripped to shreds by an eagle gone crazy. When the time comes, the ruler of Wozzle will leap into action, but for now, why not enjoy the sunshine and muse on the alterations to the castle that will need to be made once he moves in.

In successive steps, the two prongs of the Wozzle army approach the river defense lines at Fowler's Bridge. The Wozzle jaws, after months of planning, are closing at last. They are within arrow range of the bridge, the last defense before they reach the castle walls. The assault troops have been practicing at Lyminge Castle, and these walls are certainly no higher.

Upon and behind the bridge, the massed defenders are protected behind their shields. A first volley of arrows flies high into the attacker's vanguard. Several goblins fall, and Wozzle shields suddenly go up. They hesitate a few moments to regroup and spread out sideways. They move to occupy the side of the river bank that is open before them on their side of the bridge.

King Rufus signals to the ambush troops to join the main body of defenders at the bridge before they get cut off by Wozzle troops coming between them and the castle. Responding immediately, they come running down the hill from Dayko's house towards Fowler's Bridge to join the king.

The Wozzle troops do not understand why the defenders are charging down the hill towards the bridge before they themselves have reached it. However, confident in their huge numbers, the goblin soldiers surge forward in a race to meet their enemy at the bridge. Both forces arrive at the same time. By now, the king has pulled back his men to allow room for his own ambush troops to cross the bridge and join them, but the leading Wozzle attackers are just ahead of them. Hand-to-hand fighting breaks out on the bridge itself, which is narrow, barely wider than a wagon. The Wozzle soldiers are brave, motivated, and determined to achieve personal glory and earn promised rewards. Their swordsmen and axmen engage in battle with strength and determination fueled by adrenalin.

Overhead at the bridge, streams of arrows are flying in both directions. King Rufus spurs forward, cutting and thrusting, sweeping widely with his great broadsword. Soldiers from both sides are falling around him. Others are pitched over the sides of the bridge into the river beneath.

The enemy spearmen launch a fusillade of javelins towards the king over the heads of their own vanguard.

King Rufus deflects the spears with his shield. He is not hit. He seems to have eyes in the back of his head and bears a charmed life. He shouts his battle cry, "OUT, OUT. TRUTH WILL OUT!" His men take up the cry. It energizes them with renewed strength. "OUT, OUT. TRUTH WILL OUT!"

The Wozzle forces falter and hesitate.

Gyminge defenders surge forward to link up with their ambush soldiers, cutting their way through to join them.

The Wozzle soldiers, those who have not fallen, are fighting enemies in front and behind and are separated from their fellows. Their desperation leads to prodigious acts of valor. It is hand-to-hand combat with axe and sword. The ringing of metal against metal fills the air. Sometimes, men are fighting bare-handed, shouting and screaming. The wounded fall where they are hit and find themselves being trampled on by the melee above and around them.

The king's stallion, nostrils flared, neighs loudly as his rider guides him with his knees into the thick of the fighting. There is no break in the fighting as the struggle sways to and fro. Slowly, Gyminge drives Wozzle back from the bridge. The returned ambush troops become the front line of the bridge defenders as they join up with their fellow defenders.

At last, the Wozzle survivors of the first attack on the bridge break and run back to the main force to regroup for another assault. They have fought with great bravery and will come back time and time again until they achieve their objective.

Up the hill on the ridge stands Dayko, the high seer, both hands raised high as a blessing for those battling below, almost as though while he stands thus, the enemy will not prevail. He is alone.

Gerald has wanted to be with him but has been ordered by the high seer to remain in the house under cover until the eagle comes to take him away. He is too valuable to risk. Nearly everything that must go with him has been readied.

GERALD LEAVES HOME

On an order by their officer, the Wozzle bowmen form two ranks, the first kneeling and the second standing behind the kneelers. They are aiming at a distant, but clear target: the old man in white on the hill. A hundred arrows cleave the air. They only need one volley. No need to reload. Three arrows hit their target. Dayko crumples to the ground. The wounds in his leg and arm are not mortal, but the wound in his chest is. From that arrow wound, he will not recover.

Gerald runs from the house, but the enemy will waste no further arrows on him. There are better targets than an apprentice seer. He pulls with great gentleness and care, one by one, the arrows out of his beloved master. They do not come easily and tear the flesh. The one in the chest has penetrated between the ribs and must be rotated to be removed. The old man is conscious. His face is twisted with pain. He is bleeding from all three wounds.

Gerald gathers Dayko in his arms. He is heavy, but at the second attempt to lift him, Gerald finds the strength he needs. Tears run down his face as he stumbles with his master into the house. After laying the wounded seer gently on his bed, Gerald begins tearing at a sheet to make bandages and a tourniquet to stop the flow of blood.

Dayko halts him. His breathing is difficult, and he has few words left. He knows that there is not much longer. He just needs to see Gerald on his way, and then he can go where seers go when they die.

He gasps. "Go, Gerald. You are the future. Go while you can. You have the Lore in the box, my son. Save that at all costs. Guard it with your life. Hold ever to the truth. That alone can bring you back. You will come back again. I promise you. I see you returning. The eagle will carry you away, but it is not he that will bring you back. There are long, long years in exile ahead of you, and slow they will be to pass. Children from the Beyond will bring you back, and I hear them singing as they come. It is their own song they sing. They are your friends. Find them, and treasure them. Do not try to return until you have found them. You will need them in order to return. All the clues for your return are in the Rime I have written. You must study it carefully and hold fast to it in your mind. What it says will not become clear to you until the time of the return is near. But then you can use it as your guide.

"I will call the birds one last time before I am gone. Some may yet remain. They too must go. They must flee for their lives. They must not remain or they also will be destroyed. If you can gather companions as you go, that is well, but you must waste no time in the gathering. You have minutes, not hours."

The old man is close to his end. He is having trouble breathing. His mouth is dry. It is hard for him to whistle. Gerald pours between his master's lips a measure of water. It will be the high seer's last drink, and it is sweet to the taste. A few bars of a tune of strange properties pour forth in a cracked, almost inaudible, whistle from Dayko's lips. As the first response of birds fluttering nearby shows his call has been heard, he sends Gerald to see who has come and unbuckles with difficulty the broad, decorated belt around his waist that holds his bloodied, white cloak in place.

Running from the bridge up the hill towards the seer's house are a dozen or more goblin soldiers. Slightly ahead of them, easily recognizable in his seer's robe, is the traitor Zaydek, who betrayed King Rufus, putting Gyminge into the hands of Wozzle. Another traitor, Haymun, is only a little further behind him. Zaydek's frantic cries reach the house. "The Lore, the Lore! We must get the Lore! Faster! Faster! Don't let them escape." Spurred by his own anxiety to get his hands on the Lore, he is outstripping the others.

Gerald returns to Dayko, panting. "There are a few other birds, but it's Crusty, the eagle, who's come. There are already five on his back. The man from the north you described, Jock the Scot, is there. He says they cannot wait. They must be gone. But I cannot leave you, father of my spirit. Here. Let me carry you."

Dayko shakes his head and gasps his last words. "No, just hold me in your arms and bid me farewell. Take the wooden chest and also my belt. You will know who to give that to when the time comes. Be on your way, my son. Let Jock be your leader, and give him your loyalty. It is the king's appointment. You must leave me and go. I am bound elsewhere. Farewell, my son. Farewell." The old man's head drops back. Gerald takes him into his arms and straightens his head. It is too late. The high seer has gone.

Outside, the shouting increases both from the eagle's passengers and from the soldiers running up the hill. The second runner shouts to his leaner and faster companion, "Get the Lore, the Lore! The wizard wants the Lore. Let them all go. Just get the Lore!"

Jock has come running to collect Gerald. They must hurry. He halts in the doorway, and groans as he sees the still body of the high seer in the arms of his weeping disciple. Sprinting now to cross the room, Jock grabs Gerald by the arm. Gerald lays the old man gently down. Passing Queen Sheba's treasure chest to Jock, he reaches for and catches hold of the seer's belt as Jock tugs at him. It comes free, and they flee together. Outside, the others pull them onto the eagle. Crusty has turned to face the oncoming soldiers and is ready to join battle with them.

From the back of the bird, Barney takes careful aim with his catapult. His aim is true. His stone strikes the foremost runner in the middle of his forehead. A few stumbling paces forward, and Zaydek is flat on his face, spread-eagled, unmoving. Haymun and the others, ignoring him, run on. But they are too late.

Crusty, heavy laden, lumbers into the air as spears and arrows fly past, missing him. The bird gains height and, as he does so, veers towards Fowler's Bridge. The fighting is fast and furious. In the middle of the bridge is the king, the only man among them who is mounted. Crusty yells to the passengers on his back, "Hold on tight."

He is under orders to leave at once, but he will give a little last assist to the king's troops before he does so. He plans to snatch the nearest and most dangerous Wozzle goblins away from beside the king, and drop them into the lake. He is probably going to get a barrage of javelins and arrows, but he will risk that.

He screams a mighty "Kaa!" of warning. As he swoops in low over the bridge, he sees the king twist awkwardly to one side in his saddle, slump helpless, and begin to slip from his horse.

THE WOUNDED KING

Crusty's reaction is split second. He ignores the Wozzle spear-man he has been too late to reach and swerves slightly to clutch tightly the king as he slides from his horse. It is a clean lift. The king's feet slip free of the stirrups without getting tangled in the harness or the saddle. Jock saw the look of agony on the king's face as Crusty lifted him out of harms way. An exuberant yell goes up from the Wozzle goblins. Victory is within their grasp.

The eagle turns low over the lake, the king dangling from his right claw. Jock leans forward and yells, "Well done, Crusty! Get ta th' castle, ta th' north wall. Find th' room th' cuckoo entered. When we get there, 'over beside th' wall, low down. I'll show ye just where. Jordy 'n' I will jump off 'n' take th' king. Cymbeline, ye better cum too. Crusty, ye go back 'n' 'elp a' th' bridge 'til I whistle for ye ta cum 'n' pick us up. Take care ye do nae get 'urt."

The king is almost unconscious. The pain is intense. A javelin has been thrust behind the shield and into the king's left shoul-der, through the cuirass. Crusty's claw is pressing the weapon into the wound. It pulls at the flesh. The king's shield, battered and dented with marks of the fray, slips from his useless left arm and splashes into the lake.

The bird clears the top of the wall, crosses above it at the place where Jock directs, and hovers to one side. He is just above the walkway along the battlements. Jock leaves his sword with Cleemo, runs along the outspread wing where it overhangs the wall, and jumps. Jordy leaves his axe with Gerald and does likewise. Both land easily and then turn to steady Cymbeline as she also jumps.

The bird rises higher and comes round in a short circle so that the king can be caught and held by the two men on the parapet. Crusty is guided by the directions of Cymbeline in front of him and hovers with little movement as the two men, facing each other with linked arms, steady themselves to take the load of the king clad in armor.

First, the king throws the great, bloodied sword he still holds in his right hand. There's no way he can sheathe it with Crusty's claw where it is. *Drops* is perhaps a better word than *throws*. He pitches it awkwardly and horizontally into the angle formed by the wall and the parapet, hoping it will not be damaged. It rings as it hits the parapet and falls unbroken onto the walkway.

Jock whistles. Crusty spreads his claw and releases the king. Clad in all his armor, he is massively heavy, almost double his usual weight. The two men stagger a few paces backwards as though dancing together and then gently lower the king to rest against the battlement wall.

Crusty beats his wings and lifts off. It is up to those on the wall to see to the king. The men at the bridge need help, and he must get back there. It will be just this one errand more, and then they will have to be on their way to the Beyond.

Jock and Jordy try to make the king more comfortable against the wall. His wounds need immediate attention. They can't even think about trying to get him inside just yet. They have no idea what's happening outside near the bridge. They can hear the noise, but they are on the north side of the castle, and their interests are more immediate: dealing with the wounded king.

The king's face is grey as he grits his teeth and endures the immense pain. He remains conscious through it all, drawing on his reserves of strength and courage. First, the two northerners take a look at the wound itself. The javelin, being a light attacking weapon used more often in throwing over a long distance than for hand-to-hand combat, is a metal-tipped, wooden shaft. This one, driven with deadly force, has pierced through the plate of the cuirass just below the shoulder blade. Fortunately, it comes out as cleanly as it went in. It does not have hooks to prevent its removal.

Neither Jock nor Jordy have acquaintance with the fitting of body and head armor. Once the helmet is off, they follow the directions of the king himself on removing the remainder of the armor. Jock, with all the patience of a nurse, removes the bloodied cuirass by releasing straps and buckles. Slowly, the armor is peeled away and stacked in a pile against the wall. Next, they begin removing the layers of thick undergarments that have protected the king's body from the chafing of metal parts pushing and rubbing against the skin. Blood is everywhere, and the flow does not lessen as they work to divest the king of much of his clothing.

Cymbeline has turned away from the men and slipped off her petticoat from beneath her skirt. She tears this into bandages. One she forms into a plug that she packs into the wound. It is not enough. Another and yet another is packed in. The flow of blood slows and almost stops. The king must not move his arm, she instructs him, forgetting for the moment that she can hardly bear the sight of blood. All of her petticoat goes to truss up the king's shoulder and left arm into a block of crisscrossing bandages. By this time, her own clothes are also covered in blood.

For the first time, the king looks easier in himself. He is extremely concerned about the fighting, however. The shouting seems to be increasing. Something is happening at the castle gate. He suspects the worst, and well he might. A host of men are running into the courtyard from outside the castle, Gyminge men. Wozzle goblins are chasing them. The portcullis drops with a great bang that rattles the walls of the castle itself. There is shouting and hand-to-hand fighting at the gate. Swords flash. Men are shouting and falling back, wounded by arrows fired in through the portcullis. Arrows fly high over the wall into the courtyard. The gates are pushed shut. All the defenders have made it into the courtyard. Only the Wozzle enemy is trapped between the outer portcullis and the tightly closed gates inside.

Jock can smell hot oil being poured down through the murder holes in the roof of the door passage. He knows, too, that the defenders on the roof will be flinging stones and firing arrows down at any trapped attackers who might have survived the hot oil. He must concentrate on the task immediately before him. Time is running out and it's going to be a close-run thing. He tries the door from the battlements to the king's chambers, but it's bolted from inside. He had himself seen the king close it when he and Dayko visited those few hours ago. He doesn't hesitate. Though glass is rare, he smashes first one and then a second of the small panes. Reaching through, he slides the tower bolts to release the door, and quickly pushes it open. Jordy and Cymbeline already have the king to his feet. His right arm is about Jordy's shoulder, and the smaller man is carrying much of the king's weight as they limp inside.

Leaving the door open, Jock wastes no time in running across to the fireplace. He reaches up to where he had seen the king reach previously. The king's reach must be far longer than his. Jock can't reach far enough. Pulling a chair into the fireplace, he jumps on it and again reaches back beyond the stone shelf. He pulls with all his might on the protruding ledge that is up out of sight. Once again, the whole inner side of the fireplace swings open and aside. To Cymbeline's astonishment, as the pivot stone turns almost noiselessly on its oiled oak beam, the fireplace has opened into a small room. Gathered there are lights, clothes, footwear, weapons, foodstuffs, and drinking water.

Jock pushes the chair he had stood upon into the secret room, placing it against the wall beside the table. Jordy and Cymbeline help the king forward and ease him down onto it. The king slumps over. His face has an unusual pallor, and he looks fit to faint. Cymbeline pours some precious drinking water onto the corner of the tablecloth and washes the king's face. To support his bandaged left arm, she fashions the tablecloth into a triangular sling and ties it behind his neck. *We surely cannot leave him as he is,* she thinks.

Escape from

the Castle

Jock is urgent, "Jordy, go gather all th' armor. Get everythin' tha's outside, includin' th' javelin. Bring it all inta this room. Be quick! Cymbeline, we 'ave per'aps ten minutes. Run ta th' kitchen, through tha' door o'er there. Bring all th' food ye cun find. Ye will just 'ave time fur one trip. Run. Bring wha' e'er ye cun."

The girl is on her way. She knows what's needed: food supplies for the injured king until he can move. She'll bring what she can, mentally including for the king's use some kitchen towels that the men would not have thought about.

Jock busies himself striking the flint to the tinder to make a flame. Touching it to the candle wick, the first feeble flicking catches hold and the candle gives forth its light. He is anxious that there be no trail of blood across the carpet from the door to the fireplace. Retracing his steps across the room and back again, he is satisfied that no one will ever suspect the king has disappeared into the fireplace.

Jordy bustles into the room with all the armor he has managed to carry. There is now blood over his clothes also. Still, the sword, the scabbard, and a few other items remain for a second journey, which is soon completed.

Jordy takes one look at the king and confirms what Cymbe-line has been thinking. "Jock, someone must stay and help the king. It had best be me. I'll stay, and we'll try to make our escape later. We might be able to tunnel under even if there is a curtain. You must leave us here and go before it's too late. I'll take care of the king. He can't be left by himself. Do those steps lead to a tunnel to the outside? Show me how this thing closes, and be on your way. We shall make do somehow."

Jock does not reply to Jordy. He knows in his heart that this is probably what needs to happen, but there are other things to do first. He grabs two dresses hanging beside the table and wipes the cuirass clean of all blood with them. He makes them as bloody as he can by wiping anything that has blood on it. They're permanently ruined for regular use. Jock offers no explanations for his actions.

"Jordy, help me put this cuirass 'n' back plate on quick. We must make th' enemy think th' king is leavin' with us. They will nae know how many o' us were on Crusty afore we picked up th' king a' th' bridge."

The king grits his teeth and struggles himself upright on his chair. "Good thinking, Jock. Come here. Let me help you do it." He forces himself to his feet, leaning against the wall. Jordy follows the king's instructions. After slipping the cuirass on Jock, he straps and buckles as instructed.

Pointing towards the sword, King Rufus tells Jock, "Leave the great sword for me. I might yet use it to advantage. Take one of the others." Now the king points to his crowned helmet. "You'll need that too. My own crown is in this bundle here. I shall not be needing the helmet for awhile, but take good care of it until we meet again."

The king is right. Jock will need to wear the helmet also. There are one or two things left to do before he puts it on. "Jordy, tear those women's clothes into pieces 'n' throw them o'er th' wall inta th' lake. Quick! We must make th' wizard think tha' th' queen 'n' th' princess 'ave drowned in th' lake."

Cymbeline runs back across the main room with her skirt as a basket loaded with whatever she has been able to find in the way of food. She's found bread, dried fruit and some fresh fruit, biscuits, dried fish, a cabbage, carrots, and a turnip. She has dipped a large jug of water from the barrel. Although a little of it has spilled from the awkward way she has had to hold both it and her laden skirt, the jug is still almost full as she stumbles into the room. She dumps her prizes on the table, last of all the towels, but has no time to explain anything. From the water jug, she removes the large kitchen knife the king might need. Her eyes widen as she sees Jordy tearing to pieces a royal gown streaked with blood, but she says nothing. The shouting outside is getting nearer.

The king, still leaning against the wall, struggles once again to draw himself upright. He places his hand on Jock's shoulder and turns the little Scot to look him squarely in the eye. Jock sees how deathly pale the monarch looks. King Rufus speaks sternly, with great emphasis. "Listen now, Jock! I am still the king. I order all of you, I *order* you, *all* of you, to leave immediately. The future of the Twith is at stake, and it lies with you, not me. Go! I will manage or I will not manage. Go *now!* I'll push the door shut behind you. Make sure it's fully closed, and then flee for your lives. Here. Don't forget the helmet, Jock. And take that broadsword with you. Farewell, and thank you! Prosper in the truth."

Jock looks at the king. He admires this man, willing to die alone in a lightless, airless room for the sake of his country and a faint, perhaps futile, dream of a far-distant future. There's a struggle going on within the little Scot, but he recognizes that the king is probably right. At a time of difficult choices, he's giving the rest of them a chance for freedom. The king pushes them out of the room. Jock nods to Jordy to be on his way back to the wall outside and to take the shredded clothing with him. Jordy grabs the clothes he has torn and scurries off. Jock gives the helmet to Cymbeline to hold. The back of the fireplace swings shut as the king pushes from the other side and the lock clicks. Jock pushes hard to try to reopen it. It will not budge. It's like pushing at a solid wall. There's no give at all.

There is not much time. "Cum on, Cymbeline!" They run out to join Jordy on the parapet. Each of them wonder, *Will we ever see this place or the king again?*

Out, Out.

Truth Will Out!

From the pile of stones gathered for defense that are stacked by the castle wall, Jordy selects some of the larger ones and wraps the torn clothing around them. He doesn't want any of the material to be caught by the wind and get blown back against the wall before it reaches the water. He throws as hard and as far away from the castle wall as he can into the lake.

Jock struggles to see out of the king's helmet visor now that he has the helmet on his head. The king is a big man, and his helmet is far too large for Jock, who is having trouble seeing anything. He's probably never been more oddly clad than now—a crowned helmet, a cuirass, and a kilt. He takes off the helmet and carries it under his arm instead of wearing it.

Crusty has returned to the castle without having been whistled for. Things have gone badly for Gyminge. It's time for them all to be moving on quickly. He hovers beside the wall as he had done previously with his left wing lightly fluttering a step or so above the wall. Jock, Jordy, and Cymbeline run towards him. His passengers have varied considerably as the day has progressed, but the end of the changes is now at hand. Jordy bundles Cymbeline onto Crusty's forward wing feathers. She picks herself up and scuttles over to Cleemo, who is holding out a steadying hand to her. Cleemo gasps as he sees her bloodied clothes.

Gerald has run up along the wing to help. He sees that Jock is awkwardly clad and can't move easily. Jock throws the king's helmet to Gerald, who catches it and hurries it back to Barney to hold. Cleemo and Gerald are both now forward on the wing. They grab hold of Jock's uplifted hands. A great heave, assisted by a push from Jordy, brings him on board. Jock scrambles along the wing to safety. Jordy, not encumbered with body armor, is also hauled up. The three men scurry back to join the others settled on Crusty's back. Crusty finds his feathers touching either the walkway or the parapet at the side and needs to be a little higher to be comfortable treading air.

"On yur way, Crusty!" Jock yells. As the bird lifts away, he passes over the castle itself. Archers below take aim. Barney fires at any enemy he can see within catapult range. Crusty wants to be careful with so many passengers on board. He flies slowly and steadily, gaining height only gradually. Jordy is down on all fours, making a stool for his friend to stand on. Jock climbs onto Jordy's back to stand as tall as he can. Disguised as King Rufus, this is the time he needs to be seen by the Wozzle troops. He is again wearing the king's helmet, so he can see nothing of what's going on below. Gerald and Cleemo are kneeling, steadying his legs lest he lose his balance and fall. Jock waves the king's broadsword in his right hand. His left arm he keeps folded in front of his chest. The enemy will know that the king has been wounded in the shoulder and that his shield has fallen into the lake.

As Crusty turns south, they can all see that Fowler's Bridge is lost. The Wozzle engineers have improvised battering rams and ladders. The portcullis is breached, and the castle gate splinters under repeated blows. Their engineers show superb attacking skills. The air rings with shouting and banging. The defenders battle to keep the enemy out, but they are losing the fight. The first goblins are on the wall on the south side of the castle, and as they fight, others are tumbling over the wall after them. Archers still outside are firing arrows over the castle walls towards the king's chambers. Hopefully, those are still in Gyminge hands.

Barney continues to fire at any target that presents itself.

From inside the helmet comes a muffled booming of the king's war cry, "OUT, OUT, TRUTH WILL OUT!" Jock's companions take up the call. "OUT, OUT, TRUTH WILL OUT!"

The Gyminge men fighting on the ground hear that familiar cry from the sky above them. It gives them renewed vigor, although their cause is already lost. The eagle swings back over the castle for one last look, gaining height in a slow spiral. Barney puts his catapult to one side. Few stones remain, and they are moving out of range.

There is continued fighting on the walls. The vanguard of Wozzle troops is storming the castle. They pour over the walls from tall, improvised ladders. They fight foot by foot along the battlement walls towards the tower in the northeast corner. The attackers move down the narrow, twisting stairways from the walls above to the courtyard below while others behind them surge along the battlements. Clusters of defenders are overwhelmed by goblins. Knights and guards are cut down. Gyminge fighters are still defending at the gate, but it can't hold much longer. Waves of Wozzle goblins fight their way towards the king's chambers. They are aware that the king might have escaped, but his family may have been left behind. The wizard has said that he wants them taken alive.

Fires have been set, and flames break loose, spreading from the kitchen into the mess hall used by the troops. The tattered flag, a rampant horse and castellated crown above a crouching lion, has been torn by arrows. Between his tears, Gerald sees that the flag still flies above the castle, but now the gate splinters open. Cymbeline is also crying, crying for her lost love and for her lost country. If it weren't that Cleemo and Barney will be helpless without her, she would have stayed to help the king, no matter what orders he gave.

Outside the castle, the bulk of Wozzle's attacking army pours over Fowler's Bridge. Fighting still persists in patches, but now the men swimming across the brook seeking escape are the Gyminge troops.

The soldiers from Wozzle stream in through the castle gate. The torn and battered flag of King Rufus comes down. Goblins are at the foot of the flagpole, cheering. The black flag of Wozzle is tied to the halyards and slowly ascends the pole. The desperate but unsuccessful stand of the brave Gyminge warriors is almost over.

A toad, relaxing on a great lily pad with his arms behind his head, sees the great golden eagle soar above the castle wall. He is completely contented as warm thoughts swirl through his mind. *That looks like the king on board, shouting his stupid war cry. Fat lot of good that has done him! Just let him try to come back, and he'll get a sharper lesson than the one he's just had!*

The eagle disappears over Blindhouse Wood in a straight line, heading south towards Gibbins Brook. The toad gives a long sigh of satisfaction. *I've become master of Wozzle, and now I'm master of Gyminge. It's time to make my next move.*

Where is Rasputin, anyway?